I0690550

Destiny Reclaims HER
A Druidess Legacy Novel
Machelle Hanleigh

Contents

Destiny Reclaims HER

A Druidess Legacy Novel

Copyright © 2023 by Machelle Hanleigh

This is a work of fiction. Names, characters, places, and incidents either are the product of the author's imagination or are used fictitiously. Any resemblance to actual persons, living or dead, events, or locales is entirely coincidental.

All rights reserved. No part of this book may be reproduced or used in any manner without written permission of the copyright owner except for the use of quotations in a book review. For more information, write to: machelle_hanleigh@outlook.com.

First Edition, (2023, December)

Special thanks to:

Covers by Christian for an amazing cover!

ISBN 978-1-7348458-8-4 (Paperback)

Dear Reader

Thank you for embarking on this journey through the first installment of the **Druidess Legacy** series. The unfolding relationship between Da'fydd and Amber promises to grip and intrigue you. While my stories and trilogies can be enjoyed in any sequence, you might find it enriching to start with my foundational **Druidess Trilogy** if you have not yet done so. Although it's not a requirement, it could enhance the emotional depth of this story's conclusion.

My storytelling often employs third-person, past-tense, intimate narration. What this means for you, the reader, is a story filtered through the lens of the main characters. If they're unaware of something, you'll be in the dark as well based on their perspectives.

This narrative style allows for a nuanced presentation of individual viewpoints that eventually merge into a shared duality as the characters' destinies and bonds intertwine. It provides a uniquely engaging reading experience that transports you to another realm and Universe altogether.

Each tale adds new dimensions to my ever-widening fictional Universe, crafting a rich tapestry of interlinked narratives for you to lose yourself in. Your delight in navigating this intricate literary landscape inspires me to continue weaving complex and captivating stories. Please choose how you would like to join the conversation by visitng my linktree site at https://linktr.ee/machellehanleigh.

Enjoy the Journey!
Machelle Hanleigh

Trigger and Content Note from the Author

As noted on my Amazon profile, my storytelling often leans toward implication rather than explicit description. While that style persists, this particular tale delves into adult themes, focusing on emotional repercussions and character growth. Although explicit details are limited, the subject matter may trigger emotional responses based on your sensitivity to traumatic events.

Chapter One

"Stop struggling," a voice hissed into Amber's ear, each syllable etched with a gravelly harshness that made her skin crawl. "I won't hurt you as long as you cooperate."

Amber's muscles tensed as she twisted, straining against the unyielding grasp that held her. The more she fought, the more his grip solidified, like iron clamps refusing to budge. The warm caress of his breath ghosted over her neck, sending a shiver down her spine. A knot tightened in her stomach, an unspoken signal of the danger she faced.

"Who are you?" Amber's voice quivered despite her best efforts to sound defiant. Though his appearance straddled the line between youth and age, a deceptive vitality surged through his movements and tightened grip.

"That's not important." His words carried an air of finality as he yanked her forward. "What's important is that you come with me. Someone will be wanting to see you, lass."

Amber's thoughts raced, each one a frenzied blur, as she measured the iron grip confining her. She needed a plan, a moment to break free.

Summoning a shaky breath, she went limp. "Fine, I'll cooperate. Now get your hands off me."

Almost instantly, she sensed the tension in his grip loosen. As he began to release her, she pivoted to face him, breaking his relaxed hold. Her eyebrow arched in a silent challenge. "Where to now?"

"Follow me, lass," he said, his aged eyes a cryptic maze she had yet to decipher. He turned, leading her toward the same door she had stealthily entered to find refuge.

Every step forward churned a swirl of uncertainty and dread within her. But one thing was crystal clear: keeping her wits about her was her only way out of this labyrinth of peril.

"What'd we be havin' here, Bren?"

Amber's steps faltered as she came to an abrupt stop. Her gaze locked onto a new figure. The man before her exuded malevolence; his eyes, pools of icy disdain, bore into her like jagged shards. A lump formed in her throat, making her swallow involuntarily. The man who had seized her first seemed a far lesser evil than the newcomer.

Bren glanced at her. "Nothing you need to concern yerself with, Rory."

A sudden grip closed around Amber, snatching her from behind. A startled squeal escaped her lips before she could stifle it.

Bren's eyes narrowed into a fierce scowl, fixated on the man daring to lay hands on her. "Hands off, Gavin."

"You stoppin' us, Bren?" Another man sauntered in, casting a querying glance at Rory as he joined him.

Bren caught sight of the new arrival but merely lifted his shoulders in a nonchalant shrug, a mask of indifference hiding the calculations whirring behind his eyes.

Amber wriggled frantically to free herself from Gavin's vice-like grip. His grip loosened briefly, and Amber took the opportunity to lash out, kicking at his shins. But he quickly regained control, his grip tightening around her arms.

"She's to be brought before the Master and thus not yours to play with, Rory."

"Why?" Rory's eyes narrowed. "What would the Master care about a chit like this?"

Amber shot Bren a fiery glare, her eyes a confluence of defiance and apprehension. In that fleeting exchange, she silently vowed not to go down without a fight.

Summoning her resolve, she squirmed against Gavin's imprisoning grip. With a quick shift of her weight, she tried to stagger him off balance. But Gavin was an immovable force, his grip tightening like a vise around her, thwarting her attempts to break free.

Gavin's grip remained unyielding as he pulled Amber toward Rory and the other one. Despite straining against his hold, she found herself advancing, as if tethered by some invisible force she couldn't combat.

"She's a trespasser." Bren's words poked at Amber. She most definitely didn't like the sound of that.

In a desperate gambit, Amber attempted to drop her weight to the ground, seeking the element of surprise. For a split second, her arm broke free from the unrelenting grip. Before she could capitalize on her fleeting freedom and take even a single step, she was snared again, her hopes dashed as fast as they had ignited.

"Yer so wee," Rory hollered with a hearty laugh. "Where did ya think you'd get off to?" His breath, foul as a dead fish, made Amber want to retch. He ran a grimy finger down her cheek. "An' when did the Master start takin' an interest in trespassers, like?" Rory demanded.

Bren glanced at Amber, and then back to Rory. "Since this one."

"Get your grubby hands off me!" Amber scowled at Gavin and the other two with fierce determination, although dread took hold inside her. She was not a match against one brute, let alone three. She wasn't sure where Bren fit into this awful scenario, but she was confident the other three had nothing good in their heads where she was concerned.

Amber shook her arms against the one holding her and let out a blood-curdling scream. "Help me!" she screamed at Bren.

He turned his head towards her.

Amber's heart sank as she saw pity in his eyes but nothing more. She'd get no help from that man.

The laughter of the other three rankled her nerves.

"We'll be takin the chit to the Master." Rory told Bren.

Bren crossed his arms over his chest. "See that you do, straight away and unharmed."

Her mind raced, skirting around the question of what these men could possibly want with her. The enigmatic "Master" they mentioned took a backseat in her thoughts. Escape was her foremost concern.

As if tuned into her internal debate, the man holding her emitted a low, dark chuckle, sending a shiver down her spine. It was as though he could peer into her swirling vortex of thoughts, making her skin crawl with unease.

"Don't bother trying to escape, girl. You won't be gettin' away," Gavin sneered, yanking her closer.

The overpowering scent of sweat and grime assaulted Amber's senses as she was held captive, causing her nose to crinkle in revulsion. She strained against Gavin's vise-like grip, but her efforts were futile.

Focusing her attention on Rory, who seemed to command a certain deference from the others, she leveled her gaze at him. "What do you want?" Her voice was a taut wire, barely holding back the tremor of rising panic.

Rory's laughter cut through the air, a cruel sound bouncing off the empty cobblestone street. "'The Master will be decidin' yer fate." He spun on his heel. His boots clacked hard against the cracked stone as he quickened his pace, each step a declaration of his dominance over her.

Caught in a vise between her two captors, a grip tightened on each of Amber's arms, pulling her along like she was nothing more than chattel. Any hope of slipping free vanished as they moved further away.

She threw a desperate glance back at Bren, who stood his ground as he did nothing more than watch. A harsh scowl marred Amber's features, a silent, burning reproach aimed his way.

"Eyes forward," Gavin growled in her ear while forcing her head to swivel forward. Her eyes landed on the looming stone castle ahead.

As they drew closer, she noticed towering spires and intricately carved windows. She couldn't help but wonder how she had come to be on this forsaken world. Technically, she knew how, but damn, her luck was abysmal.

Amber couldn't help but scoff at her own calamitous misfortune. Hurled through the Universe, she'd landed on Earth, a supposed safe haven, despite their primitive technology.

Now she'd ended up on a world with even less technological advancement all because she'd trusted Ethan and Symon. They'd promised her an escape, safety, and look where that had gotten her. From one terrible situation to another. She cemented a promise in her mind: to never be that gullible again.

As the looming silhouette of the castle edged closer into view, Amber's thoughts pivoted back to escape and survival. Every step closer toward this mysterious "Master" tightened the knot of dread in her stomach. Eyes darting, she assessed her surroundings, cataloging potential routes of escape or objects that might serve as makeshift weapons.

All the while, she hustled to keep pace with her three captors, their long strides setting a relentless speed. Given her recent string of misfortunes, she wouldn't put it past fate to make this Master even more malevolent than the men dragging her to him.

The streets lay in haunting stillness, yet an unsettling sensation gnawed at Amber. She sensed invisible eyes scrutinizing her from every hidden crevice. Her heartbeat crescendoed when they reached the castle gates, where two imposing men in chainmail armor stood sentinel. Without a word, merely a nod from the trio, the guards unhitched the massive gates, granting them entry into the castle's shadowy courtyard.

When they entered the foyer, Amber couldn't suppress her awe. The entrance burst with grandeur, an oasis of affluence contrasting the grim journey thus far. They led her towards massive oak doors, their intimidating presence guarded by another set of two stern men armored head to toe. With a nod, the doors groaned open, revealing a spectacle that elicited an involuntary gasp.

Before her lay a room draped in intricate tapestries and ornate furnishings, each item echoing tales of unimaginable wealth and power. Scenes of conquest and battle brought the walls to life, although she quickly turned her eyes away. She had no appetite for glorifying violence; her life had served her enough of that already.

Occupying an elaborate throne-like chair at the room's far end was a man who could only be the Master. Despite his regal yet understated attire, he made the shabby garb of her captors look like rags pulled from a waste heap. As her eyes met his, Amber fortified her resolve, pressing down the quiver of fear that sought to unsteady her. She needed to maintain a facade of unyielding determination if she was to survive in this unforgiving world.

Chapter Two

The moment Da'fydd's eyes locked onto the despised trio, a surge of unexpected protectiveness overtook him. It was the woman they brought forth who triggered it, and he knew Rory was behind this ploy. Another tiresome attempt to curry favor. His patience with Bren for permitting such a spectacle had reached its limit. There would be repercussions.

His gaze detached from the loathsome trio, finding sanctuary in the woman they had ushered into his presence. Although he'd sensed a distinct disturbance ripple across his region when she arrived, he was wholly unprepared for the emotional maelstrom that engulfed him as she stood there. Words failed him. Her visage presented an enigmatic dichotomy: framed by cascading dark tresses, her face was delicate and recalcitrant. A compelling paradox that left him grappling with newfound, inexplicable emotions.

Her appearance might have been disheveled, but an other-worldly beauty emanated from her. For the first time in ages, he found himself entranced, ensnared by a foreign emotion he couldn't identify. It was an overwhelming desire to shield her, to make her well-being his priority. Without even needing to scent her, an intrinsic knowledge imprinted itself onto his very soul: their destinies were irrevocably entwined.

His attention shifted to Rory. "Why have you come before me?

Rory glanced at Amber. "Thon wee lassie was found trespassin' in the dog pens, m'Lord."

"And?" Da'fydd asked. "Why did Bren not bring her before me himself?"

Rory dipped his head. His eyes darted to his two companions.

Da'fydd pinned him with a piercing glare, daring the man to speak an untruth.

Rory uttered no response.

"Approach," Da'fydd's voice rang out, a mix of authority and intrigue. As the men led her towards the elevated platform, his eyes never wavered from hers. They were windows to a soul he found himself unexpectedly fascinated with. The unyielding glint in her eyes was a silent challenge; her upright posture an unspoken declaration of her resilience. Da'fydd found himself unexpectedly respecting her tenacity, a quality he rarely encountered. "Why were you in the dog pens?" His voice was hushed but carried an unmistakable undercurrent of command.

Her lips pressed into a taut line, but she remained steadfast under his unrelenting gaze. "I needed refuge," she retorted, her voice threaded with defiance and fatigue. "A place to gather my thoughts and figure a way off this forsaken world."

A single eyebrow arched on Da'fydd's forehead, intrigued by her audacity. "And why would you want off this world?"

"Because I don't belong here." She clinched her fists, the tenor of her voice laden with unshakeable resolve.

A twinge of unexpected empathy resonated within Da'fydd. He too had tasted the bitter draught of alienation, had yearned for a sanctuary where he could simply belong without conditions or judgments. "And where do you belong?" he asked, curious despite himself.

The woman's eyes flickered for a moment before she answered. "Somewhere else," she replied.

Da'fydd's brow furrowed. He yearned for a more thorough explanation from her, but the time and audience were inappropriate for such probing. His gaze shifted to the three men. "Dismissed." His tone left no room for dissent, imbued with an authority that couldn't be questioned.

The silence hung heavy, each second ticking away like a challenge. A latent desire stirred within him, craving for them to misspeak and offer him an opportunity to mete out justice, or perhaps merely to vent his own frustrations.

The men, however, offered nothing more than a deferential nod and bow before retreating from his presence.

His throat tightened with a tinge of unfulfilled expectation. Shifting his focus, his eyes found the woman once more. "What are you called?"

"Amber," she answered, a visible frown creased her features, caught off guard by the subtle shift in his tone.

Da'fydd gave a curt nod. He gestured with a flick of his wrist, summoning a woman who had been waiting in the wings. "Prepare Amber for the midday meal," he ordered, his tone ringing with authority.

Amber's expression shifted, a flash of resistance crossing her eyes. Da'fydd simply lifted an eyebrow, a silent challenge.

Her lips, poised to form words of objection, sealed themselves shut. A fleeting smile graced Da'fydd's lips. His silent command had been heeded, and it pleased him.

As the servant woman led Amber away, Da'fydd couldn't peel his gaze away from her retreating form. His heart agitated within him, stirred by the mystery she presented. It made him resolve to dig deep, to unearth whatever secrets lay in the hidden recesses of her past which brought her to him; even if it meant venturing into the darkest corners of her mind.

Chapter Three

A mber trailed behind the woman, her thoughts a swirling vortex centered around the man she'd been brought before. His gaze had been so intense it was as if he could reach into her, bypassing her built-up defenses to touch the core of who she was. An unfamiliar sensation fluttered inside her at that thought. A disquieting vulnerability she did not like one bit.

She shook her head, as if the physical act could scatter the troubling emotions he had stirred within her. At that moment, they arrived in a modest chamber, dominated by a large washbasin set upon an ornate wooden stand. Here, at least, she could cleanse herself of the grime and perhaps the unsettling emotions that his scrutiny had roused.

Remembering her goal to remain steadfast in the face of peril, she took a deep breath. The key to navigating this alien world, with its archaic customs and technology, was to maintain her focus and stay true to herself. If the 'Master' was to play any role in her story, it would be on her terms not his! She glanced into the washbasin as if seeking answers, then turned to the woman awaiting her next move. It was time to prepare for whatever came next, and she could only hope her will would be strong enough to see her through it.

"Strip down, lass," the woman instructed as she filled the basin with water from a spigot. She pulled open a chest and set out a pile of clean clothes on a bench. "I'll help you clean up."

A momentary pang of discomfort coursed through Amber at the thought of disrobing before a stranger. The notion struck her as invasive, but her options were limited. The filth that clung to her after her narrow escape from Ethan and a regrettable night spent in the dog pens had to go. It wasn't merely about personal comfort; she also needed to look presentable if she was to navigate this unfamiliar setting with any degree of control.

Amber's fingers hesitated for a moment over the hem of her tattered dress before she finally lifted it over her head. As the fabric pooled at her feet, her thoughts swirled with recent memories of escape, deception, and now, captivity. But as she stepped toward the large washbasin, she cast those thoughts aside. The warm water enveloped her, cleansing away not just the grime but also, momentarily, her myriad worries.

She closed her eyes, allowing herself this brief respite, this one simple pleasure in a life that had become increasingly complicated. And for that fleeting moment, as the water trickled down her skin, she felt almost at ease. Almost.

But the sensation was short-lived. Her eyes popped open as she suddenly became aware that she was not alone. The nonchalant woman had been silently working, preparing towels and clothing for her. The mundane domesticity of the scene contrasted sharply with the volatile uncertainties that clouded her mind, most notably the enigmatic man she would have to navigate around somehow.

She stepped out of the basin, drying herself quickly. The woman helped her into fresh clothing, a simple but well-crafted dress that somehow seemed perfectly suited for her. As she glanced at her reflection, Amber had to admit that she almost looked the part of a young woman of this world; Celtan as Ethan had called it, if she remembered correctly. But appearances could be deceiving. Amber knew better than anyone that appearing to fit in was not the same as belonging.

Dressed and somewhat refreshed, Amber steeled herself for what would come next. Her thoughts turned to the man on the throne. His gaze had been unsettling, yes, but also intensely focused, as if he saw something in her that she herself had not yet discovered. What that something was, Amber didn't know. But she was increasingly certain that her journey to understanding it would be as unavoidable as it was uncertain, much to her dismay.

Amber took her seat, her senses still on high alert. The food, although it appeared sumptuous and abundant, carried an odd undercurrent to its aroma; like an unfamiliar spice or perhaps something more elusive that she couldn't quite place. It was slightly jarring, and for a moment she questioned whether she should eat anything at all. In a world that already seemed tilted off its axis, even the seemingly mundane had the potential to be detrimental.

As her eyes swept across the crowd, she caught the stares of a few onlookers who hastily averted their gaze when she locked eyes with them. At that moment, the realization of her not fitting in pressed upon her. She felt like an ill-fitting puzzle piece in the context of not just this hallway and castle, but possibly this entire world.

The doors to the hall swung open and the man entered. The room seemed to shift with his presence, a silent acknowledgment of his power and status. He ascended to the raised platform and settled into the ornate chair. His eyes swept over the gathered crowd before resting briefly on her. Something in his gaze; curiosity, perhaps, or maybe even concern, made her heart skip a beat. He gave a subtle nod to someone at the side of the room, and then servers began filling plates with food.

Despite the odd scent that had initially caught her attention, Amber realized she was famished. But as she reached for her fork, she also realized her journey into the heart of this strange world and the mysteries it held, especially in the form of the enigmatic Master of the castle, was only just beginning. With a deep sigh, she steadied her nerves. Uncertainties lay ahead, but she'd faced peril before and emerged stronger for it.

Seated there, tension tightening every muscle, Amber's thoughts swirled back to her interaction with the man she only knew as the Master. She couldn't help but replay the intensity of his gaze.

What kind of person was he behind that resolute mask? What secrets resided in the depth of those eyes that had momentarily locked with hers? Despite her usual discernment, she found herself uncharacteristically intrigued. Even with her pressing need to escape, it was as if some invisible tether anchored her to that room, to the moment when he entered, capturing her.

Amber had always navigated relationships cautiously. Any semblance of romantic attraction had been with Michael, back on Earth, and that turned out to be an exercise in futility and disappointment. But this man before her was different in some way she didn't understand. The way he held himself, the quiet authority that emanated from him. It set her nerves alight in a way she hadn't experienced before, and not certain she desired to continue experiencing.

She had been a lone wolf by choice, skeptical of the intentions of males who tried to get close. Yet this one, in mere moments, had inspired a new, complicated desire to be near him. It was an enigma, a sensation that exuded foreign essentials, like stumbling upon a forgotten melody that she couldn't get out of her head.

Her contemplation was interrupted by the subtle sound of metal against hard wood. A servant had placed a plate and cup in front of her. It was only then she realized she'd been so consumed by her thoughts that she had neglected her immediate surroundings. The food, despite its aromatic allure and unfamiliar spices, remained untouched; a culinary tapestry she didn't have the heart to dismantle. Her drink sat idle, its liquid hue reflecting the ambient torchlight.

Amidst her internal whirlwind, the rest of the hall and its occupants seemed a world away. As though through a fog, she was aware of their eyes on her, but her focus remained steadfastly fixated on the man on the throne.

Chapter Four

The dining hall unfurled before Da'fydd, a magnificent spectacle where the tenebrous corners held hints of intrigue, and ethereal shafts of light sliced through the gloom of the interior from the outside. A swell of pride surged as he swept past the enigmatic silhouettes lining the chamber. Although he once had reservations about retaining a personal retinue of guards, their imposing presence now served as a formidable deterrent to those who might provoke turmoil.

As Da'fydd progressed toward the dais, the resonant cadence of his footsteps reverberated against the stone floor, drawing the gazes of those in his presence. Unfazed, he maintained regal dignity, gracefully settling into his seat.

His keen eyes scanned the assembly and alighted on Amber, a recent arrival in his region. Seated in solitude, her meal remained untouched. The subtle scent of her presence filled the air, and Da'fydd found himself inexplicably drawn to her. However, he swiftly suppressed the sensation, acutely aware of the villagers' presence at this daily mealtime gathering.

Seated at the expansive, timbered table, Da'fydd's gaze swept across the room with frosty disinterest. Although he recognized his attendance as indispensable for upholding order among his people, he found the communal repast vexing. A maelstrom of fragrances from various spices and herbs inundated the atmosphere, churning Da'fydd's stomach. With distaste, he observed those surrounding him indulging in their meals without restraint, utterly disregarding etiquette, or propriety.

His personal attendants remained at a discreet distance, vigilant and dutiful, yet mindful not to proffer food or drink without an explicit request. A gesture they had learned never transpired. Da'fydd maintained a stony composure, perceiving himself as confined to his own table, surrounded by subjects who failed to comprehend the extent of his true nature.

As the repast unfolded, Da'fydd's reverie wandered to the alluring newcomer. Amid the din, he found his gaze inextricably drawn to Amber, her very presence a beguiling riddle that ignited a fervent curiosity and the promise of uncharted realms of connection within him. Their eyes met, and for a fleeting moment, the world beyond faded, leaving only the shared intensity of their unspoken yearning.

Abruptly, Da'fydd rose, the screech of his chair reverberating through the hall. Da'fydd's steps halted just before Amber, his towering presence seeming to eclipse everything else. For a moment, the tension in the room was palpable, as if the very walls leaned in, yearning to hear what would be said.

Amber's gaze drifted downward. Da'fydd sensed his intensity pressing against her like a physical force.

"Look at me," he softly commanded, a thread of earnest curiosity woven through the fabric of his authority.

Raising her eyes to meet his, a jolt of electric recognition passed between them, momentarily forgetting the crowd of onlookers.

Da'fydd found himself momentarily disarmed. His gaze bore into hers as if searching for something he had long yearned for but never quite found. His defenses, typically unyielding, wavered under the soulful earnestness of her gaze.

Without a word, he extended his hand toward her, an unspoken invitation laden with promise and complication. The hall remained suspended in hushed stillness, each individual's attention riveted on this pivotal exchange. The silence strained, the Universe holding its breath as Amber stared at his outstretched hand, then back into his intensely dark eyes.

Da'fydd waited as he sensed hesitation within Amber, and how heavily the room's gaze weighed upon her. He silently coaxed her to gather her courage.

Amber finally placed her trembling hand in his.

Da'fydd's fingers encircled Amber's with a steadiness that belied his inner turmoil. Elation swelled within him as she allowed him to guide her to his table. Their footsteps reverberated in the room, a solemn counterpoint to the silence that hung heavy in the air.

As they settled into their seats, the murmurs began to resume, filling the hall like the distant rumble of an impending storm. The tension in the room seemed to breathe, fueled by the curiosity of the onlookers. Amber and Da'fydd exchanged glances, strengthening a connection barely conceived.

With conversation swirling around them like a tempest kept at bay, the pair sat together in a pocket of stillness. The energy that pulsated between them was almost tactile, drawing the eyes of those nearby. Amidst the chatter and clatter of dining, the two became the hall's enigmatic focal point, subjects of whispered speculation and barely concealed fascination.

As the meal continued, Da'fydd leaned in, his voice quiet. Yet the intensity of his words reached Amber's very core. "There is something extraordinary about you," he confessed, his gaze searching her eyes for an echo of his sentiments.

Flustered by his candid admission, Amber hesitated, her heart fluttering as she considered her response. "I could say the same about you," she replied, her voice tinged with caution.

Da'fydd, captivated by her sincerity, could not help but feel a deep sense of protectiveness toward her. "Who brought you to Celtan, little bird?" His tone was a velvety caress.

"I arrived here of my own volition," Amber lied, her voice resounding with clarity amidst the hushed hall.

Da'fydd's penetrating gaze scrutinized her, sensing the falsehood in her words. Despite her bold assertion, he could detect a trace of dishonesty in her tone. He narrowed his eyes ever so slightly, taking note of her evasion, but chose not to challenge her further, for now.

"Hmm," he murmured in response, his voice tinged with a hint of suspicion.

Amber shifted under his scrutiny but remained silent.

Da'fydd signaled for one of his servants to approach. "I noticed that you have yet to partake in the meal, little bird," he observed, his eyes scrutinizing her.

"I'm not hungry," Amber responded, her stomach protesting loudly in contradiction to her declaration.

Da'fydd arched an eyebrow, his gaze fixed on her. He could sense that she was not being entirely truthful. He leaned in slightly, his voice a low, penetrating murmur. "I insist."

Amber's breath caught in her throat, her gaze locking with his.

Da'fydd sensed the shift, the momentary withdrawal almost palpable. It was as if a veil had been pulled back, allowing a glimpse of vulnerability before it was hastily drawn closed again. His gaze lingered on Amber, probing, as if waiting for her to lift the curtain once more. And though she looked away, he sensed a hidden fire in her, a fierce autonomy that intrigued him as much as it challenged him. The room around them blurred into insignificance; for that stolen moment.

"Perhaps a stroll might help ease your nerves," Da'fydd suggested, his tone warm and inviting.

Amber considered his offer for a moment before nodding in agreement. "Yes, a walk would be nice," she replied softly.

As her fingers met his, Da'fydd felt a subtle charge, an electric pulse that whispered promises of destinies to be claimed. His grip was secure, yet gentle, as if each finger that held hers spoke a different tale of protection and intimacy. He guided her away from the table, their departure as silent and compelling as their presence had been.

The atmosphere in the hall shifted subtly as they left. Conversations resumed, but under a new light; as if everyone sensed that something pivotal had just occurred, something that could not be easily undone or explained. The walls seemed to listen as Da'fydd and Amber walked, their footsteps echoing soft tunes of change and anticipation.

They moved through a series of corridors, each adorned with ancient artifacts and tapestries that told stories of a world both strange and familiar to Amber. Da'fydd led her through a set of ornate double doors, which opened to reveal a secluded garden, bathed in the soft glow of the afternoon light.

The cool air almost held a hint of a sweet aroma. Here, away from prying eyes, Amber turned to face Da'fydd, her eyes questioning.

Da'fydd looked at her, his eyes softening. He guided Amber's hand into the crook of his elbow, steering her wordlessly toward his chosen destination. When they reached the dog pens, the canines erupted in joyful barks and wagged their tails.

Amber's face softened, a smile breaking through. "Thank you for bringing me back here." While she hadn't appreciated her earlier treatment, she'd found a measure of comfort among the dogs.

He paused, letting his gaze linger on her face as if memorizing its contours. "You're welcome," Da'fydd finally said, his voice noticeably softer. "And in time, I aim to uncover the truth about your sudden appearance." His words, though veiled, carried the weight of a promise, or challenge.

Amber met his eyes briefly, then her gaze drifted to the energetic dogs.

"Would you consider staying?" Da'fydd's intense gaze held her. He knew from her earlier words she had no intention of remaining on his world. He wasn't quite willing to let her go, not yet, maybe not ever. He waited for her answer, not certain how he would respond if she refused his request.

Amber seemed to waver, her eyes searching his for a moment. "I'll stay for a bit," she finally replied.

Da'fydd exhaled, a subtle release of the breath he hadn't realized he'd been holding. "It's a start," he said, his voice tinged with a newfound warmth.

Da'fydd could feel a pull to keep her near him, but catching the flicker of joy in Amber's eyes when she glanced at the dogs tipped the scales. "Would you like to spend more time at the pens?" He personally didn't understand the appeal of these beasts.

"Would that be okay?" Amber's eyes sought his, a question lingering there.

Da'fydd's eyes darted to the dogs and back to Amber's. He gave her a curt nod.

Amber's eyes softened. "Thank you," she said, a simple phrase laden with a depth of gratitude that warmed his heart.

Da'fydd signaled to Bren, who promptly approached them. He sensed Amber tense beside him as her gaze settled on the other man. "Ensure she returns safely to the castle in time for the evening meal," Da'fydd instructed.

"Of course, my Lord," Bren responded, bowing his head briefly. His eyes met Amber's, but only for a fleeting moment, as if aware of the unspoken tension lingering from their earlier encounter.

Lifting Amber's hand, Da'fydd placed a chaste kiss on its back. "You'll be safe with Bren," he reassured her, his eyes meeting Bren's in a stern, unspoken command.

Amber hesitated, her hand seeming to linger a beat longer than necessary. Encouraged by his reassuring smile and the subsequent release of her hand, she returned the smile. Then, her eyes sought out the mother dog and her pups, the furry companions that had offered her warmth in her sleep.

Da'fydd's attention turned to Bren when Amber was engrossed in showering the beasts with her affection. "How is it Rory and his cohorts escorted your charge to me?"

Bren shifted from foot to foot. "My apologies, my Lord. They insisted."

Da'fydd's stern expression showed his dissatisfaction with Bren's answer. Before Bren could utter any more excuses, Da'fydd sharply raised his hand. He knew that, in truth, Bren was aging and wouldn't be able to hold his own against the trio. As much as he loathed to do it, he knew he would have to deal with them before too long.

Da'fydd had always found solace in maintaining a certain detachment from the villagers, supplying them with the necessary resources they were too lazy to procure but otherwise keeping to himself for his own tranquility. His presence and subsequent role on Celtan, after all, had been imposed upon him, not chosen.

"I'll arrange for a guard to watch over her." Da'fydd's voice carried a tone of resolute finality.

"Thank you, my Lord." Bren bowed his head in a gesture of deference.

Da'fydd gave a curt nod before he turned and moved away without a glance in Amber's direction. He would allow himself such an indulgence after the evening repast. As he walked back to the castle, he contemplated Amber's presence on Celtan. He wondered if she knew anything about the lineage stones or her ties to this world.

He had not realized that Kaily had initiated the return of the Druidesses. Although, he hadn't paid much attention to the self-proclaimed High Druidess when she'd summoned the Council for her proclamation. Not that anyone paid attention to who was supposed to rule Celtan. He certainly didn't. Now, with Amber here, he wished he had. Her scent alone told him all he needed to know. He suspected Amber wasn't even aware of her own importance to Celtan, let alone to him personally.

Chapter Five

As the sun dipped below the towering spires of Da'fydd's castle, the encroaching twilight signaled the approach of dinner time. Bren hinted that the villagers would soon congregate for the evening repast, subtly recommending that Amber attend to satiate her hunger and to satisfy Da'fydd's expectations. The notion of bending to the will of the 'Master' irked Amber. She'd sworn never to let anyone wield such power over her again.

However, her stomach chose that moment to grumble, a corporeal reminder of her growing hunger. It had been quite a while since she'd eaten anything, and the tantalizing prospect of food gnawed at her resolve. After a moment of internal debate, she chose to acquiesce. The allure of a warm, filling meal was too compelling to ignore any longer.

Passing through the castle gates and entering the dining hall, Amber and Bren were immediately enveloped by a bustling crowd. The atmosphere was a lively blend of animated conversations and uplifting melodies, a stark contrast to her earlier dining experience. Long tables groaned under the weight of a bountiful spread, and the rich scent of smoked vegetables beckoned to her. Could this opulent meal really be a nightly affair?

Despite her amazement, Amber experienced a twinge of guilt. Enjoying such extravagance felt wrong when she knew so little about this world, its customs, and its people. But as her stomach issued another plaintive growl, she gave in to her body's demand. With Bren as her escort, she delved deeper into the communal warmth.

With an air of natural elegance, Da'fydd approached Amber. "Please, sit here," he indicated, nodding toward a table near the raised platform before making his way to his own elevated seat. His formal manner left Amber with an unsettled curiosity. As she eased into her seat, her mind spun with questions: Why had he singled her out? Why did he seem so oblivious to the other diners around him? Why had he not escorted her to the high table as he had earlier?

Irritation and disappointment washed over her. She had naively expected to share the meal with Da'fydd, and the reality stung. She told herself the distance was a blessing, an obstacle to keep her from another entanglement of lies with Da'fydd. Yet the separation between them, no matter how logical, pierced her. She stubbornly forced her attention to focus on her surroundings instead of the irritant on his throne.

A sigh slipped through Amber's lips as she observed servants weave through the various long tables with trays of food in hand. When a plate was set before her, she glanced up and realized that Da'fydd had yet to be served. Her eyebrows knitted together in curiosity before she remembered herself and adopted a neutral expression. Absently, she poked at the roasted vegetables, her thoughts turning to Bren's absence. A quick scan of the room revealed no familiar faces among the throng of villagers. She had no idea where Bren had gotten off to.

As the meal wore on, Amber's discomfort deepened. Strangely, no one approached her for idle conversation or took the seats next to her. Normally she preferred solitude over pleasant platitudes. Yet, tonight it left her feeling alone. Was she meant to sit alone and be kept under watchful eyes like a prisoner? The bounty on her plate suddenly seemed less appetizing. She forced herself to eat, each bite tasteless, her gaze carefully avoiding the high table where Da'fydd sat.

Unfortunately, Amber's eyes inadvertently met Rory's from across the room. She swiftly averted her gaze to the serving girl, who had just set a silver cup before her. Yet when she risked another glance, she found Rory still watching her, his stare icy and filled with undisguised hostility. It was as if he were cataloging each of her movements, looking for an excuse, any excuse, to bring her harm.

Struggling to keep her composure, she tried to look away, but the malevolence in his eyes felt almost like a physical force. His stare seemed to carry a weight, a promise of vengeance yet to come, that sent a shiver crawling down her spine. A fleeting glance revealed his friends nearby, leering and chuckling at her expense. The thought of ever being alone with Rory and his companions filled her with a dread that soured the taste of her food completely.

Amber's attention shifted to the dynamics unfolding in the dining hall. A pattern emerged that she found increasingly jarring. Aside from a smattering of young boys, all the servants were female, while the number of women seated was conspicuously low. The men appeared jovial, engaging in light banter and playful exchanges. Yet, something in their demeanor struck a discordant note, a subtle undertone revealing a deeper, less amicable attitude toward females.

The situation evoked memories of her own world, where the subservient role of women was an unspoken but well-understood fact. Yet, on this world, the ambiguity was unsettling. The conflicting signals were a veneer of joviality masking an underlying tension. Her unease intensified, making her question the seemingly genteel facade of Da'fydd's society.

A servant woman startled her out of her inner ponderings. "Are you finished, milady?" Amber cast a brief glance at her plate, where most of the food still lay untouched. With a heavy sigh, she nodded in confirmation. She'd consumed enough to merely quiet her hunger pangs since her appetite had deserted her. As the woman picked up the plate, she leaned close to Amber. "Don't stare at them, especially that one," nodding in Rory's direction.

"I wasn't," Amber lied.

"Keep to yourself and don't attract too much attention," the woman advised, her words laced with a warning that Amber understood all too well.

Resolving to keep a low profile, Amber focused her gaze downward. It hadn't proven effective in the past, but she clung to the notion that someday it might. Despite her resolve, her eyes were irresistibly drawn to the high table, where Da'fydd presided. She quickly averted her gaze, hoping he hadn't noticed. Lately, it seemed she had a knack for attracting unwanted attention.

The memory flashed through her mind of that night at the bar, failing to escape the notice of Ethan and Symon, a lapse that ultimately hurled her into this bewildering, unfamiliar world. Each furtive glance and subtle scrutiny now felt like a heavy chain, linking her to a past decision she couldn't reverse but continued to pay for.

As the meal neared its end, Amber's peripheral vision caught Da'fydd rising from the high table. Her pulse quickened. Was he coming her way? Did his approach have anything to do with her, or was he merely passing through? She tried to keep her focus away but could feel his eyes on her. Despite her resolve, she risked a glance.

The servants near her table scattered, nearly upsetting her drink as they made way for Da'fydd's deliberate approach. His effect on the hall was more potent than she'd anticipated. Conversations stopped mid-sentence. One man's jaw hung open, as if he had forgotten how to close it. A woman at another table closest to Amber's emitted a soft gasp, like the fluttering wings of a startled bird. The weight of the room's attention settled on her shoulders like a cloak of bismuth, and she resented Da'fydd for summoning this unwelcome spotlight with just a few steps.

Finally, he halted before her, his eyes capturing hers with an intensity that sent a shiver down her spine. Ignoring the palpable tension swirling around them, he extended his hand. "Will you join me in my private quarters for the night?" His words were quiet but carried a timbre that seemed more like a command than a request.

Amber's throat tightened. Here was yet another man exerting his will, yet the strange magnetism she felt toward Da'fydd muddied her thoughts. She gazed up at him. "I appreciate the offer, but I must decline," she managed to say, keeping her voice steady. For once, she felt as though she had regained some semblance of control.

His response was as cold as the metal of a sword left overnight in the winter frost. "As you wish," he intoned, pulling back his hand as though he had touched a flame, each word laced with a veiled yet unmistakable chill.

Da'fydd's swift departure left Amber feeling a mix of relief and disappointment. She had stood up for herself, but she couldn't deny the pull of desire that coursed through her very being for this man. As she watched him speak with one of the guards by the entry doors, she couldn't help but wonder what he was planning next. The tension in the air was palpable, and Amber held her breath, waiting for the next move in this strange dance between them.

None came. Da'fydd left the dining hall without a backward glance in her direction.

Amber nibbled on the tip of her finger, frowning as she wondered if she'd made a mistake.

The dining hall gradually emptied, its chatter giving way to a quiet stillness. A young woman, seemingly the same age as Amber, moved toward her. She leaned in, her voice low and tinged with urgency, as though imparting a confidential truth.

"If the Master hasn't assigned personal quarters, find someone to share a space with tonight," she suggested.

Amber's brow furrowed, caught off guard by the stranger's unsolicited counsel. The importance of paired slumber eluded her, and she couldn't fathom why it might be desirable, let alone imperative. Though she had spent many nights in solitude, resting on unforgiving ground or tucked into cramped spaces, she hesitated to dismiss the advice.

In her experience, women refrained from forming such alliances, as they often invited peril rather than offered protection. "I appreciate the advice," Amber responded, her voice soft yet tinged with caution.

The young woman nodded, her smile a brief earnest flash, before she melted into the dwindling crowd. Amber mulled over the stranger's words, questioning her wisdom in refusing Da'fydd's proposition. She shook the thought away, redirecting her focus on securing a sleeping spot for the night. As far as she was aware, the 'Master' hadn't set aside any quarters for her. He probably wouldn't if his swift departure and reaction to her declining his offer was any indication.

Her glance swept across the remaining occupants of the dining hall and, almost as if magnetized, landed on Rory. She quickly averted her eyes, but an unspoken tension pulled her gaze back to him. He was seated by the hearth among his companions, and she felt the intensity of his stare as though it were a tactile force. He swept his disheveled hair back from his face, his eyes never wavering from hers, locking her into a stare that seemed predatory, almost malicious.

How she wished he had chosen another seat; somewhere Da'fydd might have caught his unsettling demeanor. Then again, would Da'fydd have cared? He had, after all, left her to fend for herself, albeit after she'd rebuffed him. She mentally chastised herself, cursing her complicated circumstances.

Engrossed in her internal debate, Amber remained oblivious to her surroundings until the table subtly shifted, rousing her from her reverie. She glanced up to find the woman who had assisted her in dressing earlier now seated across from her. A flicker of recognition passed between them, accompanied by subdued smiles. "That door leads to a hallway connected to the kitchens."

Amber frowned.

The woman leaned in, her voice dropping to a whisper tinged with a hidden agenda. "There's another door off that hallway, one that leads directly to the Master's tower. If you decide to go to him, it's wiser to avoid being seen." The implications of her words hung heavy in the air, insinuating that Amber could choose to spend the night with Da'fydd after all.

Amber's frown deepened but she held her tongue, her mind awhirl with questions and doubts. As the woman retreated, her departing words clung to Amber's thoughts. She didn't know if the woman's guidance was purely informational, or an underlying motive behind her seeming kindness.

After last night's unsuccessful endeavor to secure a safe haven, Amber was acutely aware that she needed a more defensible spot to sleep. The dog pens had failed her, lacking the security she'd hoped for. She'd been unknowingly exposed to discovery. A lesson she'd learned the hard way. The challenge now was to weigh whether seeking refuge with Da'fydd would make her more or less vulnerable.

Her gaze inadvertently settled again on Rory and his group. A shiver of unease slithered down her spine, reinforcing her need for a better solution.

The servants had long since cleared the tables, and the music that had previously filled the air was now dwindling to its final notes. A few people remained, savoring their drinks, or staking out sleeping spots, but the hall was largely empty. She suspected Da'fydd had exited early, possibly stung by her rejection of his offer.

The thought of hurting his overinflated ego briefly crossed her mind, but she quickly dismissed it. Her own safety trumped any concern for his feelings. Amber remained resolute in her determination. She would not resort to intimacy as a means of self-preservation.

Caught between her internal struggle and the waning atmosphere of the hall, Amber pondered her limited options. The suggestions and unspoken possibilities hung in the air, leaving her with decisions that could reshape her immediate future in ways she could scarcely predict.

While keeping her head angled away from Rory, Amber flicked her eyes just enough to gauge his condition. He seemed deep in his cups, clinging to his friends as though he couldn't stand upright on his own. Maybe his intoxicated state would hinder him, or better yet, render him unconscious. She needed to exit the dining hall, but it was crucial she did so without catching his attention. A sense of unease expanded within her, magnified each time her eyes darted back to Rory.

Finally, an opportunity presented itself. Rory, now engrossed in a playful wrestling match with his friends, had his back turned. Seizing the opportunity, Amber rose and moved away, her pace steady to prevent arousing suspicion. Once she stepped out of the dining hall, she exhaled a sigh of relief. The outdoor air was invigorating, a welcome contrast to the castle's stifling ambiance, and she relished the touch of the cool breeze on her face.

However, the cold was more biting than she'd anticipated, her dress ill-suited for the chill. A thought crossed her mind: maybe Bren had some spare blankets in the stables. Even if she didn't intend to bed down there, she could still check on the dogs and secure some extra cover. As she traversed the modest village, the inhabitants seemed to pay her no mind. The dying twilight had surrendered to a starlit darkness, and she grimaced at the idea of being out after dark again, knowing too well the dangers that lurked in the shadows.

As Amber pushed open the door near the dog pens, she was met with enthusiastic tail-wagging and excited panting from the resident canines. She'd expected them to be asleep, given their laborious day.

These dogs were not the cuddly pets she'd come to know on Earth. They were working animals, trained to perform an array of tasks. Bren had demonstrated earlier how the dogs could sniff out spoiled food, chase away pests, and even deliver small buckets of water or clean rags on command. Although the notion of animals serving as labor didn't entirely sit well with her, she found solace in the fact that Bren treated them kindly. She'd gained a newfound perspective of him apart from her earlier experience.

A smile broke across Amber's face as she reached out, patting the heads and backs of the dogs that gathered around her.

Their simple presence, devoid of judgment or ulterior motives soothed her soul. When she moved toward the rear of the stables, the dogs trailed behind her, their tails swaying in apparent delight. She hoped to find Bren somewhere back there.

Her search for Bren proved fruitless, but she did discover what appeared to be a spare blanket. Next to it was a cot with bedding that seemed untouched. As tempting as the cot appeared, she chose not to disturb it. It could very well belong to Bren, who hadn't yet turned in for the night. Instead, she grabbed the blanket she deemed to be extra, draping it over her shoulder as she pondered her next move.

As she stood there, lost in thought, a surge of reluctance washed over her at the idea of leaving the dogs unattended. Their warm presence had provided her with a small measure of security and comfort, a fleeting connection in a world filled with uncertainty. But she steeled herself with the thought that they had fared well before her arrival and would continue to do so.

As she stepped away, an uneasy realization lingered: her nightly sanctuary required better fortification than the dog pens. An inner voice urged her to stay close to the canines. She quashed the temptation. Remaining there would make her all too vulnerable.

Her fingers clenched around the fabric of the spare blanket she carried, its coarse texture serving as a minor comfort. Amber considered her options. She could either head back to the castle, admitting defeat but potentially finding safety, or she could press on, trusting her instincts to guide her to a secure hiding spot. Neither option was without risk, yet standing still was the worst choice of all.

Gathering her courage, Amber decided to move forward but altered her path slightly, veering off into the sparse forest that bordered the village. Her eyes adjusted to the darkness, scanning her surroundings as she moved cautiously. The idea was simple: if someone was indeed following her, the uneven terrain and natural obstacles of the forest would slow them down or reveal their presence.

As she ventured deeper into the woodland, her ears remained alert, sifting through the nocturnal symphony for any sound out of place. The woods seemed to embrace her, and for a moment, she allowed herself to savor the serenity that nature provided, its woodsy aroma filling her lungs.

Finally, Amber stumbled upon an abandoned hut, its wood weathered and door slightly ajar. With a sense of cautious optimism, she approached and peered inside. The interior was spartan, but it appeared dry and serviceable. Most importantly, it was secluded.

Amber froze, her hand on the door. A shiver ran down her spine; her stomach clenched. Slowly, she turned, only to collide with a solid form. She let out a startled yelp and stumbled back, but a firm grip on her arm kept her in place. "Where do ya think ya be goin', lass?"

Rory yanked Amber closer and leaned into her face. Amber shoved against him and tried to turn her head, but it was too late. Rory forced his lips against hers in a painfully sloppy kiss. Amber jerked her head to the side and tried to headbutt him. When she missed, Rory shouted in laughter. "I likes that fire, but I'll have to break ya. Ya won't be disrespectin' me again." He ran a grubby finger down her cheek. The dark leer in his eyes made Amber's stomach roll harder. "Since ye've spurned the Master, ye're mine to play with now."

Gavin and the other male, whose name she didn't know, smirked and chuckled as they watched Amber struggle against Rory. She was disgusted by them.

"Screw you!" Amber jabbed her knee into Rory's groin. He cried out in anguish, letting go of her to clutch his crotch.

Amber pulled herself away from his reach just as Gavin and the other male rushed to Rory. Dropping the blanket, Amber booked it towards the dog pens, sprinting with the full force of sudden adrenalin. She heard Rory yell at his friends behind her. "What are ye at? Seize her!"

Amber's legs burned as she raced past the dog pens and stables, focusing solely on the rear of the castle. Each stride took her closer to what she hoped was a service door to the kitchen.

As the door loomed in her sight, she hurled herself against it. The lock shattered under the force, sending a jolt of pain through her shoulder. Gritting her teeth, she propelled herself into the dimly lit kitchen.

The room's stillness wrapped around her like a shroud, and for a moment, she paused to regain her breath. Then the servant woman's directions flashed through her mind. Fueled by a new sense of purpose, she bolted towards the far door, her footsteps echoing on the stone floor.

Amber's eyes darted around the hallway as she searched for any indication of the path to Da'fydd's tower. Her sprint took her past rich tapestries and lifeless suits of armor, her gaze jumping from one detail to another until she found it; a narrow, door-like panel hidden in a dim alcove. Taking a steadying breath, she made her way to it and nudged the door open.

The door creaked, revealing a spiral staircase shrouded in darkness. Her eyes probed the void, uncertainty coiling within her. She shook it off, tightened her grip on her resolve, and started ascending the staircase. Each step lifted not just her body but also her determination; it surged through her like an unquenchable fire. She couldn't afford to fail; not when the stakes were this high.

The distant clangor of heavy footsteps and agitated voices reached her from the kitchen below. Her heartbeat quickened. She was still not safe, and this tight stairwell offered no exit. Compelled by the urgency, Amber quickened her ascent, committed to escaping the trio closing the distance behind her.

Her pace quickened, her breaths came in short gasps as she darted up each painstaking step. The men's roaring commotion echoed through the confining space, making her stomach churn with fear. She could hear them getting closer, their boots thudding against the cold stone steps.

Trembling with adrenaline and nerves, Amber fought to keep her wits about her. She had to stay focused and find a way to outmaneuver the men and escape their grasp. She could feel her legs growing weaker with each passing moment, but she refused to give up. She had come too far, too close to what she hoped was safety, to let them catch her now.

With her heart pounding in her chest, Amber hurried up the winding staircase, her footsteps echoing off the stone walls. As she passed through the second level, the grandeur of the castle's halls, with their vaulted ceilings and intricate carvings made her stop in her tracks. The alcoves lining the walls were filled with statues and tapestries, giving the space a sense of history and importance that Amber found awe-inspiring and intimidating.

Despite her wonder at the castle's magnificence, the clamoring below made Amber regain her focus on her goal. The woman who had given her the information about Da'fydd's whereabouts had indicated he resided on the third floor, which made sense. Amber trusted her own instincts enough to follow those instructions.

Relief washed over Amber as she stepped into the dimly lit hallway of the third floor. The air, redolent with the mingling scents of incense and aging parchment, seemed to hum with the soft echoes of distant chanting, or perhaps it was just the thumping of her own heart. She moved forward cautiously, eyes darting through the interplay of shadow and light. The slim possibility that Rory could be lurking here made her more vigilant. She was in too deep to falter now.

As she drew closer to her destination, her thoughts circled back to Da'fydd. Would his offer still stand? And how would he feel about her sudden, uninvited appearance at this hour? Her reverie was shattered by the sudden reverberation of footsteps echoing through the corridor behind her. Panic snaked through her veins, urging her to quicken her steps. Had Rory and his friends closed the distance already? She fought to dispel the panic rising inside her, concentrating instead on locating Da'fydd's secluded chambers.

The echoes swelled in intensity as she reached a lone door at the hallway's end. Her pulse throbbed in her ears. She extended a shaky hand to grasp the doorknob, but her foot snagged on an uneven stone in the floor. Momentum propelled her forward, and she collided with the wooden door. Pain erupted in her hands upon impact, but surrender wasn't an option. Wincing, she righted herself and turned the handle, hoping she had found the sanctuary she so desperately sought.

Chapter Six

Da'fydd paced back and forth in his room, his eyes fixated on the variegated brown rug beneath his feet. The rejection from Amber, still fresh in his mind, stung more than he cared to admit. He thought they had made a real connection.

As he gazed out the window, his eyes fixated on the stragglers below returning to their disheveled and fallen-apart dwellings. He knew others would bed down in the castle. He cared not where they slept, as long as they stayed out of his way.

His eyes drifted to the surrounding forest that once boasted abundant life, now reduced to spindly trees and sparse vegetation. It might as well have been a barren wasteland. With a frustrated sigh, he yanked the drapes closed to block out the dreary sight of the village. What did Amber's refusal mean? And why did he feel like everything around him was slowly withering away?

Da'fydd's reflection in the mirror sneered back at him. Why couldn't Amber see how much she needed him? Every fiber of his being screamed out for her, to claim her. He ran a hand through his dark hair, pacing back and forth as he tried to think of a way to make her understand. He could feel the weight of the castle walls closing in on him, suffocating him with their silent judgment. With a groan of frustration, he slammed his fist into the stone wall.

Da'fydd forced himself to take a deep breath and tried to push aside his desperation. He knew there had to be a way to make Amber see that they belonged together, to make her understand the depth of their connection. But how?

As he paced back and forth, his thoughts consumed by the image of Amber's face, a sudden surge of energy from Celtan infused him. Without thinking, he reached out and effortlessly lifted the chair next to the mirror, his fingers moving as if spinning a ball. But as rapidly as the energy had come, it slipped out of his reach, leaving him even more frustrated and powerless.

With a growl of anger, he hurled the chair against the wall. The legs shattered, and the seat exploded, sending slivers of wood flying across the room. How could he possibly get that wretched woman out of his head?

Da'fydd stood amid the splintered debris, his chest heaving with emotion. He couldn't stand the thought of being apart from Amber, not now that he had found his true mate. It didn't matter that he hadn't been searching for her.

She was within reach, unmistakably his. Yet, the more she occupied his thoughts, the more he grappled with a sense of impotence. He needed to channel his focus, to make her realize they were destined for each other, but the task loomed insurmountable. Frustration welling up, he slumped against the bed's edge and buried his face in his hands, succumbing to his feelings of helplessness.

After a time, Da'fydd lifted his head, and his eyes darted to the mess he'd created, the shattered chair symbolizing his inner turmoil. He drew in a deep breath and focused his energy, waving his hand in a fluid motion. The dust and debris flowed into a neat pile near the door, ready for the morning servant to clean up. Da'fydd had no patience for messiness, not when it reminded him of his chaotic turmoil.

Da'fydd's thoughts drifted to his past, to the endless years of hopelessness and despair that had consumed him. He could feel the weight of his father's judgment bearing down on him, crushing him under the weight of the man's perceived view of his son's inadequacies. But as his thoughts drifted back to Amber, a small smile tugged at the corners of his mouth. With her by his side, he believed he could face anything. She would give his Universe forsaken life meaning.

He stood up from the bed, his movements slow and deliberate, as if savoring every moment. He crossed the room to the window, pulled aside the heavy drape, and gazed at the star-filled sky. The cool night air wafted against his skin, and he closed his eyes, breathing deeply. For a moment, he forgot about his troubles, about the weight of his past or present. All he thought about was his Amber and the way her scent permeated his every fiber.

With a renewed sense of purpose, Da'fydd turned away from the window and strode back to the bed. Energy coursed through his veins, a sense of clarity and determination that he had not experienced in some time. He knew he couldn't let Amber slip away, not when their connection was so strong and undeniable.

He reached out and picked up a piece of the shattered chair, turning it over as if searching for inspiration. He would find a way to show Amber that they were meant to be together, to make her see the depth of their connection. And he would do whatever it took to make that happen. With a fierce determination burning in his chest, he tossed the piece of wood back onto the pile of debris. He began to pace back and forth across the room, his mind racing with ideas and possibilities.

Da'fydd's concentration was shattered by a loud thud against his chamber door, followed by frantic pounding. He jerked his head up, irritation flooding through him at the intrusion. Who would dare disturb him at such a late hour?

He crossed the room in long strides and yanked open the door without bothering to first scan with his Druidic abilities. His temper had him ready to unleash his fury on whoever was on the other side. But his anger gave way to surprise when he saw the figure standing before him. It was Amber, her eyes wide with fear and desperation.

Da'fydd acted on pure instinct, reaching out and pulling Amber inside his sleeping chamber, slamming the door shut behind her. As he turned back to face her, he saw her trembling and gasping for breath.

Before Da'fydd could say anything, Amber threw herself into his arms. He frowned and wrapped his arms protectively around her. Amber clung to him as if her life depended on it. The notion that Amber might share his yearning to be close electrified him. Had she been consumed by thoughts of him, just as he'd been with her?

Excitement rushed through him as he wondered if their connection could already be strengthening. He tightened his arms around Amber and held her close, pulling her with him towards the bed. He sank onto the soft mattress with Amber still securely enclosed within his protective embrace. Da'fydd pictured himself sliding his hand up the small of Amber's back and coaxing her to lay back with him. He resisted the temptation. He would take things slow to savor the moment with her.

Amber lifted her head and gazed into Da'fydd's eyes. He reached for Amber's cheek, cradling her warm face in his hand, and inhaled deeply to take in a lung full of her scent. Instead,

Da'fydd was hit with the pungent odor of another male. Recoiling from Amber, he glared down at her in pure disgust.

"What have you done?" Da'fydd hissed between ragged breaths as he twisted out of her grasp. He wanted to shake Amber until her body went limp. It angered him to know she'd been with another man first before seeking him out. She was his! She should have realized this!

Amber's eyes widened as she gazed up at Da'fydd, a frown creasing on her brow. "What have I done?" She stood to move closer to Da'fydd, but he swiftly held his hand up and stepped backward.

"How dare you enter my chambers with the scent of another male on you!" Da'fydd spun around and yanked open his door. "Out!" He stood with a tight grip on the door's edge, his knuckles turning white.

Amber stepped closer to him, her eyes darting out into the hallway. "Please, no. Don't turn me away. Please." Amber's eyes filled with tears.

Da'fydd remained unmoved, his sympathy obscured by the fury her betrayal sparked within him.

She had attempted to deceive him as though he would never find out. His anger intensified, not only because of her betrayal but also because her unexpected arrival had caught him off guard, delaying his realization of the male's scent on her.

Amber's tears streamed down her face as she crumpled to the floor at his feet, seemingly pleading for him to let her stay. "I said out!" he commanded.

Amber's voice wobbled as she spoke, and Da'fydd heard nothing she uttered, nor did he care to. He wanted her gone from his sight. Amber stood and cried harder. She finally formed words Da'fydd could understand. "Please. Let me explain."

Da'fydd face heated with his growing anger. "Out!" He slammed his closed fist on the side of the door. Amber jumped at his outburst and ran out of the room.

Chapter Seven

Tears clouded Amber's vision as she clung to the stone wall outside Da'fydd's chamber, bewildered. Her heart pounded in her chest. She'd nearly tripped down the stairs she'd failed to notice earlier. She cast a fruitful gaze at his chamber door, her hopes shattered to pieces. Tears streamed down her face as she shuffled through her options.

The backstairs she'd come up was a potential encounter with Rory and his cohorts; a risk she couldn't afford to take. She dragged herself to a standing position and hurried down the stairs, her hand skimming the coarse wall for stability. Da'fydd's refusal to listen to her pleas for assistance had left her awash in emotional turmoil.

Reaching the second level, Amber fell to her knees, unable to continue. She gasped for breath and wiped angrily at her tears while fear coursed through her veins. Her face throbbed in sync with her pounding heart. She'd hoped that the subtle connection she felt with Da'fydd, and his earlier invitation would lead him to help her.

Instead, she'd faced rejection that left her enraged and bewildered. Although Amber had just met Da'fydd, she believed he was different. As it turned out, he behaved much like the countless men who had come and gone throughout her life. Men who lived without a moral code or honor.

As her breaths steadied, Amber swept away the remaining tears with the sleeve of her borrowed dress. Her vision began to clear, though the dim hallway still presented a challenge to her sight.

Amber's eyes settled on the staircase, likely a path to the main floor. She needed sanctuary for the night, though where to find it remained elusive. Venturing outside the castle was out of the question. No one there would offer aid, not that it mattered. Her eyes flicked back to the stairs she'd just come down, a flare of anger warming her gaze. She nibbled on her fingernail, mulling over her next step.

Further down the corridor, Amber spotted an alcove. It wasn't perfect, but the thought of facing others downstairs or braving the world outside the castle walls made it a preferable option for the night. A wave of disillusionment washed over her. Despite being in a new, unfamiliar world, she found herself resorting to the same survival tactics she'd honed during her difficult upbringing.

Head bowed and arms crossed, Amber edged toward the alcove, seeking a pocket of darkness for refuge. The recess offered minimal shelter, but she nestled into a corner on the chilling floor, drawing her knees up to her chest. Clasping her legs, she tucked her face into her arms, in an attempt to retain her dwindling warmth.

The castle's cold penetrated her bones, deepening her regret over abandoning the earlier-found blanket but retrieval was too risky. She resigned herself to the icy embrace of the night. With measured breaths, she relaxed her tensed muscles, allowing her thoughts to drift toward uneasy sleep.

A rigid set of hands gripped Amber and painfully yanked her to her feet. Her head flew up, and she squinted to make out the face of her intruder. She could not see well, but she sensed precisely who it was by his voice. "There ya are, girl." Rory's words were echoed by the laughter of his two friends behind him.

Dread and panic took over Amber's entire body, and she began to scream for help. Her words bounced off the walls. Despite her earlier assessment, she fervently hoped the castle walls were not too thick and that her call for help would reach Da'fydd.

Rory shoved his dirty hand over Amber's mouth. "Be silent, girl. No one's comin for ya." His biting words made Amber cringe, and her heart plummeted as the truth of those despised words took hold.

With renewed determination, Amber attempted to bite Rory's hand. She was able to nip the lower part of his palm, and he cried out in pain. Rory shook Amber hard and shoved her at his friends. "Gavin, Hamish, hold her down!"

The two males grabbed Amber's shoulders and arms and held her tight. She wiggled and kicked at them, but it was no use. They were immensely stronger than she was, and she was already exhausted. Rory squeezed her cheeks hard against her teeth, forcing her eyes to meet his. "Ye do tha' again, an' I'll be knockin' yer teeth out before I'm finished."

The full weight of gravity bore down hard on Amber as the trio forced her back against the freezing stone. Her head hit the floor like a hammer. Her eyes fogged over, and staticky white stars danced in the blackness. Amber's eyelids drifted shut as she was unable to keep them open.

Her mind drifted to a distant memory as she welcomed the bliss of unconsciousness.

A water fountain trickled water from its top-down two tiers back into the bottom and bubbled into the small circular pool. It was somehow always cold to the touch. Amber dipped her fingertips in and playfully disturbed the ripples. She glanced over her shoulder at her mother, whose smile warmed Amber's heart and brought life to her soul. She could stare at her mother for hours. When Amber turned back to the water, her reflection of a much younger self stared back, smiling. A hand entwined with her own as her mother guided her further into the gardens.

Birds sang atop red-flowering bushes, and some sort of lizard stealthily approached the walkway. The green of each leaf among the vast vegetation glistened in the sun. Light water droplets still clung as if the garden had just been watered. Amber remembered daydreaming of floating on a sea of tranquility in that lush garden.

Amber's mother let go of her hand and sat on an elegantly designed bench. Each carving was masterfully and carefully placed, and the details always awed Amber. She sat next to her mother and scooted close. A loving arm wrapped around her shoulders. "You, child, are destined for great things," her mother would say, kissing the top of her head.

Not knowing what she meant, Amber asked the same question she always did. "What do you mean, mamma?"

"You'll see, little princess. You'll soar across the Universe to find yourself, and when you do, remember me."

Amber still had no inkling about what her mother's words meant, but her answer had always been the same. "I'll never forget you, mamma." Amber slipped under her mother's arms and wrapped her arms around her waist, pulling her close.

Chuckling, her mother hugged her back just as tightly. "And I'll never forget you, my darling daughter."

Chapter Eight

Typically, Da'fydd detested the presence of servants while he occupied his chambers. Yet, soon after expelling Amber, a chambermaid's unexpected knock resounded at his door, asking if he required anything. His first inclination was to send her away, but then he reconsidered.

She could handle the disarray he'd left behind. It occurred to him that her arrival might not be random, perhaps prompted by Amber's complaints following her abrupt eviction. It would be like a woman to complain of such things.

He observed the chambermaid kneeling as she gathered the splintered wood into a worn-out bag. He clenched his teeth, imagining venting his frustrations on her.

His temper was still very close to the surface. He took a deep breath, his eyes never straying from her figure. He could seize her and toss her onto his bed, and she might even enjoy every second of it as she had on the rare occasions he'd indulged her.

However, Da'fydd had grown weary of her. She no longer provided the entertainment he desired. He couldn't even recall her name or if he had ever inquired about it. The names of the women he had taken to his bed eluded him. In his mind, they were merely fleeting moments of pleasure in his seemingly endless existence.

Da'fydd averted his gaze from the chambermaid, kneeling at his feet, and turned his attention to the hearth on the wall opposite the bed. The embers had diminished to the point where the room had grown noticeably colder. Cold temperatures rarely troubled him, as he could manipulate the surrounding air to maintain his comfort. More often than not, he ignited fires simply for the cozy atmosphere they created.

Da'fydd's gaze returned to the chambermaid, realizing that Amber's presence had ignited more than just his temper. The chambermaid swept the remaining dust into a bag and secured it with a knot. Rising to her feet, she lowered her head deferentially in his direction. "Do you require anything else, m'Lord?" She exuded a playful charm that Da'fydd had once found alluring, albeit briefly.

Approaching her, Da'fydd extended his hand. He rarely engaged in conversation with villagers or servants.

As expected, she offered him a beguiling, coy smile, set the bag aside, and readily placed her hand in his.

He led her towards the bed. He turned her around when he reached the edge and placed her hands on the mattress. "Not a word," he warned as he lifted the hem of her long dress.

The chambermaid nodded as she glanced at him over her shoulder.

"Eyes on the bed," he ordered.

She obeyed just the way he liked it. He didn't tolerate disobedience. Something his servants and villagers had learned over the many long years since he first arrived on Celtan and took over the Lailoken Region.

"Not a sound," he repeated. The woman was always too noisy for his taste which is one of the reasons he hadn't deigned to touch her in quite some time. Da'fydd locked his mind with hers as he exposed her heated core. Not surprisingly, she was already wet for him, and her mind filled with desire. He intensified her desire, freed himself, and slowly filled her. She would do to expel some of his temper and longing for another.

She cried out in pain or pleasure as he surged harder into her. He didn't bother to determine which; his mind focused on Amber and her rejection of him. She would regret discarding him before he taught her what it meant to belong to him: mind, body, and soul.

Da'fydd glanced over at the chambermaid as she sleepily ran her fingers annoyingly down his arm. He placed her arm on her stomach and rolled her to her side while sending a compulsion into her mind to sleep. He wanted to shove her out of his room, but she could hardly keep her eyes open, and despite the rumors, he was not such a cruel Master to serve.

While he had sated himself late into the night, sleep illuded him. He'd hoped the distraction would have quieted his desire for Amber. If anything, it had merely intensified it. He hadn't encountered such a connection with anyone since leaving his home world. He drew in a deep breath. It was his mother's home world, not his, he corrected within his thoughts. A reminder that rankled him to no end.

He would have become the ruling Prince of that world if his cursed Druidic genetics hadn't surfaced. He had thought his people's genetic code could override all other species, but he had been wrong. It hadn't overridden the Druid code coursing through his veins. The longer he fought the pull of the Druid calling, the harder it became for him to exist in that world. He had come close to waiting too long.

Da'fydd had left voluntarily to avoid the stigma of being banished, something that would prevent him from ever returning. His cousin had shown him kindness in that regard.

A sad, sardonic smile crossed Da'fydd's features. He didn't begrudge his cousin for assuming the position of ruling Prince. The cousin, a half-sibling on his mother's side, now governed his preferred home world, while Da'fydd's cursed blood kept him tethered to Celtan.

Despite his own desires, he understood that his destiny lay elsewhere, away from the throne and the responsibilities that came with it. It was a bittersweet realization, knowing that he could only visit his birthplace for short periods, never truly belonging there again. For a brief moment, Amber had given him back some of that connection.

Da'fydd exhaled a heavy sigh as he glanced at the chamber-maid, snoring loudly in her slumber. The thought of rousing her and insisting that she leave crossed his mind, but he dismissed it as too laborious. Instead, he placed his forefinger on her forehead and concentrated. As her snoring subsided, he removed his finger.

Casting aside the covers, Da'fydd perched on the edge of the bed, his naked body welcoming the invigorating chill that enveloped him. He approached the window with pur-poseful strides, drawing back the drape to reveal the twi-light hour—neither morning nor night. Restlessness coursed through his veins, urging him to abandon any hope of sleep.

Allowing the drape to fall back into place, he turned towards the bed and retrieved a clean pair of trousers from his chest. He opted to forgo a shirt, confident that few villagers or servants would be awake at this hour and those awake would not dare take notice.

Stepping out of his chambers, Da'fydd sought something to quench his thirst, resolving to deal with the chambermaid later if she remained upon his return. As he ventured forth, the chilling embrace of the stone floor crept into his bare feet. Cautiously descending the ancient flight of stairs, each soft, deliberate footfall resonated throughout the shadowy corridor. The hushed echoes bounced off the age-worn walls, returning to his ears as faint whispers of a forgotten past.

Upon reaching the second-floor landing, Da'fydd halted and lifted his nose, inhaling deeply. He detected a familiar scent tinged with notes of iron. Quietly, he crept toward the edge of the landing, and the smell grew stronger. He recognized it as blood, and there was an abundance of it. His eyes were irresistibly drawn to the alcove on the tower's second level. Compelled to follow the scent, he left the landing, and with each stride, the odor became more distinct.

Da'fydd wished his eyesight were as sharp as the keen sense of smell he had inherited from his mother. The alcove was shrouded in darkness, but with a wave of his hand, the torches lining the walls burst into life, casting their light upon a body lying on the floor ahead in a crumpled heap.

He rushed to the figure, stopping just a foot away. The long, dark hair veiling the woman's face was unmistakable. Da'fydd knelt by Amber's side, gently brushing her hair with his fingertips. Blood had soaked the strands, tangling them and they clung to her neck. A pool of blood surrounded her lower body, and her thighs were covered in scratches and bruises.

Another scent assaulted Da'fydd's senses, followed by a few others. They were the smells of men who had inflicted such damage on his Amber that an intensely fierce urge within Da'fydd rose.

If it wasn't for the fact that Amber required immediate healing, he would have given in to his desire to hunt down and extract retribution from the perpetrators. After being satisfied they had suffered enough, then, and only then, would he gift them with death.

He realized his fists were clenched against Amber's blood-saturated dress, and he released the ruined material. Staring at her chest, Da'fydd confirmed the rise and fall, indicating she lived, although her breathing was far more labored than he cared for.

He swallowed hard, shoving his anger deep as he reached underneath Amber's knees and upper back, cradling her in his arms. He raised a leg to support her as he rose to his feet.

Amber didn't flinch or make a single sound at the quick movement. He reached into her mind, which surprisingly was not easy to do. He pushed harder to connect his mind with hers to find Amber's mind floating near oblivion. Da'fydd knew he had to act quickly or risk losing her forever.

Da'fydd navigated along the wall, rushing from the alcove to the landing. Running up the stairs to his room while holding Amber tight to his chest, Da'fydd burst inside, sending the door crashing against the wall. He repositioned Amber as her body began to slip from his grasp from the slipperiness of her blood.

"Get out!" Da'fydd bellowed at the chambermaid still sleeping in his bed.

Amber stirred in Da'fydd's arms as the chambermaid jolted awake, startled by his booming voice. She scrambled out of bed, almost tripping on the blanket caught around her bare legs as she grabbed her clothes. She covered the front of her naked body and ran from his bedchamber.

Da'fydd noticed Amber's eyelids flutter open but then closed just as fast. He suspected the movement had been reflexive as he couldn't sense a consciousness within her mind that would indicate awareness.

He kicked the chamber door shut with a loud bang. He placed Amber on his bed, not caring about the blood. He held out his hand and called forth a towel. He carefully wiped away Amber's blood as he divested her of her dress. Once he'd cleaned up what he could with the dry towel, he gathered the discarded garment and towel and tossed them into the hearth. He hurled a fireball into the pile to incinerate them. He entered his bathing chamber and returned with another towel and basin of water. He finished cleaning up the dried blood off his Amber.

He sat beside Amber and cradled her head in his lap. Her pale skin appeared almost translucent. He buried his renewed anger at what had been done to her. He would deal with those who did this later. In this moment, his Amber required his full attention.

He pierced the vein in his wrist with his sharp incisor. He gently coaxed open Amber's mouth and held his wrist to her lips so his blood dripped onto her tongue. She tried to turn her head away. He smiled down at her. Even unconscious, she was too stubborn. He issued a silent command to accept his life's blood. While his genetics was predominantly Druid, his blood was still Dia'Kharn. It would help heal Amber faster than his Druid abilities would do alone.

Da'fydd gently withdrew his wrist from Amber's lips, the wounds sealing with a faint shimmer. He hesitated, his eyes locked on her still form for a moment before his hands glided over her body in a tender, intimate dance. The warmth of his touch spread like an invisible flame, dissolving the remnants of blood that the towels had missed, leaving her skin nearly pristine and unblemished. There would be telltale signs, but they would fade soon enough.

As Da'fydd's healing energy pulsed through Amber, her injuries faded before his eyes. Her once-marred skin felt supple and delicate beneath his roughened touch.

Amber shivered involuntarily, the fine hairs on her arms standing on end as goosebumps cascaded down her limbs. A thrilling current of electricity surged between them, and Da'fydd couldn't help but feel his skin tingle in response, an unspoken connection growing stronger with every passing breath.

With a sudden urgency, Da'fydd tore away the tattered remains of Amber's undergarments, revealing more areas of damaged skin requiring his healing touch. He divested himself of his trousers and covered her body with his, connecting them in every way possible as he continued to mend her, their shared energy creating a bond that transcended their physical forms, drawing them closer in their vulnerable yet powerful embrace.

Amber's muscles unwound beneath Da'fydd's palms, the tension ebbing away as her pain dissolved under his ministrations. He carefully traced his hands up her thighs and across her abdomen. He watched with sorrow as her wounds sealed shut, leaving only a faint yellow hue, like the ghost of old bruises. He knew some traces of the damage would need time to heal naturally and wished he could do more.

Da'fydd's heart ached with the desire to envelop Amber's mind and erase her suffering, to share his life force and take away all her pain. The depth of his longing reminded him why he rarely healed others, even using ancient Druid techniques. There was a price to be paid for such healing.

Regardless of the cost, Da'fydd was determined to help Amber heal as completely as possible, so he ventured into the labyrinth of her mind. Her memories were veiled, but he sensed the crushing weight of anguish beneath the surface. Her psyche was a maelstrom of sorrow, regret, and hatred, and Da'fydd knew he had to tread carefully as he sought to mend her soul. He wouldn't remove the memories that made her who she was, but he would soften their impact.

He completed the ritual healing of his people just as Amber's body twitched, signaling the beginning of her transformation. Da'fydd jerked away reflexively. Her eyelids fluttered open to reveal dark irises that darted around the room before locking onto his gaze. Her initial grogginess gave way to an intense stare as she bolted upright, the rapid healing clearly taking effect.

Becoming aware of her naked state, Amber instinctively crossed her arms to cover her chest and stomach. With a quick motion, she snatched the edge of the disheveled blanket on the bed, wrapping it around herself for a semblance of modesty.

A hint of amusement flickered across Da'fydd's face. For a brief moment, he considered drawing attention to his unclothed state just to have the pleasure of her reaction.

"What did you do to me?" Amber's voice trembled with shock and panic, her eyes wide with disbelief.

"I healed you," Da'fydd patiently replied, his gaze lingering on the exposed curve of Amber's neck, a spot previously hidden by her hair.

"What's wrong with my memory?" She rubbed her head as if in pain, though physically, it would have been impossible. His healing had been quite thorough.

"I healed you," he repeated. Da'fydd's patience began to wear thin, but he fought to maintain his composure.

"No!" Amber's voice rose in anger, her worried face flushed with heat. "You did something to me. What did you do?" The fury in Amber's words was palpable. She repeatedly tapped on her forehead with her palm.

Da'fydd rose to his feet, taking a few purposeful strides away from the bed, then turned and closed the distance between them. He leaned in, his face mere inches from Amber's, and enunciated each word. "I. Healed. You." He wondered if she was being ungrateful or offended by his assistance. Either way, he didn't care to be asked the same question when his answer would remain the same.

Amber's breathing grew labored, and she shook her head in denial. "You did something else. I..." Her gaze wandered, lost. "I don't feel right." Her eyes returned to him, pleadingly searching his face for an explanation.

Da'fydd pivoted and moved to sit on the edge of the bed. Amber unexpectedly shifted to accommodate him. As he settled down, he inhaled deeply. He understood that he should feel remorse for intruding on her body and mind intimately, but he harbored no regrets. He sensed the question she truly wanted to ask, almost as if he could read her thoughts. He could prolong her frustration by waiting for her to voice it or simply give in. With a heavy exhale, he decided to relent.

"The healing process of your mind and memory quiets the emotions of the harmful memories," Da'fydd informed Amber. He was sure she wouldn't understand what he meant.

"Explain," Amber frowned, staring blankly at him.

Da'fydd couldn't help but smile just enough to irritate her. He was not accustomed to being ordered around, especially not by a woman. She will have to learn in time, and he will be the one to teach her. "The memory remains intact without emotional attachment."

"I want my emotions back!" Amber shook her head at him in disapproval. "It doesn't feel right."

A mocking laugh erupted from Da'fydd in response to her demands. It was foolish to him that anyone would want emotional attachments to the most horrid or saddening parts of their lives.

With all the turmoil in Amber's life, why would she disagree? Did she long to feel the misery of her past encounters? It was an unfathomable notion to Da'fydd.

"I want them back." Amber's breath caught in her throat. Tears swam in her eyes. "I need them back," she insisted in a subdued voice.

"Do you?" Da'fydd mockingly asked. He ignored the daggers shooting from Amber's eyes.

Da'fydd put his hand on Amber's head without giving her a choice. He flooded her with all the emotions of that moment, for which he would dole out punishment to those responsible for hurting her later when Amber was better. Her breathing grew more labored. The tears she stubbornly tried to hold back slipped from her eyes and down her delicate cheeks. Da'fydd pulled his hand away but left the emotional storm within her mind.

"Do you?" Da'fydd prodded again, challenging her to plead with him again for those despised feelings.

The emotions would be quieted for Amber, but for him, they would remain fresh. Especially the aftermath of healing her and taking on a portion of her injuries until his natural healing process would silence the injuries he'd absorbed within himself. He had taken a part of her and given a piece of himself in the process.

"No." Amber's reply was soft, like a whimper of someone emotionally defeated.

Da'fydd abruptly withdrew the emotional torrent he had unleashed upon Amber and straightened his posture, causing the bed to dip slightly beneath him. He couldn't help but wonder if he had been too forceful with the emotions, but he believed she needed to experience their intensity to comprehend his actions. Tenderly, he brushed aside her tangled hair and cleared away the glistening tears with the pads of his roughened thumbs. He knew she would require a thorough cleansing, but for now, she truly needed a chance to rest.

"Sleep," Da'fydd commanded.

Amber frowned in confusion. She opened her mouth as if to say something.

Da'fydd watched as Amber's eyes, glistening with unshed tears, grew heavy and finally closed. Her breathing slowed, becoming soft even as she succumbed to a deep, restful slumber. He knew she lacked the strength to resist his compulsion. His gaze followed her chest's rhythmic rise and fall before he leaned in closer. Carefully, Da'fydd hovered over her serene visage, opening his mouth to delicately trace the corners of her eyes with the tip of his tongue, tasting the saltiness of her tears before they dried. He pondered what he would do with her next.

Da'fydd was certain that Amber would struggle against the intimacy forged between them in this moment. As much as he wished she wouldn't, he relished the prospect of the chase. He yearned to play with her emotions in a way he'd never done before, at least not with such intensity or intimacy.

Alternatively, he could let her distance herself, biding his time until she inevitably sought him out. In either scenario, Amber would become his bonded mate. She had no choice—the Universe had determined her destiny.

Perhaps he could keep her confined to his room until she finally accepted her fate. Amber's destiny was inescapable; she just didn't possess the knowledge he did. Not yet, anyway. It seemed increasingly likely that Amber was the type to learn through adversity and not through the wisdom of others.

The sight of Amber asleep captivated Da'fydd as the lingering traces of her sorrow on his tongue tantalized him like an exquisite delicacy. He shifted away from her and slid off the bed. Standing at its foot, he recognized that remaining so close to her any longer would stir emotions and desires he wished to avoid.

At the same time, she required time to fully heal. The more he dwelled on Amber's anguish and the feelings she evoked within him, the more he craved her presence. The connection may have been disconcerting for him as well. Still, he staunchly denied any burgeoning infatuation he did not control. Yet, in the recesses of his mind, he sensed himself plummeting into a chasm of uncertainty.

Protecting someone had never been a priority for Da'fydd, and his failure to shield Amber gnawed at him. Rather than blaming himself, he redirected his ire toward a decision already made. He vowed that those who had harmed her would suffer at his hands. But first, he would have a word with the guard he'd assigned to her earlier.

Chapter Nine

As Amber opened her eyes, a veil of fog seemed to lift from her mind, gradually replaced by the soft light filtering through the curtains. For a moment, the room was a blur; then her vision sharpened. What had been a space shrouded in the hearth's flickering shadows now lay revealed in daylight. She noted every line in the stone walls, the fine layer of dust settling on the wooden furnishings.

The room carried an unmistakable masculine aura, likely undisturbed by any woman's presence, aside from the periodic cleaning by a maid or servant. She pondered whether the shadowy figure she'd thought she'd glimpsed the previous night was one of these women or simply a trick of her imagination, a product of her failing vision from her disoriented mind.

Amber's eyes drifted to the window, tracing the origin of the soft light filling the room. There, ensconced in a chair with its front legs lifted slightly off the floor, sat Da'fydd. His arms folded and his ankles crossed, he rested his feet against the bed's edge. The possibility that he had maintained this vigilant stance throughout the night struck her with a complex blend of unease and comfort.

Despite his assistance, a residual disquiet persisted in her, as if her very cells resisted ease. Memories of the assault still hung like a haze, their invasive touch almost palpable. Yet, her emotional response seemed abstract, hovering at the fringes of her consciousness. While she recognized that anger and sorrow should flood her, those torrents remained frustratingly out of reach.

"Who attacked you?" Da'fydd demanded, his gaze fixed intently on Amber without a blink or the slightest hint of movement in his body. His presence in the room was harsh and chilling, reminiscent of the aura one might associate with a ruthless, dangerous individual.

Amber sat up, clutching the covers tightly to her neck. "What do you care?" she retorted, her glare aimed directly at him.

"Don't make me ask you again," Da'fydd warned, his jaw set.

Amber took in the flawless balance of his features—the chiseled indentations flanking his nose and the prominent cheekbones framing his eyes. His gaze wielded a magnetic pull, each element contributing to the image of a formidable warrior. A silent struggle of resolve unfolded between them. Despite her best effort to maintain her glare, Amber finally broke the contact, diverting her eyes. "I don't know their names," she lied, exhaling deeply. An undercurrent in his voice warned her against revealing the identities of her assailants.

"Then you will point them out to me when the time comes," Da'fydd stated, his tone allowing no room for argument.

Amber bristled, ready to protest, but something in Da'fydd's eyes stopped her. In truth, she knew two of their names but felt a pang of guilt at the thought of revealing that fact. As the room fell silent, Amber focused on her hands, fidgeting with the thick fabric of the blanket in her lap. "Will you harm them?" Amber questioned softly.

"Punishment will be doled out." Da'fydd's gaze remained steady on Amber. She met his eyes for a fleeting moment before averting her own.

"What kind of punishment?" Amber asked, her concern about Da'fydd's capabilities evident in her tone.

"The proper kind." Da'fydd offered Amber a subtle nod, as if expecting her to grasp its meaning.

Amber exhaled, her frustration evident. Her eyes locked with his. "The death kind?" She asked, the words feeling wrong on her tongue.

Da'fydd stared at her without answering, his gaze sweeping over her as if sizing her up. He tilted his head back, the cords of his neck standing out prominently beneath his tanned complexion. "You would have me spare their lives?"

"I didn't say that."

"You didn't say otherwise." Da'fydd's words came out as a matter-of-fact statement without any hint of emotion.

Amber's gaze shifted towards the door, her thoughts trailing off. "I'm not sure," she finally confessed, torn between wanting to protect them and her reluctance to admit aloud what she desired.

Maybe if Da'fydd hadn't muted her emotions when he healed her, she'd have had the courage to speak her mind, or perhaps not. Causing others harm was something she inherently avoided. With a furrowed brow, she worked to dispel the internal chaos that clouded her thoughts.

In truth, she wanted them dead for what they had done to her, but what kind of justice was that? She couldn't bring herself to cause pain, no matter the circumstances. She refused to be the one who named them for death, for it would be no different than if she pulled the trigger herself or carried out whatever punishment was customary on this backward planet.

Suddenly, Da'fydd sat up, and the chair landed on all four legs with a loud thud. He stood up, fixing his gaze on the chamber door. "Stay here," he ordered.

Amber opened her mouth to inquire about his abrupt behavior, but Da'fydd had already stormed out, slamming the chamber door behind him. She sat, her gaze fixed on the door.

Her mind raced to grasp the reason for his sudden exit. Already uneasy since waking, his swift departure intensified her anxiety. She sprang from the bed to the door, pausing with her hand hovering over the handle, uncertain of her next move. For a moment, she sensed his presence on the other side of the door, but the sensation quickly evaporated, leaving her in lingering disquiet, devoid of answers.

Chapter Ten

With purposeful strides, Da'fydd entered the throne room, each step resonating through the stone walls. Disregarding Ethan, Kaily, and Moto, who trailed him like specters. He ascended the dais to his imposing chair and sank into it. Lines of irritation marred his features as he leaned back, elbow perched on the armrest, chin cradled in his hand. His posture radiated indifference, and he regarded the trio before him with unspoken impatience.

Despite the invitation his manner offered, Ethan and the others remained unmoving, their eyes locked on him yet offering no words. Exasperated, Da'fydd gestured for them to proceed, his hand cutting through the air dismissively. "Well?" he demanded, breaking the silence. "What do you want?"

The throne room was sparsely populated, its quiet atmosphere unusual for this time of day. Da'fydd suspected that most had migrated toward the dining hall given the hour. Yet, he was aware that every present ear would be finely tuned to the forthcoming exchange.

Out of his peripheral vision, he spotted Rory and his constant companions lurking in a shadowy corner. The trio
appeared far too engrossed in this unwelcome interrup-
tion. Rory, who usually exuded a boisterous energy, seemed
uncharacteristically subdued. The fool couldn't resist casting furtive glances in Da'fydd's direction, as though seeking something unsaid. Annoyed but not swayed, Da'fydd
brushed off the distraction and refocused on Ethan, Kaily,
and Moto. Whatever game Rory was playing, it could wait.
The immediate matter demanded his full attention.

Ethan strode stiffly towards the dais, his gaze fixed on
Da'fydd. "What have you done with Amber?" he demanded,
his voice laced with anger.

Ignoring Ethan's question, Da'fydd turned his attention to
Kaily, who stood slightly behind his little brother. "Why have
you come here unannounced?" he asked coolly.

Ethan's face flushed with anger as he advanced, closing the
gap between himself and the raised platform where Da'fydd
was perched on his throne. "Show the High Druidess some
respect!" he snapped, his fists clenched.

Da'fydd fixed Ethan with a look of disdain. "What makes
you think I would recognize her right to rule when I did not
recognize Deykin's?"

Although Kaily had claimed the title of High Druidess, Ethan had no right to come to the Lailoken region and make demands, especially that one. Lailoken was his domain, and so was Amber. Ethan had been a fool to retrieve a Druidess that was not his to claim. Da'fydd could almost pity him for his stupidity if he didn't harbor anger at him for bringing Amber to Celtan in the first place.

"How dare you!" Ethan's face flamed with rage. "You've always acted as if you were better than the rest of us, not bound by Celtan's laws."

"Why would you concern yourself with someone who isn't even yours?" Da'fydd asked instead of verbally rising to his brother's bated words. He took pleasure in watching Ethan's face contort with confusion. "You couldn't claim her in truth because she wasn't yours to claim. You've made a mess that I will have to clean up."

"She's my bonded mate! I did what I was supposed to do, and I'll not let you take that from me!" Ethan's voice bellowed throughout the halls. "How dare you say she doesn't belong with me!"

Da'fydd steepled his fingers, resting his elbows on the arms of his ornate chair that resembled a throne, leveling his younger sibling with a stern glare. "And yet you are wrong," he coolly responded. "She was not yours to find but mine."

Ethan's face contorted with anger as he glared at Da'fydd. "I don't believe you," he spat out. "You can't just take what's not yours and claim it as your own. Give her back to me now."

Da'fydd's eyes locked onto Ethan, reading the turbulent mix of anger and underlying pain that filled his brother's gaze. From where he sat, Da'fydd could almost taste Ethan's simmering jealousy. His brother had unintentionally handed him a true mate in Amber. Yet, it was a complex entanglement that Da'fydd had never sought.

"No." With a single word, Da'fydd punctured Ethan's inflated sense of triumph. A perverse sense of satisfaction unfurled within him as he watched Ethan squirm, grappling with his own foiled expectations and the unintended consequences of his actions.

"Enough!" Kaily's voice sliced through the tension like a finely honed blade. She extended her hand toward Ethan, her eyes locking onto his with an intensity that seemed to transcend words. In that prolonged moment, a silent exchange transpired between them, opaque to Da'fydd yet laden with meaning. Whatever communication took place, it was potent enough to momentarily still the currents of discord that had overtaken the room.

A smirk crossed Da'fydd's lips as he sensed Kaily's palpable ire. He entertained himself with the thought of Ethan's potential reactions should he learn about the intimate bond already forming between Amber and Da'fydd. The mere notion added a delicious layer of complexity to an already tense atmosphere, heightening Da'fydd's anticipation for what would unfold next.

Da'fydd's eyes narrowed as Moto approached, clutching the stone Ethan had reluctantly surrendered to Kaily. He'd been mildly surprised when the Kahoali warrior had divested her of the stone.

As he glanced at Kaily, he couldn't help but smirk at her visible agitation. The High Druidess shuffled her feet, arms crossed, biting her tongue but clearly yearning to unleash her thoughts. The visible struggle brought a flicker of amusement to Da'fydd's stern expression.

As for the stone, its significance remained a veiled puzzle piece in a game Da'fydd had little patience for. His eyes met Moto's briefly, a silent exchange of wills. They all had to understand that Amber was his concern, a destiny that would be shaped by his hand alone.

His gaze turned icy, his posture exuding an air of sovereign authority. In his region, his word was law, and he'd make sure everyone present came to understand that fact. None would contest his dominion here. Especially not when it concerned Amber.

"That is Amber's lineage stone," Kaily said, unable to hold her tongue as Moto handed the stone to Da'fydd.

As soon as he took it, the stone began to glow and pulse with energy, like a beacon calling forth its rightful owner. Da'fydd knew exactly what the stone signified, but he didn't reveal that to Kaily or Ethan. He wondered why they were so interested in Amber, but he knew it was his prerogative to decide who had access to her. "The stone is meaningless to me." He dismissed with his words their attempt to claim authority over her. "Amber is under my protection, and I alone will decide her fate."

Da'fydd's gaze shifted from the stone to Kaily as he slipped it into his pocket. "Anything else?" Da'fydd responded with imprudence in his voice.

Kaily visibly bristled at Da'fydd's condescending tone.

Ethan glared at Da'fydd, his eyes narrowing with rage. "We have a right to see Amber!" He started to move closer to the dais, but Moto reached an arm out across Ethan's chest to stop him.

Da'fydd shook his head. "You have no right to her." He turned his stern attention back to Kaily, who appeared to be just as agitated. "Does the stone not confirm as much?"

Ethan's face twisted with anger as he glared at Da'fydd. "You can't keep her here against her will!" he spat.

Moto tightened his grip on Ethan's shoulder, holding him back from further approaching Da'fydd.

Da'fydd's eyes flicked back to Ethan. "Against her will? She's been tended to and is resting comfortably," he sneered. "Besides, it's not like she was taken from you unwillingly."

Kaily stepped forward. "Show us that she is well cared for," she said, her voice shaking slightly.

Da'fydd's attention was diverted from their bickering by a familiar energy approaching. He cursed to himself for his distracted mind. He realized too late that he should have secured his chambers before dealing with the unwanted guests. Apparently, even being naked without female clothing was not enough of a deterrent.

Chapter Eleven

Amber's heart thudded as she frantically searched the room for something to wear. She felt exposed and vulnerable, standing naked in a man's chamber. Panic set in as she realized there was nothing in sight. How could she leave the room without something to cover herself?

She attempted to calm her agitation, but a sense of dread crept up her spine. She shivered, the coldness of the stone walls seeping into her bones. She could still feel the hands of her attackers on her body, their vile words ringing in her ears. Her eyes darted around the room, searching for any clues as to what had happened to her borrowed dress. But there was nothing.

Amber discovered a chest and eagerly lifted the lid. As she did, the scent of woodsy soap mingled with leather filled the air. For a moment, she closed her eyes and indulged in a rare smile. She hadn't permitted herself the luxury of savoring time alone in Da'fydd's presence.

Shaking her head, she refocused, determined to dispel those distracting thoughts. Her hands quickly sorted through the clothes, settling on drawstring pants and a loose shirt. A frown crossed her face; they would undoubtedly be too large. Nonetheless, they were far preferable to navigating the castle in her current state of undress.

Amber pulled the shirt over her head and stared at the edges that practically fell to her knees. She let out a heavy sigh and slipped on the pants. She pulled them up as far as she could, wrapped the drawstring around her waist, and tied it as tightly as possible. The waistband hung loosely around her hips. She shook her head as she knotted the edges of the shirt in an attempt to secure both. She stopped in front of the mirror and studied her appearance. She touched the yellowing bruise on her cheek and frowned. It could be worse, she thought. She took a deep breath and squared her shoulders.

Ignoring Da'fydd's explicit orders, Amber couldn't fight her desperate need for freedom from the confines of his chamber. Her fingers quivered against the chill of the door handle as she nudged it open. Slipping out into the dim hallway, she crept barefoot over the icy stone floor, each footfall reverberating in the stillness.

Amber skidded to a halt on the second-floor landing. Her heart thudded rapidly in her chest as her eyes slid of their own accord to the alcove where the attack happened. A frown marred her features as she stared at the alcove. She waited for a flood of emotions to hit her. None did. None would. Da'fydd had muted her emotions in relation to that memory, and others. She didn't know just how far back he'd muted her feelings. She made a point of not revisiting unfortunate events she has lived through. She glanced at the floor and willed her heart to slow its frantic beating. With a deep breath of determination, she forced her gaze to the stairs and began making her way down the rest.

She skirted past the hidden entrance to the kitchens, her heart racing with a mix of dread and curiosity. At least, Da'fydd hadn't muted her ability to feel, although, her current flood of emotions was not welcomed at this time. Her eyes darted from wall to wall, corner to corner. Uncertainty sent a frisson of anxiety through her, but her need to understand why Da'fydd left so abruptly overwhelmed her. She required answers.

As she neared the dining hall, tingling at the back of her neck drew her attention. The sensation compelled her to redirect her footsteps down a different hallway. She 'followed' the otherworldly sense down one hall and another, her curiosity heightened. Soon, she came upon a door framed by two guards. It was the same room she'd been brought to. Her instincts flared; she knew Da'fydd was inside the throne room even though she couldn't say how she knew. It was just a feeling.

After pausing for a moment to steel herself, she sucked in a deep breath, arranging her features into an expression of unyielding determination. To her astonishment, the guards stepped aside and swung the doors open without a word. As she crossed the threshold, the muffled discussion inside crystallized into recognizable yet indiscernible words. However, the tones were unmistakably charged, laced with an anger she couldn't ignore. Mustering an additional surge of courage, Amber moved through further into the expanse of Da'fydd's throne room, ready to confront the unfolding scene and sage her curiosity.

Chapter Twelve

As Amber stepped into the throne room, Da'fydd's irritation spiked. She had blatantly disregarded his explicit command to remain secluded in his chamber. Yet as he caught sight of her, a cloak of protectiveness enveloped him.

The defiant glint in her eyes stirred something different within him. There was a resilience there, a courage that beckoned him to respect her autonomy. Now he found himself at a crossroads, teetering between his innate desire to shield her from harm and his newfound respect for her unyielding spirit.

Da'fydd had little appetite for igniting another verbal skirmish, particularly with the three whose departure he keenly awaited. Any intervention on his part could lead them to suspect he was Amber's assailant, especially since some bruising remained despite his majikal healing. Such could give Ethan sufficient reason to involve their father, Gregori. The last thing Da'fydd needed was another clash with his already estranged father, adding fuel to their smoldering discord.

Da'fydd and Ethan's relationship was a tapestry of bitterness and open disdain, threads that had been woven from their shared paternal connection to Gregori. Their father was hardly the family man, a vagabond spirit who roamed the Universe, fathering offspring with a laissez-faire attitude. The neglect experienced by Da'fydd in his formative years still clung to him; Gregori had scarcely been a presence, surfacing only when it suited his whims. Even then, his attention was typically focused on Druid Council politics rather than the well-being of his own son.

Da'fydd had long since rejected the strings attached to his place on the Council, unwilling to be yet another pawn in his father's cosmic game. This refusal had only deepened the fractures, but as far as he was concerned, the past was secondary. Now, his eyes and instincts were trained on the present, specifically on Amber, the one person he was unwilling to compromise.

Da'fydd locked eyes with Amber, seizing the moment as an opportunity to introduce her to the concept of telepathy, albeit sooner than he'd originally planned. The urgency of the situation compelled him to bypass gentle introductions. He mentally relayed his message to her, his eyes never wavering from hers: to stand behind him on the dais, and to remain silent.

He saw her eyes widen, a flare of astonishment flickering across her face. Although the weight of the unspoken words hung in the air, he sensed a certain compliance in her gaze. For now, she understood the gravity and didn't challenge him. And for that, he was quietly grateful.

As he glanced around the room, Da'fydd could sense the tension building between Ethan and Amber. Ethan's intense stare made her increasingly uneasy and fidgety. It was clear that Ethan had not yet accepted the fact that Amber belonged to him. Da'fydd was determined to protect Amber, no matter the cost.

Did Ethan hurt you? Da'fydd expected Amber to say yes.

No. Amber stared at the floor.

Then, why are you nervous? You are safe with me, Da'fydd assured her.

Although Da'fydd communicated telepathically with Amber, she didn't reply with words. Instead, she let out a long sigh of relief that eased her mind. Despite sensing her nervousness, Da'fydd observed that she maintained a composed demeanor, assuring him that she had the situation well in hand. He briefly considered maintaining his focus on Amber's thoughts but shifted his attention back to Ethan and the others. He knew that Amber could handle the tension in the room, and he admired her strength and resilience.

Da'fydd observed Ethan and Kaily sharing a look of concern between themselves. *I wish you would have remained above in my chambers.*

Are you mad at me? Amber's eyes appeared heavy with sadness and shame.

No, Da'fydd replied with a slight shake of his head. *Nice outfit,* he teased as he stood and held out his hand to Amber to help her up the steps of the dais and placed her hand on the back of his seat. *We will talk more later.*

Kaily gave Ethan a miniscule shake of her head. It would have been nice for Da'fydd to know what they were thinking or communicating.

"Why is Amber injured?" Ethan's angry voice bellowed through the throne room, causing a hush to fall over the small crowd that had gathered. "Why is she covered in bruises under your care?" His voice rose even higher, resounding with frustration and anger.

As tensions mounted and the atmosphere in the room grew heavy, Da'fydd noticed that Amber was becoming more and more self-conscious, cowering behind his chair. She reached out and placed a trembling hand on the chair near Da'fydd's neck. He could feel her anxiety and fear as she trembled physically and mentally.

Da'fydd sensed that Amber was scared that Ethan might try to take her back, but he was determined to protect her no matter what. He wouldn't let anyone harm her or separate them.

You are not going anywhere, little bird. Da'fydd sensed Amber give a slight nod of her head.

"It's not your concern," Da'fydd responded to Ethan's questions, his voice calm and measured, despite the rage building inside him.

"It is my concern," Ethan retorted, lunging towards Da'fydd.

Moto swiftly caught him in a binding net, preventing him from stepping closer.

"Please, Ethan," Kaily pleaded, trying to calm him down. Ethan's face turned red with anger, but Da'fydd couldn't hear what he said in response.

"It's being handled," Da'fydd said, unconcerned with defending himself. He had never felt the need to and never would.

Da'fydd sensed a small chuckle emanating from Amber's mind, and he smirked to himself in response. *I'm glad you're amused,* he silently communicated, feeling her slight amusement.

Ethan scowled at Moto.

Kaily intervened, placing a hand on Ethan's shoulder and gesturing for Moto to release the binding net.

"Don't touch me!" Ethan yanked his shoulder out from under Kaily's hand. "I'm fine!" he retorted, distancing himself, breathing hard and sweating as if he had just fought in battle.

"It seems your departure is long overdue." Da'fydd gestured with a wave of his hand towards the double doors.

Ethan's eyes darted to the guards stationed along the walls, their postures tense, hands floating close to the hilts of their swords. A visible sign of his exasperation escaped as a huff, and his eyes narrowed into a glare aimed squarely at Da'fydd on his throne. Da'fydd caught the look and couldn't help but find Ethan's frustration almost amusing. His brother's inability to seize control of the room only emphasized Da'fydd's own authority here. A power Ethan would never have.

Da'fydd's eyes shifted to Kaily, who seemed engrossed in scrutinizing Amber. Her gaze was thoughtful, as though she were piecing together a complex puzzle. After taking a moment that felt like an eternity, she inhaled deeply and nodded, as if she'd come to some internal resolution. Then, with a twist of her body, she indicated her intention to leave the room. Da'fydd found himself increasingly intrigued by her actions, even as he pondered the implications for Amber and for himself.

Da'fydd couldn't ignore the ripple of unease emanating from Amber as she crouched behind his chair. She seemed like a vulnerable creature caught in a storm, isolated and tentative. It irked him that she felt she had to hide, though he understood her instinct to do so. The tension in the room had grown taut as a bowstring, a brittle quiet that begged to be shattered. Even though no one had made a hostile move, the promise of conflict hung in the air like an unspoken vow.

He was acutely aware of Ethan's influence on Amber's distress, a notion that curdled in his stomach. His mere presence acted as a bulwark for her, and he couldn't help but wonder if she sensed the lengths he would go to protect her. Even veiled behind his form, her apprehension persisted as if she felt unseen eyes dissecting her very essence.

For the moment, she had entrusted him with her safety, even if that trust was as fragile as a spider's web. The sooner he could rid the room of these unwelcome guests, the sooner he could attend to the layers of complexities that were becoming their entangled lives.

Da'fydd could sense that Ethan was still simmering with anger as he overheard him speaking to Kaily. "What are you going to do about him hurting Amber?"

Kaily's gaze turned sharp as she fixed her eyes on Ethan. "Amber is now under Da'fydd's care. It's his responsibility to handle the situation," she said, rubbing the back of her neck. "Don't interfere in their affairs." Though she didn't sound defeated, it was clear that she had come to realize the hopelessness of the situation.

As Moto nudged Ethan, guiding him towards the exit, Da'fydd caught Kaily's eye. She glanced back at him with a resigned expression, offering a subtle nod as if acknowledging an unsaid understanding between them. Clearly, she had been the voice of reason, tempering Ethan's volatility during their visit.

As the trio exited, making their way through the threshold and out of the room, Da'fydd felt an odd sense of relief coupled with a newfound respect for Kaily's diplomatic skills. The room's atmosphere seemed to lighten, as if a weight had been lifted.

Behind him, Amber moved away from the security of his chair, her hand coming to rest on the armrest. He sensed her easing tension, the cloud of her anxiety slowly clearing away. Despite the friction and the lingering questions, for that moment, a fragile peace settled in the room.

Da'fydd gave her a reassuring nod, conveying that everything would be alright.

"Thank you," Amber murmured, keeping her head down and her tone quiet.

Da'fydd turned his gaze in the direction Amber was staring, already preparing himself for another hostile confrontation. To his surprise, it wasn't the door or the possibility of Ethan's return that held her attention. Instead, her focus was on Rory and his companions, who sat at a distance, watching the unfolding drama.

As their eyes met, Rory quickly looked away, his casual demeanor shifting subtly but noticeably. A disconcerting feeling settled in Da'fydd, a realization that something was awry.

Da'fydd felt a surge of anger and suspicion, but he tamped it down with practiced control. Now wasn't the time for recklessness or outbursts. With Amber's well-being hanging in the balance, he couldn't afford to let another disturbance shatter the tenuous calm they had managed to establish.

Da'fydd returned his attention to Amber. *Was it them? Did Rory and the other two hurt you?*

Amber winced at his questions as if they had hit a nerve.

Da'fydd could tell she heard him but refused to answer, so he asked again. *Did Rory hurt you? Your silence will not save them. I have other ways of finding out, but I would prefer honesty between us.*

Yes, Amber hesitantly answered.

Da'fydd took a deep breath, willing himself to rein in his anger before addressing Amber. *Go back to my chamber and do not disobey me this time,* he warned, holding her immobile with his gaze.

Amber's eyes widened with fear. *Please don't kill them,* she begged.

Da'fydd's face twisted, his eyes narrowing and forehead wrinkling. *Why would I spare them after what they did to you?* It was an unfathomable request to him.

I'm asking you, please. I can't. I won't be able to live with myself. Amber's eyes watered.

The sight of tears welling up in Amber's eyes only fueled Da'fydd's desire to destroy Rory and his friends. It was difficult for him to understand why Amber had asked him not to kill them, and he couldn't fathom how they could have hurt her, yet she still cared if they lived. He was angry and confused, but at the same time, he couldn't bring himself to push Amber away. He wanted to keep her close and protect her from harm.

Da'fydd leaned forward, his fists clenching tightly around the arms of his chair. He furrowed his brow, deep in thought, trying to make sense of his conflicting emotions. On the one hand, he knew he shouldn't care about what Amber had to say, but on the other hand, he couldn't help himself. He had witnessed the devastating aftermath of what the trio had inflicted upon her. Moreover, he grappled with conflicting emotions regarding Amber's fear of Ethan.

As he contemplated Amber's request and her apparent sympathy towards Rory and his friends, Da'fydd couldn't help but wonder what Ethan may have done to frighten her.

Fine. I won't kill them, Da'fydd gave in. He glanced up to lock eyes with Amber. *If they so much as look at you the wrong way, I will punish them in every way they deserve, regardless of what you want. Beg, plead, cry, I won't care.*

Amber nodded, almost like a tick of the head. *Thank you.* She opened her mouth, paused, then shut it again.

What is it? Da'fydd asked.

Nothing. Amber shifted, rubbing her arm as though something was bothering her.

We've been through this before. I won't repeat myself, Da'fydd said, his gaze fixed on her as he demanded an answer.

What will you do to them, then? Amber asked, her voice quavering in her own mind.

Don't fret about it. Only know I will not kill them as you have asked. Da'fydd leaned back on his throne. *Return to my chamber. I'll meet you there after I'm satisfied with the situation.*

As Amber hesitated, Da'fydd sensed her unease, a reflection of his own unresolved tensions. With a nod meant to instill confidence, he watched her draw a deep breath and walk towards the door. Her posture was rigid, her gaze fixed ahead as if she could escape the room's heavy atmosphere by simply not acknowledging it.

Once she was out of sight, a torrent of repressed emotions surged within Da'fydd. His thoughts shifted ominously to Rory and his companions. Visions of doling out a brutal, public justice clouded his mind, a dark fantasy where he could vent his frustration and establish, beyond any doubt, the gravity of transgressing against him or against those he held dear.

But he snapped himself out of it, taking a slow, steadying breath. He knew that such measures, while emotionally satisfying, wouldn't solve the deeper issues at hand. His focus should be on Amber's safety and on maintaining a fragile peace, even if every fiber of his being screamed for vengeance.

Shaking his head, Da'fydd avoided glancing over at Rory, who sat too close for comfort. Regret flooded through Da'fydd as he realized how oblivious he had been to Rory's actions all this time. He questioned how he could have missed this about him. Perhaps he had been too preoccupied with other things or simply didn't care enough to pay attention. Whatever the reason, the thought that Amber's attack may have been his own fault made his stomach drop.

Da'fydd's burst of frustration slowly subsided, and his unpleasant thoughts faded to the back of his mind like a storm passing overhead. He knew he would have to contemplate his past actions or lack thereof, at a later time.

His attention shifted back to Rory, and their eyes locked in a cold, dark stare. Da'fydd's features contorted into a small, menacing smile as he contemplated revenge. The thought of inflicting pain on Rory and his accomplices filled him with a sense of satisfaction, and he knew he would make them pay for what they had done to Amber.

Rory took several steps backward before turning and fleeing towards the double doors leading out of the throne room, followed closely by his friends. Da'fydd couldn't help but be amused by Rory's predictability and cowardice. He imagined the thrill of hunting Rory down like a predator chasing its prey.

As Rory and his friends escaped, Da'fydd leisurely stood up, stretching his neck and arms, the joints cracking loudly. He held up his hand, summoning a broad sword that shone brightly in the light of the throne room. He drew a deep breath and let a slight, sinister grin spread across his face.

"Let the hunt begin." Da'fydd declared, stepping off the dais and moving towards the exit with a languid grace. Da'fydd knew his prey could run all they wanted, but they wouldn't escape his wrath.

Chapter Thirteen

Amber felt the weight of the stares as she exited the throne room, an unsettling sensation that normally would have made her skin crawl. However, a sense of safety accompanied her, a quiet assurance she reluctantly admitted had something to do with Da'fydd's presence. He'd thrown her out of his room earlier, an action that should have ignited a firestorm of resentment within her. Yet, that anger was clouded by a different emotion: gratitude.

He had healed her, a fact she couldn't simply dismiss. Although her emotions surrounding the memory had been muffled, as if dulled by an unseen hand, her feelings were an ambiguous blend of anger and thankfulness. She wrestled with the complexity of it all, questioning why these contradictory emotions were swirling within her as she made her way out of the room.

As Amber ascended the stairs to Da'fydd's tower, a sense of relief washed over her. She was grateful that she hadn't been handed back to Ethan and that Da'fydd had listened to her pleas not to kill Rory and his friends. She couldn't bear the thought of being responsible for another's death, no matter the pain she had endured at their hands. It wasn't precisely sympathy she felt for them but rather a deep reverence for life in general. She'd witnessed too much death in her life to have such disregard for others.

As Amber pondered the inexplicable shift in Da'fydd's attitude, she found herself grappling with a confusing mix of emotions. Guilt? On his part? The notion seemed laughable; Da'fydd didn't strike her as the type to be swayed by such a vulnerable emotion. Just last night, he'd excoriated her and booted her from his room, accusing her of wrongs she hadn't committed. No, guilt didn't seem like his modus operandi.

Yet, something had undeniably shifted in him. His guarded demeanor had transitioned into something akin to protectiveness, perhaps even laced with a subtle kind of adoration. The corners of her mouth lifted in a small, bemused smile as she recalled the way he'd regarded her earlier. It was as if she'd suddenly become something invaluable to him, an object of tenderness that required safeguarding.

But why this transformation? Amber shook her head, unable to make the pieces of the puzzle fit. While the shift was jarring, it wasn't wholly unexpected. Their initial meeting had been anything but ordinary, a tangle of awkwardness and palpable tension that defied easy explanation. Now, despite her confusion, curiosity smoldered within her, compelling her to explore the enigmatic being that Da'fydd had become.

Regardless of the reason for his abrupt change, she found herself unexpectedly drawn to this new version of him; so different from the man who had expelled her from his room just the night before. Yet, for all her fascination, she couldn't ignore a sense of caution that niggled at her consciousness.

Da'fydd had proven himself unpredictable, and the prudent course of action was to protect her heart from his mercurial nature. Even as she acknowledged this, she couldn't completely resist the allure that was pulling her towards him, causing her to question, to ponder, and, despite herself, to hope.

As she neared the slightly open door of Da'fydd's chamber, Amber was gripped by a wave of regret. She mentally chided herself for not accepting his offer earlier before the cascade of unfortunate events had unfolded. Yet, a more cynical part of her whispered that had she done so, he might have sought his own gratification only to discard her when he was done. That's what men like him did, or so her past experiences had taught her.

Still, the tender protectiveness he'd shown earlier flickered in her memory. It conflicted with her earlier assumptions, throwing her internal compass off balance. She could only hope that his newfound concern wasn't a mask for pity. That would be the final insult, one her pride might not recover from. Amber steeled herself, reminding herself that she had her own strengths.

As Amber's hand met the wooden surface of the door, she took a deep breath to steel herself, then pushed it open further. To her surprise, a chambermaid was in the midst of tidying up, her focus near the doorway. Upon seeing Amber, the maid hastily gathered her cleaning supplies, brushing past her without meeting her eyes, and exited the room.

A fleeting sense of déjà vu washed over Amber as she observed the maid's hurried retreat. But the moment she tried to pinpoint the reason, the feeling evaporated like morning mist under a blazing sun. Shaking off her lingering thoughts, she secured the door behind her, sliding the crossbar into its place.

Though the action should have provided some assurance, her instincts remained on high alert. As she surveyed the room, she made a silent vow to herself: she wouldn't be caught unprepared again, or at least she'd strive not to be. Mastering that level of constant vigilance was still a work in progress, but it was a challenge she was willing to accept.

Settling onto the edge of the bed, Amber allowed herself a moment of stillness, her thoughts whirling like leaves in a tempest. She replayed the recent horrors: her abduction by Ethan, the hair-raising flight through treacherous woods. As if being tossed into an entirely different world wasn't disorienting enough, the last few days had thrust her into a whirlwind of chaos. She exhaled a weary breath and massaged her temples, her eyes closing momentarily as if to shut out her new reality.

When her eyes flicked open again, they roamed the room, as if expecting the walls or furnishings to yield answers to questions she couldn't yet put into words. Her gaze landed on her own hands, now wrapped in fine but foreign fabrics, a stark reminder of her disorienting reality.

As Amber lay back against the bed's plush pillows, her thoughts inevitably drifted toward Da'fydd. Despite her failed attempt at a relationship back on Earth, something about him struck a chord deep within her. Her eyelids felt heavy as she considered the risks, weighing them against the tantalizing pull of the unknown.

Chapter Fourteen

Da'fydd's steps were measured and unhurried as he made his way toward the edge of the village. His sharp senses were already picking up the scent of Rory and his friends, their tracks easy to follow. A small smile played on his lips as he knew they were no match for his hunting prowess. A soothing wave of tranquility enveloped Da'fydd, instilling in him unwavering confidence that he would catch up to the trio at his leisure.

There existed no place they could flee to where he wouldn't discover them. His extraordinary olfactory prowess would ensure that tracking them during the chase would be effortless. He relished their flight, much like a cat that revels in the exhilaration of hunting down a mouse, toying with it, and ultimately consuming its prey. Not that he cared much for cats or any such animal some worlds liked to keep as pets. Still, the comparison was appropriate.

What are you doing? Amber's pondering thought invaded his mind. Da'fydd sensed that she wasn't expecting an answer and wasn't even aware that she had projected her thoughts to him.

Da'fydd's lips curled into a grin. *Hunting.* As he sensed Amber's surprise at her idle question being unexpectedly answered, his grin transformed into one of satisfaction.

He returned his focus to his hunt. A rush of excitement at the prospect of catching his prey enveloped him. With his sword poised on his shoulder, Da'fydd drew in a deep breath, sifting through the myriad scents outside his castle. The medley of odors was far from enticing, yet his sole focus was on discerning Rory's unique pungent fragrance. He meticulously sorted through the aromas until he pinpointed the foul odor, directing his attention toward its source.

The trio had already sprinted past the village and entered the forest. Now enveloped by the woodland, locating them would not prove much of a challenge, much to Da'fydd's disappointment.

What are you doing, little bird? A grin spread across his face upon sensing her sharp intake of breath. He waited a heartbeat for a reply. None came. Amber had a wealth of knowledge yet to acquire, and he was eager to impart his wisdom. This prospect provided a glimmer of anticipation for events yet to unfold.

Navigating between structures that scarcely qualified as dwellings, Da'fydd arrived at the village's periphery, pausing to gaze into the forest. He drew in a breath, verifying that he remained on Rory's unmistakable trail. The scents of Rory's companions grew more pronounced, but Da'fydd's pursuit focused on Rory as his primary target. The others were inconsequential, mere sheep devoid of independent thoughts or actions. Regrettably, their feeble-minded allegiance meant they would share in Rory's impending doom.

Entering the forest with an air of tranquility, Da'fydd's boots crushed twigs underfoot as he strode forward, the snapping reverberating off the withering trees. He could faintly discern the sounds of Rory's flight in the distance. As he ventured deeper into the woods, Da'fydd realized he had nearly closed the gap. The scent of Rory's fear-induced sweat fueled his ferocious instincts. The fleeing figures appeared like insects darting through the underbrush, but he could now see them clearly. Drawing nearer, a cliff that bisected the forest came into view. Rory and his cohorts, Hamish and Gavin, found themselves cornered between the precipice and Da'fydd's relentless pursuit. Escape was no longer an option.

No, please don't. Amber implored, but her words held no sway in Da'fydd's thoughts. Her pleas were a faint murmur, effortlessly dismissed as he zeroed in on his quarry.

Da'fydd closed in on Rory and his companions, cornering them with nowhere to flee. Terror seized their expressions, yet Rory's fear held Da'fydd's attention. He yearned for Rory to experience every agonizing moment of pain and torment he intended to inflict as partial payment for what he'd done to his Amber. With a mere flourish of his hand, Da'fydd ensnared all three men in an invisible binding net, rendering them immobile. Trapped in his sinister grip, they could only wait helplessly as he mulled over their impending doom. However, before sealing their fate, Da'fydd needed to know why.

Da'fydd, his expression cold and unforgiving, stepped forward to address the immobilized men, focusing on the main perpetrator. "Now, Rory," he began, his voice icy, "I trust you realize the consequences of your actions."

Rory's eyes glimmered with defiance.

Da'fydd knew he would have spat at his boots if he were able. Da'fydd moved his hand ever so slightly, loosening the net enough for Rory to have a smidgen of mobility. Just enough to further anger him.

"To hell with ye and yer little harlot," Rory snarled. Yet, beneath his audacious words, his trembling form betrayed his terror.

One of Da'fydd's dark eyebrows arched nonchalantly. "I've allowed you into my home, allowed you to dine at my table, and endured your incessant favor-seeking. Yet this is how you repay my kindness?" He shifted his stance and sword, pausing before continuing, "It appears I've been too lenient with you. Many of your transgressions have gone unpunished. You've taken for granted the privileges you've been granted at my allowance."

"Let me go, ye coward, and face me in a square go!" Rory challenged, his voice filled with ire. "Ye are nothin'!"

"Bold words from a man quaking with fear," Da'fydd taunted, his laughter dripping with scorn. "You won't be victorious." He briefly entertained the notion of setting Rory free from the binding, giving him a chance to humiliate himself further.

"At least I'll die knowin' I wasn't tethered," Rory growled, his eyes filled with hatred. His two friends stayed silent, their gazes fixed on the ground.

Da'fydd could almost feel pity for their wretched lives, bound to a groveling, spineless excuse of a man.

"What part did you two play?" Da'fydd directed his question to Hamish and Gavin.

Gavin hesitated before speaking, his voice tinged with reluctance. "We kept watch, m'Lord."

Hamish chimed in, adopting a similar tone, "And helped restrain her, m'Lord, but we didn't want to do it."

Da'fydd's gaze bored into Hamish and Gavin with a look of disgust etched on his features. "And yet you dared to participate in his deplorable actions against what was mine," he spat, his voice filled with contempt. "You both knew what was right and chose to ignore it. You could have stood against Rory, but you chose to partake in his twisted game instead."

He took a step forward, his sword glinting menacingly in the light. "You will learn that such actions will not be tolerated in my region. You will pay for your misjudgment."

Both men bowed their heads, their shame palpable, visibly trembling. "Please, m'Lord," Hamish begged, his voice cracking on the words. "We didn't know what we were doing. We were caught up in Rory's twisted ideas and are so sorry for what we've done."

"Aye, we beg for your mercy," Gavin added, his eyes pleading with Da'fydd. "We were fools to follow Rory, and we'll do anything to make it right. Please spare us, m'Lord."

Da'fydd tightened his grip on his sword, his eyes narrowing with anger as his gaze shifted toward Rory. "Loyalty to another should never justify such despicable actions," he growled.

Da'fydd narrowed his eyes, his gaze flicking back to Hamish and Gavin. "Your words do little to alleviate the damage you have caused," he said, his voice cold and unyielding. "You have betrayed my trust, and you will suffer the consequences."

"But," he continued, after a long pause, "I am willing to give you a chance to make better decisions. Make no mistake, if you fail, your punishment will be severe." Da'fydd released the binding net on Hamish and Gavin with a flick of his hand, allowing them to move freely. "Stay out of my sight."

Gavin and Hamish bowed their heads and darted away. Da'fydd's eyes followed them as they disappeared into the forest. They were nothing but dogs who did everything Rory expected or asked them to do.

Da'fydd's gaze flickered to Rory. His annoyance was evident on his face. The sword resting on his shoulder glinted in the light, poised for a swift and deadly strike.

"As for you, Rory," Da'fydd said, his voice cold and harsh. "Your punishment will not be so lenient. Your jealousy and selfishness have brought you to this point, and now you will pay the price for your deplorable actions."

Rory's eyes widened with fear. Da'fydd noticed him shrinking back, the man's bravado faltering in the face of his anger. Again, Da'fydd briefly considered releasing the binding net that held him captive, allowing Rory to stumble backward off the precipice upon which he'd been cornered.

Da'fydd placed the tip of his sword against Rory's chest just above his heart. He pushed the sharp end in just enough to draw blood. He prepared to sink his blade deeper when a voice stopped him. *You promised not to kill them.*

Impressive, little bird. Da'fydd responded to Amber. A sense of admiration flowed through him as he realized her silent communication had been intentional. *You learn fast.* He didn't allow her time to respond before continuing his silent discourse. *I agreed not to kill them. I never promised, little bird.* Da'fydd smirked, watching Rory struggle against the binding net. The foul stench of urine that emanated from him made Da'fydd's nose wrinkle in disgust. He took some satisfaction from his captive, being too terrified to control his bodily functions. *Besides, I let Hamish and Gavin go.*

"If only the binding net could keep you from soiling yourself," Da'fydd's tone dripped with disdain.

It's the same thing, Da'fydd. You say you won't do something, and in a way, you are genuinely making a promise, a vow. How could you break it? Amber's words grated on Da'fydd's mind.

If I say I promise, that's a promise. I said I would not do it but didn't make a vow to you. Nothing is being broken. Da'fydd's eyes narrowed.

You're parsing details to fit your own desires, Da'fydd. How can I trust a man whose actions do not match his words? Da'fydd bristled at the defeat he heard in Amber's silent voice. It irritated him that she seemed to be losing faith in him already.

In a way, she was right, and it annoyed him. He would be breaking an agreement he'd made with her. Da'fydd turned away from his prey, his sword tip dug into the soil at his feet as he let the blade drop downward. He took a second to ponder. With an angry growl, he conceded. *You win, little bird.*

It's not about winning. Amber scoffed.

Isn't it?

NO!

I will honor our agreement, Da'fydd said. *For now,* he added after a pause.

What is that supposed to mean? Amber demanded.

A smirk crossed Da'fydd's face. *It means they had better not anger me again.* Da'fydd's smirk widened at Amber's silent response, knowing he had succeeded in asserting his dominance over her despite giving in to her unreasonable request.

With a flick of his wrist, Da'fydd conjured a shimmering portal before them. Extending his hand in a swift motion, he propelled Rory into the swirling gateway, bonds, and all. A part of him relished the idea of Rory remaining restrained on the other side, but he knew the portal's nature would dissolve the binding net during transit. The entrance would deposit Rory on the barren outskirts of the volcanic badlands, a wasteland that scorned life itself. While Rory would remain on Celtan, making his way back to the Lailoken region would be difficult. That is, if the fool dared to return.

Chapter Fifteen

Amber blinked, her gaze refocusing on the intricate patterns of the bed's canopy. She found herself suddenly severed from Da'fydd's mind, unsure whether she had involuntarily retreated or if he had deliberately closed off his mind to her. The unexpected mental connection had startled her, even led her to question its reality. Yet she couldn't deny various strange phenomena she'd encountered on her journey across different worlds before arriving at Earth. This was merely another enigma to add to the growing list.

Amber closed her eyes again and focused intensely on Da'fydd. *What did you do with him?* Amber gently massaged her temples to alleviate the dull ache which throbbed in tempo with her racing thoughts.

Startled, Amber rolled forward and sprang to her feet, her eyes locking onto Da'fydd's as he materialized at the foot of the bed. The sudden appearance caught her completely off guard, and a shiver ran down her spine, intensified by the chill air he seemed to bring with him.

I sent them away. And if the trio knows what's best for them, they will remain gone. Be content that they still live. Da'fydd sat in his chair, still near the bed from that morning.

"You didn't have to sneak up on me like that," Amber glowered, her hand covering her heart, willing it to slow its frantic beating.

Da'fydd smirked. "It was faster to portal inside." He crossed his arms over his chest.

Amber shifted on the bed, her gaze lingering on Da'fydd's relaxed form. The way he sat there, at ease, was a far cry from the fierce, unforgiving man she had previously witnessed. It was like seeing him in a new light, and the realization hit her like a bolt of lightning. She wanted him. Her body hummed with a primal desire she couldn't ignore. It was as if every fiber of her being was drawn to him. She couldn't resist the urge to reach out and touch him, to explore every inch of his body. But she knew it was a dangerous game to play. She had no idea what the consequences might be, what price he might extract from her, but the pull was too strong to ignore.

No need to be shy. Da'fydd eased forward, deftly unfastening his boots. With a muted thud, they found their place on the floor. *I hear you and all you desire, little bird.*

Amber's heart pounded in her chest as she scrutinized Da'fydd's features, desperate to decipher the enigma before her.

His unspoken words seemed layered, leaving her uncertain and on edge. Was he taunting her or offering a glimpse into his genuine thoughts? Her confusion intensified the emotional chaos swirling within her. The burgeoning heat between them puzzled her even more. Why was she even contemplating intimacy? It was something she'd always steered clear of, and yet here she was, drawn inexplicably to the man whose actions and demeanor defied comprehension.

Da'fydd rose from his chair with an elegant fluidity that captured Amber's attention. Taking measured steps, he closed the distance between them. He extended his hand to take hers, gently but firmly pulling her to her feet. As he led her toward the window, a hitch caught in her throat, and her pulse quickened. The simple act of him guiding her felt charged with an undefined tension, leaving her in a state of suspended expectation.

His voice, low and imbued with a compelling huskiness, prompted her to follow his gaze out the window. "Look out there," Da'fydd urged. "What do you see?" His tone invited her not just to observe, but to deeply consider, setting her senses on high alert.

Her eyes scanned the landscape beyond the glass, but her focus wavered, upended by the warmth of Da'fydd's breath against her neck. What she uttered in response sounded disjointed, even to her own ears.

A soft chuckle emanated from Da'fydd as his arms circled her waist from behind, anchoring and unsettling her at the same time. "Do you see beauty when you gaze out upon this world?"

She hesitated, her gaze drifting over the sparse forest and distant rolling landscape. Her shoulder lifted in a tentative shrug. Yes, perhaps there was beauty, but it was overshadowed by the complex enigma that was Da'fydd, filling the room and her thoughts, making the view outside seem almost trivial.

Every world has a unique quality if one looks close enough. A sentiment Da'fydd was just beginning to experience for himself.

Catching his eyes in a brief, over-the-shoulder glance, Amber offered a small smile. She then turned her gaze back to the view beyond the window, her mind a tangle of thoughts, most of which stubbornly remained on the man standing too close behind her.

"The beauty of the Universe is all around us." He paused, his lips brushing against her ear. *But do you see the beauty that lies within you, Amber? The exquisite beauty that I see every time I gaze upon you?*

Amber's heart swelled with emotion, her body leaning back against Da'fydd's as his arms tightened around her. She knew then, without a doubt, that she wanted him, despite not wanting to feel this deep, uncontrollable desire inside her. She wanted him in every way imaginable. And from the way his body pressed against hers, she could tell he wanted her too.

I hear your desire for me, little bird.

You hear nothing, Amber countered.

Da'fydd's embrace sent a rush of emotions through Amber, a desire that excited and scared her. She attempted to push down the thrill coursing through her at his touch, but it was futile.

A soft chuckle caressed her ear. *I hear all of you, Amber,* Da'fydd's whisper flowed into her mind. *I have started the bonding process with you. I know you can feel it, as do I.* He leaned in, and Amber's body pressed involuntarily back against him. "I don't wish to fight it as you do, but I won't touch you without your consent now that you're healed."

A frown crossed Amber's features. There it was. Da'fydd had done something without her permission, but Amber couldn't find it in herself to be angry, although a part of her knew she should. Her desire for him overrode all other emotions, and the sensation of him saying her name in her head drowned her. There was something so incredibly sensual of mind-to-mind words whispered. She sighed, and her eyelids drifted shut.

Da'fydd released her.

Amber pivoted, suddenly aware of the absence of his warmth, her skin tingling where his touch had just been.

Da'fydd smoothly lifted his shirt off, the fabric gliding over his shoulders and head before landing softly beside his discarded boots. *I can strengthen our bond if you allow me.*

Amber hesitated for a moment, her desire warring with her fear. But then she leaned into him, her body pressing against his. She swallowed, the sudden dryness of her mouth making her parched. *How?* Amber whispered within his mind, too afraid to break the moment between them with the sound of her voice.

Da'fydd bit into his wrist, the same spot as he'd healed Amber. Blood dripped down his forearm. *Drink it, feel it.* He cupped the back of her head but did not force her head to dip to his wrist. She had to willingly take what he offered her.

Amber stared at his sharp cuspids that suddenly resembled fangs. Her eyes flew up to lock with his. She hesitated.

Da'fydd leaned in closer, his breath hot against her skin. "Don't be afraid, Amber," he whispered, his lips grazing her neck. "Let me show you the beauty of our connection, the depth of our bond." His hands slid down her body, eliciting a shiver that ran through her. "I promise to be gentle," he added, his voice imbued with a deep, velvety timbre. "But you must trust me."

Caught in an invisible current of emotion and desire, Amber found herself leaning in, even as Da'fydd tilted his head closer to hers. The space between them shrank until it was no more, as if some unseen force had guided them into this vulnerable but electrifying moment. Her lips met his, a soft but meaningful contact that seemed to ignite the air around them. It was as if a hidden reservoir of feelings burst forth, making her heart race, and sending shivers down her spine. She wrapped her arms around his neck, deepening the kiss. He responded in kind as his hands slid down her back and drew her in to close the last bit of space between them.

As he broke their kiss, Amber gasped for air, her eyes again locked on his. "What was that?" she whispered.

Da'fydd smiled, his dark eyes sparkling. *That, my little bird, was just the beginning.* He gave a nod of his head, and her eyes drifted down to land on the blood trickling out of his wrist.

Amber's lips parted, and she extended her tongue to the two small gashes on Da'fydd's wrist, tasting the metallic metals she expected to find in his blood. There was something else she tasted. A sweetness not unlike warm, molten chocolate coated her tongue as an indescribable fragrance invaded her senses.

In that instant, an inexplicable connection surged through her, filling her with a warmth that radiated from her core to every extremity. She didn't need to understand it; it felt as if this moment had been written in the stars long before they'd ever met. With her eyes closed, she surrendered to the emotion, allowing herself to exist, however briefly, in this perfect slice of time with him.

Fully unguarded for the first time, Da'fydd let Amber draw in the very essence of his being, opening mental floodgates that had long been sealed. Raw and vulnerable, he withheld nothing, even letting her glimpse the corners of his mind he often shrouded in secrecy. It was a gamble, this soul-exposing intimacy, but one he was compelled to take. And so, he let her see him, not just the surface but the depths, every facet of his complex self.

Her eyes flew open in astonishment. Amber lifted her head to meet Da'fydd's gaze. She'd seen him, really seen him, in a way she never thought possible. The exposure was exhilaratingly daunting, and she experienced a curious blend of vulnerability and trust in that moment. *I see and feel everything about you.* Not that she could make sense of any of it. The images cascaded through her consciousness too swiftly for her to fully grasp. It was like trying to capture raindrops in a sieve, each fleeting glimpse more elusive than the last. Yet, even if she couldn't decipher the details, the emotional impact lingered, leaving her feeling inexplicably connected to him.

He smiled at her as he encouraged her to continue taking in his life force without words but with emotions.

She complied with his wishes.

His hands emanated energy with every gentle touch of her body. He had no choice but to let her in if he wanted to fully bond with her. She would be his and would remain out of anyone else's clutches. Destiny had played a hand in his favor, and he could not have been happier despite the complications his bonded mate brought into his life.

Da'fydd slipped his ill-fitting shirt from Amber's shoulders. He clucked his tongue at her. *This exquisite body should not be clad in this way.*

Amber shrugged her shoulder, and her eyes sparkled at him.

He chuckled. *You've had enough.*

Amber lifted her head and licked the last few tantalizing drops from her lips. Her eyes followed his every move as he held his palm over the open wounds. The gashes quickly mended back together, and only tiny bruises remained.

You are mine. Da'fydd whispered into Amber's mind.

Amber's stomach clenched, and her heart skipped a beat. *Am I?* Amber touched his face and cupped his jawline, inexplicably mesmerized by this man.

His intense gaze held hers. *You are!* Da'fydd kissed Amber's cheeks one at a time. He gradually slid his trousers down her legs, his eyes never leaving hers. *Breathe, Amber.* Amusement flowed from his mind to hers.

I am, aren't I?

Da'fydd shook his head at her, eyes filled with desire so intense he knew she wanted to look away. He didn't let her. He kept his will locked with hers. When they were both suitably naked, he lifted Amber into his arms. He intended to show her just how completely she belonged to him.

Chapter Sixteen

Amber awoke with a start, her heart racing from the vivid dream that had begun to fade from her conscious mind. She blinked a few times, trying to adjust her eyes to the dim light of the room. Glancing around, she realized she was in Da'fydd's bed, snuggled under the blankets with him. The memories of last night came flooding back to her, causing a blush to spread across her cheeks. She stretched her hand toward him, sliding across his warm, bare skin. His light breathing next to her sent shivers down her spine.

For a moment, she lay there, lost in thought, contemplating what had happened between them. It was sudden and unexpected, yet she couldn't deny her intense connection with Da'fydd. A soft smile tugged at the corners of her lips as she realized she didn't want to let go of him.

Da'fydd stirred beside her, and his eyes fluttered open. He turned his head, his eyes locking with hers as a lazy smile played across his lips. "Good morning, little bird," he murmured, his voice still husky with sleep. "Did you sleep well?"

"Morning," she whispered and nodded, scooting towards him on her side. With her finger, she traced a path down his chest as she relived the previous night's events in her mind. She couldn't help but frown. "What are you?"

Da'fydd's lips curled into a smile. "What are we, would be a more appropriate question."

Amber avoided eye contact and spoke in a quiet voice. "Why was I brought here?" she asked, pushing Da'fydd's previous response out of her mind. "And why is there so much interest in me? I don't understand. I'm nobody important." She glanced around the room as if searching for clues about her situation. Why had Ethan brought her to that world? The uncertainty made her feel powerless and insignificant.

Da'fydd's expression softened as he brushed a lock of dark hair away from her face. "You, my little bird, are far from nothing." He climbed out of bed, the blanket falling from his naked body. He retrieved the stone from his discarded clothing and climbed back in bed beside Amber. He smiled at Amber's slight embarrassment from the flush in her cheeks. He handed her the stone, and it flared to life. "This is why."

Amber's eyes darted from the stone to Da'fydd's face. She furrowed her brow. "I don't understand." Her eyes were drawn back to the smooth stone set perfectly in the palm of her hand.

It pulsated with light and hummed with life. Her eyes drifted back to Da'fydd. She wanted to know everything all at once.

Da'fydd reached his hand towards Amber's and caressed the stone in her palm with the lightest of touches. An electrical current passed between both of their bodies. "From my understanding, the previous High Druidess sent all the females with Druidic abilities away from Celtan."

"Why?" Amber asked, her confusion growing as she attempted to understand it all.

Da'fydd shrugged. "Unknown and not important."

Amber sat up and scooted so her back rested against the headboard. "Where did she send them?"

"Out into the Universe," Da'fydd huffed lightly.

"Where?" Da'fydd's vague responses only fueled Amber's persistence, making her all the more determined to get answers.

Da'fydd let out a heavy sigh, raising an eyebrow. "Out, and it doesn't matter specifically where they were sent." His tone was tight with his growing frustration.

"Alright," Amber conceded. She breathed out a long exhale. "What does that have to do with me?"

"Kaily, the woman here yesterday, can return those lineages to Celtan." Da'fydd knew the explanation would be complicated, but he attempted to simplify it for her.

Amber frowned. "What do you mean lineages? How long ago were these women sent away?"

"About three thousand years ago." Da'fydd scooted closer to Amber.

"And I'm from one of these lineages?"

"Seems so," Da'fydd nodded.

"I still don't understand. Ethan acts as if he has some claim to me. Why would he act that way?" Amber's eyes searched Da'fydd's, pleading for him to provide an answer.

Da'fydd rolled over onto his back, pulling Amber gently down with him. She nestled into his side, her head resting on his chest as she listened to the steady rhythm of his heartbeat. She lifted her head and gazed at him, waiting for an answer. "Da'fydd?"

"It doesn't matter." Da'fydd turned his head as his eyes landed on the far wall.

"It matters to me. Why does Ethan think I belong to him? Why did he come for me?" Amber nudged her body against Da'fydd's.

Da'fydd gently stroked Amber's spine with a light draw of his fingertips, almost tickling her. "The stones are tied to specific lineages. Don't ask for more. I didn't stick around for a detailed explanation when Kaily summoned the Council." Da'fydd eyed the stone still in Amber's hand. "The stones respond to a true mate's touch."

Amber's eyes narrowed briefly. "My stone responded to Ethan?"

"Must have. I wasn't there when he approached the basin." Da'fydd wasn't going to bother explaining about the basin. There was already too much to cover.

"But it responds to you, too," Amber noted.

Da'fydd only nodded. He didn't fully understand it, either, so how would he help her with all this? It was something they'd have to learn and go through together.

Amber sat up, pulling the covers with her, keeping them covering her chest. "Kaily left me with you because you are my true mate?"

"Seems so." Amber was becoming increasingly frustrated with Da'fydd's terse responses.

"Seems so? Either I am, or I am not." Amber's eyes narrowed on him. "I am, aren't I?"

Da'fydd reached up and linked his fingers behind his head. His eyes remained locked with hers. "Yes."

"You had no intention of ever looking for me, did you? If Ethan hadn't brought me to Celtan, I would still be in the dark about who I am, wouldn't I?" Amber angrily demanded as she slid towards the edge of the bed. The subtle distance she placed between them was almost like a boundary, a physical manifestation of her internal struggle to comprehend this conversation.

"It's not that simple." Despite the truth, Da'fydd had no intention of confirming her accusation.

Amber's emotions flared, incandescent in her gaze as she met Da'fydd's eyes. With a swift motion, she cast aside the blanket and vaulted out of bed. A sharp exhale burst from her lips, punctuating her mounting frustration. She shook her head, almost as if trying to dislodge the confusion and the hurt. The air around her seemed to thicken with the weight of unspoken grievances.

"Amber," Da'fydd began, his voice layered with an attempt to soothe the evident tension.

"Don't Amber me." She began rummaging through Da'fydd's room, pulling open drawers and the armoire's doors.

Da'fydd sat halfway up, resting on one elbow, and waved his hand. "What are you doing?"

"Getting dressed. What does it look like I'm doing?" Amber grumbled.

"Making a mess," Da'fydd sarcastically answered, though it might have made her angrier.

Amber stood tall, her gaze fixed on him, and placed her hands on her hips. "Where are my own clothes? I don't want to wear yours anymore."

"I burned them." Da'fydd climbed out of bed. "Your dress was destroyed in the attack. There was no fixing it."

"What am I supposed to wear now?" Amber yelled, holding her forehead with her hand. "Besides, the ones I already borrowed from you need to be washed."

Da'fydd glanced around the room. "There might be something in here," he replied, moving towards a chest Amber had not yet torn through.

"You better not give me a throw-off of one of your tarts," Amber warned.

"Tarts?" Da'fydd chuckled. He closed the lid of the chest with a thump. Any female clothing in his room would be from one of his servants he used from time to time to alleviate his needs. "Can I trust you to wait here while I locate something appropriate for you to wear?" He pulled on his trousers and slipped his arms into the sleeves of his shirt as he pulled it down over his head.

Amber walked over and sat heavily on the bed, returning to clutching the covers over her body. It almost didn't matter why she was covering herself, and she failed to see why she did it when she had just gallivanted around the room butt naked.

Amber's gaze softened as she gazed up at Da'fydd. "Why didn't you come for me?" Her voice carried an undertone of plea, a subtle yearning for him to bridge the gap between them with a truth that would make sense of it all.

Da'fydd stepped closer, the distance between them narrowing both physically and emotionally. His eyes locked onto hers, revealing a softness that contrasted with his usual guarded demeanor. "It's complicated." Da'fydd gently traced a finger down the contour of her cheek, his touch light yet charged with unspoken emotion.

Amber exhaled softly, her gaze shifting downward. "Complicated? How can it be more complicated than this?"

Da'fydd's eyes clouded with emotion he didn't quite know how to articulate. "Trust me, it is."

"It really isn't," she said, her gaze lifting to meet his. She felt the sting of tears in her eyes, which only irritated her more. She was not one to be driven to tears, ever. "You have no idea what my life has been like," she added, her voice laced with frustration and sadness.

"Worse than what you've experienced here?" Da'fydd asked though he regretted the taunting question as soon as the words left his mouth. He had already seen enough of Amber's memories during their blood exchange to know the answer.

Amber looked away. "Nothing I haven't been through before."

Da'fydd frowned and reached to grasp Amber's chin. He turned her head to force her eyes back to his. "I'm sorry, I truly am. This life is not the one I wanted for myself, let alone with my true mate."

"None of us get the life we want, Da'fydd." Amber heatedly retorted.

"Is that why you fled your home world? To get the life you wanted?" Da'fydd asked, his tone laced with a combination of taunting and sarcasm.

"I had the best life I could on Earth." Amber crossed her arms and glared at him. Minus some horrible choices, but she kept that part to herself.

Da'fydd smiled down at Amber. "Why Earth? We both know it's not your home world, and it's not even all that close to the world you came from. Your scent is odd for Arkyn, not exactly a match, but close enough it must be your origin of birth."

Amber let out a humorless laugh, her eyes avoiding Da'fydd's gaze as they drifted toward the wall behind him. "Same solar system, different world," she muttered, bitterness tingeing her words. Sethre, the planet she had desperately wanted to leave behind, now seemed like a distant nightmare she couldn't escape no matter how far she ran.

Da'fydd asked with a serious tone, "It was that bad there, wasn't it?" The glimpses of memory spoke of deeper layers of pain than she might be willing to share. Despite his curiosity, he didn't want to push her beyond what she was ready to reveal.

Nonetheless, he had a strong sense that the horrors she had experienced were absolutely devastating.

Amber's eyes snapped back to Da'fydd's, flashing with hot fire embers within their depths. "Worse. I escaped when the first opportunity presented itself. Not that it mattered that much." While not as bad, her life on Earth had not fared much better. "Get me some clothes, please."

The corner of Da'fydd's mouth twitched. "I expect to find you here when I return."

"Of course you do. I'm not property to be owned and ordered about!" Amber crossed her arms.

"Oh, my little bird, such delusions will not serve you here." Da'fydd leaned in close, the warmth of his breath tickling the curve of her ear. "I've claimed you as my own; make no mistake. You would do well to protect what is mine." He straightened and held her gaze for an uncomfortably long moment.

Amber shook her head at him but failed to find the words to respond. She watched him move his hands in an odd pattern, and a brisk coldness took over the room. Da'fydd took a step and vanished.

Amber touched her cheek where his hand had been just seconds before. She tried to force her thoughts away from the intense desire that bubbled within her sparked by his touch. She was unaccustomed to feeling any kind of desire toward any man.

The idea of being owned by a man was abhorrent to her. Her world had been governed by patriarchal norms, where women were mere possessions. They were expected to serve a specific purpose. They were discarded like worthless objects if they failed to fulfill their duties. Amber couldn't bear being reduced to such a fate again.

A grin tugged at the corners of Amber's lips as she cast her gaze over to the ensemble she'd donned the day before, borrowed attire from Da'fydd. Though she'd initially balked at the idea, she couldn't deny the comfort they'd provided. Knowing Da'fydd, any replacement clothing he might offer would be woefully out of sync with her personal preferences. So, she decided to reclaim yesterday's garments, pulling them on with a sense of wry amusement.

After dressing, she caught her reflection in the room's mirror. To her surprise, her bruises were already fading, a welcome mystery in a world full of them. Picking up a nearby brush, she deftly subdued her flowing locks, coiling them into a loose bun at the nape of her neck. She took a moment to evaluate her reflection, her mind humming with thoughts of uncertainties.

In her rummaging, she'd found the shoes she'd been given the first night, thankfully. She put them on before slipping out of Da'fydd's chamber.

She couldn't help but feel a sense of relief that Rory and the others were gone. She was anxious to explore the castle and surrounding area, to quell her curiosity about where she was.

Her stomach grumbled, reminding her that she hadn't eaten much lately. As she reached the bottom of the steps, Amber decided to stop by the dining hall and grab something to eat.

But as she entered the room, she found the food surprisingly unpalatable. The aromas from the first evening meal had enticed her, not that she remembered much of the taste. Even the second one had not been so bad, although, admittedly, she'd limited her selection to the vegetables.

Groaning, Amber realized she needed to eat something, even if it wasn't to her liking. She passed through the kitchen door to see if she could find anything more appetizing.

Amber's eyes widened in disbelief as she surveyed the kitchen. Stacks of dishes teetered precariously, and remnants of meals long past were strewn about like forgotten casualties. The unsettling sight clashed violently with her previous experiences in Da'fydd's castle, little as they were. Her stomach turned at the notion of finding anything edible here.

With a furrowed brow, she stepped back, her thoughts in turmoil. The incongruity between the luxurious rooms of the castle and this neglected kitchen added another layer of mystery to an already enigmatic situation. A sense of disquiet settled over her as she resolved to seek nourishment beyond these walls.

Slipping out of the castle's rear exit, Amber was determined to forage for something more appetizing in the village. As she navigated her way through the labyrinthine of dilapidated dwellings, she couldn't help but wonder how much she truly knew about this place, and more unsettlingly, about Da'fydd himself.

Amber's eyes swept across the village, the weight of her observations settling in. She noted the fine lines etched into the faces of its inhabitants, the wear and tear on their clothes, and the scarcity of goods. The village was not thriving, but rather scraping by, clinging to each day like a vine to a crumbling wall.

While it was true that a superficial glance at the townspeople could suggest contentment, looking deeper revealed the grit and tenacity it took to get by. Now, with the illusions stripped away, Amber couldn't help but feel an ache in her chest.

Her initial perceptions, influenced by the enigmatic Da'fydd and the grandeur of his castle, had painted an incomplete picture. It became clear to her that life in the village was anything but easy. The people seemed hardworking, yet it wasn't enough. They lived under the burden of unspoken struggles.

Amber pressed on, her steps growing heavier with each revelation. She glanced back at the castle, its towering presence casting a long shadow over the community below. Somehow,

the imposing structure felt less magnificent than it had before, its walls seemingly built on the backs of the villagers.

Still determined to find food outside the castle's disheveled
kitchen, she advanced deeper into the village, considering the
dichotomy between the Da'fydd she knew and the reality of
his subjects. The truth, she understood, was always multi-lay-
ered, and she had yet to peel back all the layers.

As she moved through the village, consciously shielding her
thoughts from Da'fydd's mind in case he realized she hadn't
stayed put, she couldn't shake the feeling that her understanding of this place, and perhaps even of Da'fydd himself,
was about to deepen in ways she hadn't yet anticipated.

Walking farther into the village, Amber stumbled upon a
scene that tugged at her heartstrings. Beyond the cluster of
the tiny dwellings, she discovered a stretch of cultivated land.
It was too small to be considered a farm but bigger than
a garden. People, their faces lined with worry and exertion,
tended to the plants with hands caked in soil.

As she observed, it became painfully clear that the yield was
far from enough to sustain the castle's inhabitants and the
surrounding village. A pang of disbelief mingled with sorrow
hit her as she shook her head. Was this the best they could do
in a land filled with magical possibilities?

With a heavy heart, Amber pivoted and began her trek back to the castle. She had an errand in mind, visiting the dog pens. Somehow, the thought of spending time with those creatures seemed like a small but meaningful relief from the weight of her newly discovered insights.

As she stepped into the barn, a chorus of barks and the enthusiastic thump of wagging tails greeted Amber. The conditions of the pens were acceptable, but they didn't align with the pristine image she had formed earlier. Her eyes met the eager gazes of the dogs, their innocence contrasting starkly with the dissonance she felt.

Amber couldn't pinpoint signs of outright neglect, yet it was evident that these animals were not cherished family members. They were working dogs, tools rather than companions, and the realization weighed heavy on her. Even in their simple, joyous greeting, she found another contradiction that made her question the place she was in and the man who ruled it.

The sharp clang of metal meeting wood snapped Amber out of her reverie. She pivoted to locate the sound. Bren was at the distant end of the barn, a bucket overturned by his feet. Before she could process the situation, a flurry of movement caught her attention. She spun around, her hand clutching her heart, as two guards burst into the barn. Her eyes narrowed in irritation as their glances brushed past her, their attention fixed on Bren.

She didn't see what he did to cause them to depart as quickly as they appeared, leaving Amber bewildered by the swift sequence of events.

Turning back to Bren as his lips curled into a brief smile, offering a glimmer of camaraderie amid the day's work. She waved in response. After, he stooped to pick up the over-turned bucket and continued his tasks. Amber's eyes remained on him a little longer, her thoughts subtly weaving into the intricate fabric of her increasingly complex world.

A soft whimpering sound coming from behind the larger dogs drew Amber's attention. As she approached the group, she leaned in and saw that one of the pups had wandered away from its littermates. Without a second thought, Amber reached down and scooped up the tiny pup, admiring its adorable features and playful energy. She left the barn with the pup nestled in her arms.

When she reached the castle garden, she found a makeshift bench in the courtyard. Amber sat and cradled the young pup in her lap. From her vantage point, she could watch the castle's inhabitants go about their day. A living tableau that she found perplexing. The laughter of children filled the air until a ser-vant shooed them away, their giggles receding into the distance. Guards patrolled the area, their presence conspicuous in its silence, a stark contrast to the livelier exchanges among the castle's other inhabitants.

As Amber observed, she felt like an outsider looking in, a hidden observer in a world that was becoming increasingly difficult to understand. With each laugh, each stern face, each quiet nod from the guards, she amassed more questions than answers. What sort of leader was Da'fydd to inspire such a range of emotions and behaviors from his people? And where did she fit into this complex tapestry? The young pup nuzzled her hand, pulling her from her musings, yet her questions remained, hovering at the edge of her thoughts.

The pup wriggled free from Amber's embrace, emitting endearing grunts and soft whines as it gingerly positioned itself beside her on the bench. Gathering its puppy courage, it made the small leap to the ground, landing front paws first with a grunt of effort. The pup then settled at Amber's feet, circling once to find just the right spot before curling up, content and unprompted.

Amber watched the little scene unfold with a smile, her eyes softening. Despite the questions swirling in her mind, despite the inconsistencies she'd noticed in the castle and village, this small moment of uncomplicated loyalty warmed her. The pup seemed to offer her a snippet of normalcy in a world growing ever more complex.

Amber's gaze drifted back to the castle garden, if it could be called that, and the surrounding area. She noticed the forest was not as healthy as she'd thought. It was strange how something appeared one way but changed the more familiar the scenery became.

Amber glanced down at the sleeping puppy at her feet as she whined. She realized that they had been there for quite some time. With a sigh, she decided it was time to return the pup to its littermates. But as soon as she reached the pen, the little puppy refused to leave her side. It nuzzled against her and wagged its tail, clearly preferring Amber's company to that of its siblings.

When Amber explained the situation to Bren, he was surprisingly understanding. He told her that she could take the pup with her if she wanted to. But before leaving, Amber made sure to feed and water her. As she walked back to the castle, the little girl happily followed her, its ears flopping with every step. Even as she climbed the stairs to Da'fydd's tower, the puppy stayed content in her arms. At the top, she set the little girl on the stone floor.

Amber opened the door to Da'fydd's chamber, and the pup barreled between her feet, almost tripping her. Amber laughed out loud as the puppy attempted to jump on the bed with complete confidence but bounced off the side and fell on the floor. Amber rushed over and picked her up. She knew she'd have to come up with a name for her.

Amber held the puppy on the bed, rubbed her head, and smoothed her fur with her hands. She needed a bath. Maybe she could get one of the servants to bring up a bucket of warm water.

Amber's attention jerked toward the door of the chamber opening. She could feel Da'fydd behind it before he even opened it all the way. He entered with folded clothing in one arm.

"It took longer to find something suitable for you to wear." Da'fydd stopped in his tracks. "What's that?"

"What's what?" Amber tried to play innocent and tucked the puppy against her. She smirked to herself.

Annoyed, Da'fydd asked, "Why is that thing in my chambers?"

"It's not a thing. It's a puppy, and she's sweet." Amber held the pup at the apex of her forelegs, presenting her to Da'fydd for a closer inspection.

Da'fydd twitched his nose. He didn't exactly dislike dogs but didn't really understand his people's need to keep them. He had no idea what they did with them and didn't care to find out. His eyes narrowed at Amber. "This means you left the chamber, disobeying me."

"Well, I," Amber placed the pup on the floor, frowning. "I wanted to go outside." She straightened her spine, ready for a fight.

Da'fydd's eyes narrowed at her. "Wearing my clothes again."

Amber lifted a shoulder in a shrug.

Da'fydd was torn between irritation and amusement by Amber's audacity. She had brazenly disobeyed him by leaving the castle again. Still, he couldn't help but be entertained by the sight of her in his clothes. The trousers were too large, and she had to tie a belt around her waist to keep them from falling down. She had even rolled up the legs to make them fit. The shirt swallowed her whole, making her look like a child playing dress-up. Despite his frustration with her disobedience, Da'fydd couldn't help but be amused at the sight.

"What are you smiling at?" Amber put her hands on her hips and looked herself over. She dropped her arms. "I wasn't going to sit here the whole time naked." She glanced away, trying to hold onto her pride.

"Nothing." Da'fydd's tone sobered. "I brought you this to wear."

Da'fydd handed Amber the folded garment. She shook it out and frowned deeply at the heavy velvet gown. Despite her discontent, she remained silent, suppressing her true feelings, for now. There were other things she had on her mind.

"Why is the village in such a poor state?" Amber's question drew Da'fydd's entire focus.

"What do you mean?"

"The buildings are in poor condition, and the garden is almost bare." Amber pointed out.

"The villagers have food. We trade with our neighbors." Da'fydd passively answered Amber as if she was stating something he had no interest in.

"They don't look taken care of." Amber crossed her arms. "Don't you care about their well-being?"

"It's not my fault if they can't care for themselves. They can work and see to their own needs." Da'fydd replied defensively. "Foods provided in the castle for those too lazy to fix their own meals."

"How? How can they take care of themselves without the proper necessities?" Amber demanded. "Where do they bathe, and how do they make the means to build better homes or to feed their children?"

"It's not my concern. I feed them every day in the dining hall. Is that not enough?" Da'fydd's voice bellowed.

"It's not!" Amber's rage exploded. She glared at the dress. "And this, this is the ugliest thing I've ever seen." She threw the offending garment on the floor.

Amber stabbed a finger at it, and before Da'fydd could stop it, Amber's hand radiated energy, setting the dress ablaze. Da'fydd hardly flinched as he put it out with a snap of his wrist. He frowned at Amber, curious as to how fast her power reacted to her emotions.

"What the," Amber stood agape at what happened before her eyes. She held her hand with the other, and her eyes widened. "What was that? Did I do that?" Amber backed away.

"You need to be trained," Da'fydd said, which only further confused Amber.

"Train me for what?" Amber demanded.

"To use mind majik."

Amber frowned, staring at the scorched dress, still holding her hand in awe. His words made no sense to her.

Da'fydd shuffled through the chest and tossed something at Amber.

She missed catching it.

"Now you'll have to wear a handoff from one of my 'tarts'." He turned and pointed to the pup. "And that is not staying here."

"We'll see," Amber smirked. She would not be deterred.

Da'fydd stared at her, then turned on his heels and stormed out of his chamber.

Chapter Seventeen

Amber's eyes stayed glued to the closed door, her irritation mounting with each passing second. She shifted her glare to the garment at her feet, the one she refused to catch when Da'fydd tossed it at her. Her outfit, a makeshift assembly from Da'fydd's wardrobe, was ill-fitting. While somewhat comfortable, she'd become increasingly frustrated with pulling up the pants. She realized she needed more suitable clothes, but with Da'fydd's uncooperative mood, she figured she was on her own in procuring them.

Her mind made up, she exited the chamber, the heavy door closing behind her. She was unsure what her resolve would entail, yet she was unwaveringly determined. Leaving the castle's stone walls behind, she ventured back into the village, hoping to find some kind of marketplace she missed spotting earlier. The issue of local currency didn't weigh heavily on her mind. She decided to cross that bridge when she came to it, if she could find what she required.

Her search for a market proved fruitless as the day wore on, not that she'd harbored a great deal of hope in the first place.

With the light fading, she grew uneasy about being out at night, but the thought of returning to the castle empty-handed was equally disheartening. She muttered to herself as she leaned against a nearby building, hoping the dilapidated wall would hold her slight weight.

Suddenly, a woman appeared, leaning nonchalantly on a longbow. Amber squealed in surprise. "Who are you?" she demanded.

"They call me the Huntress."

Amber's eyes roamed over the woman before her, a figure of towering height. Her form was athletic, resulting from countless hours hunting in the forest if the longbow she leaned on gave an accurate impression. Her attire was practical and rugged: leather pants, a vest over a tunic, and wristbands. One of the bands had a leather loop and a strip that covered part of her palm. Amber thought it might have been a protective bow guard.

A quiver with arrows was slung across her back, and leather boots encased her feet. A dagger was strapped securely at her waist. Her appearance was such that she resembled a maiden of the forest or even a goddess.

Her hair was a striking reddish-blonde, flowing long and loose. But her eyes genuinely captivated Amber. They were an intense blue, radiating wisdom that surpassed anything Amber had ever encountered. It was these eyes and the woman they belonged to that intrigued and intimidated Amber. This was a woman of immense experience and power, and Amber couldn't help but be drawn in by her presence.

"What brings you to the village?" The Huntress repeated her question.

Amber blinked, snapping herself out of her deep thoughts. "Uh, um..." She frowned, glancing down at her makeshift attire. "Clothes." She glanced back up to meet the Huntress's gaze. "I'm searching for something that fits me better, something that isn't a damned dress."

The Huntress responded with a simple nod, her silence giving away nothing. Her blue eyes held Amber's gaze for a moment longer, an understanding smile tugging at the corner of her lips, allowing Amber to continue.

"Can you direct me to where the marketplace is located?"

"The village doesn't have one," the Huntress stated, casting a sweeping gaze over their sparse surroundings for emphasis. "They barely have enough to survive here."

Amber's expression tightened, a knot of perplexity forming within her. "But the castle seems well-provided for," she said, a note of hesitation flavoring her words. She'd observed the lackluster state of the village and its gardens earlier but hadn't fully comprehended the depth of its resource struggles.

A knowing smile graced the Huntress's lips. "It would appear so, wouldn't it? I may be able to assist you."

Amber's expression registered confusion, but a bag materialized at her feet before she could voice her question. "What's this?"

"Clothing," The Huntress explained. "They might be a bit large for you, but it's certainly a better fit than the oversized garb you're currently wearing."

Amber peered inside the bag, finding clothes that bore a striking resemblance to the Huntress's own attire. Warmth spread across her face, morphing into a wide smile of gratitude. The garments seemed to promise a better fit plus warmth. "Thank you," she said, her gaze brimming with appreciation as she glanced up at the Huntress. "How can I ever repay you?"

The Huntress's gaze briefly strayed towards the castle before returning to Amber. "Your presence here is repayment enough," she declared.

This left Amber frowning in confusion.

"Oh, and you'll need this. It will guard against the chill of the night."

Amber accepted the long cloak the Huntress offered. Like wool, the fabric felt thick and warm yet had the softness of cashmere. She shook her head, at a loss for words. "I don't know what to say."

"Thank you is enough."

Amber glanced back down at the bag. "Thank y-" she began, but the Huntress had vanished when she lifted her gaze again. She scanned the humble street and its rudimentary buildings, but the woman was nowhere to be found. Wrapping the cloak around herself, Amber felt a surge of gratitude for her unexpected good fortune. She set off towards the castle, eager to change into her new attire.

Amber's eyes fell on the puppy amidst the disorder as she entered Da'fydd's chamber, and her heart sank. A mess from the little canine stained the clothes she had discarded earlier. She mentally chided herself for overlooking the pup's basic needs like food and a place to relieve itself. In her preoccupation, she had entirely forgotten to arrange anything for the little girl. With a sigh, she nudged the soiled clothes towards the door's edge, uncertain of a better immediate solution.

Amber draped her cloak on the back of a chair near the hearth. She reached into her bag, drew out a fresh set of clothes, and changed into the better-fitting attire. The Huntress had been correct in that they were a bit big on her but not nearly as oversized as Da'fydd's garments had been. With her new clothes on, she scooped up the pup, intending to find food for the little creature. She was just about to leave the room when the door creaked open, and in strolled Da'fydd with his usual swagger.

Da'fydd's gaze raked over Amber, his eyes narrowing in disapproval. "What in the world are you wearing?"

"Clothes," Amber retorted, raising an eyebrow at him.

His nose crinkled as he sniffed the air, his frown deepening. "What's that foul stench?" he demanded.

Feeling her cheeks burn, Amber cast a quick glance at the soiled clothes she'd set aside. "There was a... mishap."

His gaze darted between her and the puppy, suspicion creeping into his eyes. "What sort of mishap?"

Amber gestured nonchalantly towards the pile of discarded garments.

Upon closer inspection, Da'fydd recoiled, a string of curses under his breath. With a wave of his hand, the messy pile vanished, leaving no trace of the incident. "Get that beast out of here!" His voice had risen, carrying a note of anger.

"No!" Amber cradled the puppy closer to her chest, her protective instincts flaring.

Da'fydd inhaled deeply, attempting to compose himself. "Where did you get those clothes?" His gaze fell on the cloak draped over the back of the chair. Before Amber could respond, he called out, his voice reverberating through the room. "Ravenna!"

In an instant, the woman who'd gifted Amber the clothes materialized in the room.

"Yes, princeling?" Her voice was sweet and melodious, but Amber detected an undercurrent of mockery.

"You're like him," Amber said, glancing at the Huntress.

Ravenna cast her a smile. "Not quite."

"Don't call me that!" Da'fydd's voice was sharp.

Ravenna's attention returned to him. "Then don't summon me like a child throwing a tantrum."

With a scowl, Da'fydd stormed over to the chair, grabbed the cloak, and thrust it into Ravenna's hands. "She doesn't need this."

Unfazed, Ravenna returned the cloak to Amber. "She's a Druidess, Da'fydd. You need to accept that. Besides, she'll have one of her own soon enough."

His face hardened, but he remained silent.

Ravenna's eyes narrowed. "Unless you intend to deny this woman her heritage."

Confusion washed over Amber as she tried to keep up with the conversation happening around her, as though she weren't standing there. Da'fydd had already said she was of a Druidic lineage, but what did that entail?

"Ravenna, this isn't your concern. We had an understanding." His accusing finger pointed at Amber. "And you've crossed the line."

Ravenna responded with a bark of laughter. "Firstly, princeling, she was in the village when I gave her the clothes and the cloak. Secondly, as a Druidess, she is my concern." With that, Ravenna turned to leave, her hands moving in a familiar gesture.

"Don't you dare turn your back on me, Ravenna," Da'fydd warned.

Ravenna glanced back over her shoulder, a sardonic smile gracing her lips. She winked at Amber. "Her heritage, her choice." And with that, she vanished.

A low growl escaped Da'fydd. He turned cold, hard eyes on Amber. "Return that beast to the pens."

"And what if I don't?" she challenged.

He remained silent, his stare unyielding.

Amber steeled herself, refusing to let the man intimidate her. "Well, she needs to eat anyway," she said after a long silence, crumpling under the intensity of his glare. She spun on her heels and stormed out of the room, the door slamming shut behind her.

As she ventured towards the dog pens, Amber replayed the conversation with Da'fydd in her mind, each word echoing with a weight she hadn't initially grasped. The chill of the evening air caressed her cheeks, the comforting rustle of leaves in the distant forest providing a soothing backdrop to her tumultuous thoughts.

The evening light cast long shadows that danced and swirled around her, reflecting her whirlpool of emotions. Her fingers tightened around the soft bundle of the puppy in her arms, its warmth reassuring amidst her unsettled feelings. Her thoughts drifted to the Huntress, the cloak, and the cryptic conversation. Was she indeed a Druidess, as they claimed? What did that mean for her future in this strange, backward world? Her heart pounded in her chest as she approached the pens, the quiet night amplifying the questions swirling in her mind.

Chapter Eighteen

Da'fydd stirred, the emptiness beside him rousing him from his slumber. He awoke alone for the second morning in a row despite retiring to bed with Amber. As his weary eyes adjusted to the dawn's light, thoughts of her, elusive as ever, pervaded his awakening senses. Despite his persistent efforts, she'd rebuffed his advances, leaving him to wrestle with the specter of her silence.

His senses twitched at the residual scent of the puppy lingering in the room, his eyes falling on the makeshift bed Amber had fashioned near the hearth. He could make it vanish with little effort, but the thought of Amber's fury held him in check. Her insistent plea for the pup to share their bed had earned a firm refusal from him, and ever since, her words had been sparse and curt.

With a flick of his wrist, Da'fydd made the leftovers from last night's meal vanish. Despite his growing irritation, he couldn't ignore the concern that Amber had barely touched her food. Her pointed remarks about the disorder in his domain were reminiscent of Gregori's infrequent but biting criticisms, touching a sensitive spot he'd rather not confront.

Shaking off the covers, he rose, moving to splash his face and chest with water from the basin. It was cold from the night before, but he cared little. As he dressed, his mind whirled with thoughts of Amber. The need for reconciliation with her was growing urgent, and he thought he might finally have a plan.

Stepping through a portal, he entered the former dungeon, now transformed into a flourishing greenhouse. The cool, damp air carried the scent of the Dia'Kharn plants, a food source for his people. Selecting a round, spikey fruit from a nearby bush, he bit into it, savoring the sweet and spicy liquid within. As a luminous leaf drifted to the stone floor, he picked two more fruits, a smile spreading across his face as he considered Amber's likely whereabouts.

The emotional wall of Amber's growing ire made it increasingly challenging to connect with her mentally. Still, Da'fydd closed his eyes and reached out with his senses. He managed to pick up a faint impression of her being near the dog pens, but her exact whereabouts eluded him.

Exiting the greenhouse through a portal, he found himself before the dog pens. Amber was not immediately visible, and the clacking sound inside the barn only led him to Bren, the caretaker. A wave of annoyance washed over him as he approached the man, the rift between him and Amber widening with each passing moment.

"Where is Amber?" Da'fydd's voice echoed through the barn, an unmistakable edge of impatience in his tone. Bren, startled, nearly dropped the feed bucket he was holding.

"Mistress Amber? She was here a moment ago..." Bren trailed off, glancing around, not quite meeting Da'fydd's gaze.

Da'fydd frowned, scanning the area. The barn was bustling with dogs, yet Amber was nowhere in sight. His heart clenched with a strange feeling he couldn't quite place. He shook his head, discarding the disconcerting feeling.

"Never mind," he muttered, unwilling to admit his concern to Bren. Turning away, he strode towards the barn exit, his mind reeling with unanswered questions.

As Da'fydd stepped outside, the morning breeze touched his face, clearing his thoughts momentarily. He swept his gaze across the yard once more, hopeful for a sight of Amber's raven hair or even a stray echo of her laughter, although he had yet to hear her laugh genuinely. Instead, he found only an empty courtyard and the distant sounds of the village waking, a subtle reminder that life moved on, whether or not he found what he was seeking.

Letting out a sigh, he made an uncharacteristic decision to wait. He figured Amber would eventually return, and he intended to be there when she did. Clutching the fruits in his grasp, a sort of peace offering, he strolled to a nearby bench and settled down. His eyes remained locked on the pathway that led towards the dog pens.

Da'fydd allowed his thoughts to drift, replaying their recent interactions. The silence, the tension, the barely concealed anger; all foreign sensations to him. He was used to command and control, orchestrating the world to his liking. But with Amber, it seemed the usual rules did not apply. As the morning light ascended, he found himself engrossed in contemplation, pondering ways to bridge the gap between them, to rekindle the vivacious spirit he'd initially encountered in her. He'd felt a flicker of hope for the first time in what seemed like an eternity.

With these thoughts occupying his mind, Da'fydd wove his way through the village's cobbled paths, each step leading him closer to the gardens. Restlessness gnawed at him. He was never one to remain idle. As he entered the area, his first scan didn't reveal Amber, stoking his simmering irritation. Exhaling slowly to quell his rising temper, he took a more careful perusal of the surroundings.

Finally, his eyes landed on his quarry, busily plucking ripe produce to eat straight from the vine, seemingly indifferent to the castle's offerings for the morning repast. With his intended peace offering in hand, Da'fydd advanced toward her, reining in his frustrations for the moment.

"There you are, little bird," Da'fydd murmured. He winced inwardly, frustrated at his struggle to modulate his tone. Years of unquestioned authority had left him unused to softening his voice, especially when his temper was simmering beneath the surface.

Amber shot him a venomous glare, her eyes flitting back to the task. The silence that followed her dismissive gaze surprised Da'fydd, causing a scowl to creep onto his features. A flush of annoyance warmed his cheeks as he swallowed back his anger, inching closer to her. He took note of the stiffening of her posture, the rigid line of her back as he neared.

"What are you doing?" He asked, eyeing her as she plucked at the stubborn vines.

"What does it matter to you?" Amber retorted, her words sharp and biting.

His hands tightened around the fruit, his knuckles paling. Drawing in a deep breath, he forced his fingers to relax. "I noticed you didn't eat again last night," he said, trying to inject a casualness into his voice that he was far from feeling.

Amber pivoted towards him, crossing her arms protectively. "The food wasn't edible... again."

Da'fydd offered her a forced smile, his eyes betraying his irritation. "So you've mentioned."

"Have I?" Amber's words were laced with mockery, each syllable grinding against his patience.

"If you're unhappy with the food, then do something about it," he said, his grip on the fruit once again tightening.

"How? I can't cook, and why would your servants listen to me if they won't even listen to you?" Amber challenged.

His laughter reverberated with a jarring edge. "What makes you think they don't listen to me?"

Amber raised an eyebrow, a smirk playing at the corners of her lips. "Oh, that's right. You don't eat, so why would you care about fixing something that doesn't directly affect you."

The air between them crackled with tension as Da'fydd stepped towards her. His hot breath stirred the loose tendrils of hair framing her face as he pinned her against the unyielding stone wall. "I don't tolerate disrespect from them," he pointed vaguely in the direction of the village, his gaze flicking down to the ruined fruit in his hand. Discarding it, he muttered, "What a waste."

Amber gasped, a soft whimper escaping her lips. His attention snapped back to her, his rage abating as he stepped back.

"What were those?" she asked, her voice slightly louder than a murmur.

Regret gnawed at him as he noticed the slight tremor in her body. "A peace offering," he admitted, locking eyes with her.

"Oh." The softness of Amber's voice skimmed the surface of silence.

Reaching out, he conjured two more fruits, cradling them carefully in his palm. "Come," he said, extending his free hand towards Amber.

Reluctance clouded her eyes as she hesitated, her hand hovering in the air between them. Da'fydd forced himself to remain still, to wait for her to make the move. He wasn't used to waiting but knew he couldn't rush this.

"I won't hurt you," he assured her, watching her eyes flicker to meet his. His words hung between them, a promise he needed her to believe.

"Please," he implored, the plea torn from somewhere deep within him. "Trust me."

Her gaze shifted to his outstretched hand once again. With a shaky breath, she finally placed her hand in his.

Amber gave him a tentative smile and nodded, signaling the allowance to lead her away. Da'fydd guided her to a bench under an almost alive tree. It was surprising that it hadn't fallen susceptible to its environment as the others had.

"This," Da'fydd held up one of the fruits, "is what sustains a Dia'Kharn." The other one rested on his thigh.

Amber frowned. "Dia'Kharn? I thought you might be part vampire."

Da'fydd's hand whipped out and grabbed Amber a little too hard by the throat. Her eyes went wide with fear, and her breath became jagged. "Don't ever call me a Vam'Peer again. Not even a poorly pronounced version," he growled.

"Remove your hand, princeling." A woman's voice, they both recognized, intruded.

Da'fydd's eyes remained locked with Amber's, still full of terror. "Not your concern, Ravenna."

"I told you, she is a Druidess, which makes her our concern," Ravenna repeated what she'd pointed out only days before.

Amber's breath hitched in her chest as Da'fydd withdrew his hand. Rising to his full height, he turned to face Ravenna, maintaining a facade of nonchalance despite the deadly arrow poised in her longbow, pointed directly at his heart. He mentally reached out to Amber, his voice echoing in her thoughts without glancing in her direction. *If you think of fleeing, don't, you won't make it far.*

"You think we would not know when one of our own steps onto this world? Or that we would not protect her from the likes of you?" Ravenna's gaze remained steely, her arrow unwaveringly trained on Da'fydd.

Da'fydd's laugh was harsh and cruel. "Protect her? You didn't protect her!" Ravenna's countenance altered in response to Da'fydd's words, indicating that he'd struck a nerve.

"You are violating our understanding, Ravenna." He held up his hand, and a red fireball manifested in his tense palm.

Two other women materialized on either side of Ravenna as if on cue, their hands held out defensively towards Da'fydd. "Are you sure this is the path you want to tread, princeling?" Ravenna's question was laden with an audacious challenge.

Stepping up to Da'fydd's side, Amber implored, "Please." She gestured at him, her hands upraised, her eyes filled with apprehension. She didn't utter another word, yet the deep-set sorrow in her eyes seemed to quell Da'fydd's anger more effectively than any words could. He responded by closing his fist, snuffing out the flame, and allowing the pent-up energy to dissipate back into Celtan. His hand dropped to his side.

"Amber is safe with me." Da'fydd declared, his voice calmer. He slipped an arm around Amber's waist, pulling her closer. She flinched subtly yet didn't resist his gesture; an unspoken acknowledgment of her role in defusing the situation.

Ravenna, her arrow still nocked, though no longer trained on Da'fydd, lowered her longbow. A silent exchange occurred between her and the other two women, who vanished into thin air. Ignoring Da'fydd, Ravenna addressed Amber directly. "If you ever find yourself in need, call out my name. I will come," she vowed, her gaze flitting to Da'fydd one last time before she, too, disappeared.

Da'fydd remained silent, his eyes fixed on the spot where Ravenna had stood. Amber moved to intercept his gaze. "I'm sorry for any offense caused," she murmured.

Da'fydd's gaze met Amber's, and he held her tightly against his chest. They both embraced each other, savoring the moment. "That word is a grave insult to Dia'Kharns." He rested his chin on Amber's head and inhaling her scent deeply. "My father is Druid, my mother was Dia'Kharn. I may tell you the sordid details someday, but not today." Da'fydd's eyes darted to the peace offerings on the ground, and with anger burning inside him, he conjured small fireballs and threw them at each item, all while holding Amber close.

Amber's confusion was evident as she furrowed her brow, but Da'fydd shook his head subtly to silence her. Although clearly curious, Amber remained silent as Da'fydd created a portal to transport them back to his chamber.

Chapter Nineteen

Rousing from her slumber, Amber found herself enveloped in the warm sanctuary of Da'fydd's embrace, a haven of comfort and protection. With delicate fingers, she traced intricate patterns on his bare chest while her gaze lingered upon the face of the man who seemed lost in slumber. It was a fleeting moment of serenity, allowing her to delve into the depths of her emotions for Da'fydd and untangle the complexities of their intertwined experiences over the past few days.

Da'fydd treasured this tranquil interlude with her, recognizing the significance of allowing her the solitude to gather her thoughts. Slowly, he conveyed his awakened state, sharing a tender glance that brought warmth and desire. Their eyes locked in a silent exchange, speaking volumes that words could not capture. Yet, amidst the tender connection, Da'fydd gently nudged her. *Get dressed, little bird. I have something to show you.*

Amber emerged from the shelter of Da'fydd's embrace, her thoughts still entangled with the warmth of their intimate connection. "What do you want to show me?"

Da'fydd beamed a playfully taunting grin at her but didn't answer.

Amber frowned, although a smile spread across her lips. Her nimble fingers fumbled with the buttons of her blouse as her mind played out countless scenarios of what awaited her beyond the confines of his chamber. Curiosity and trepidation surged through her veins, igniting a sense of anticipation that quickened her heartbeat.

Last night had brought a profound sense of peace between them, a tranquility that seemed to permeate their souls. As Amber reflected on those cherished moments, a warmth spread across her cheeks, ignited by the intimate connection they had shared with each other.

She stepped into her pants, her eyes straying to Da'fydd, who remained as silent as ever. The room seemed charged with ineffable energy, as if the walls themselves held secrets yearning to be unveiled.

Once she'd donned the vest and secured it, Da'fydd took her by surprise when he draped the cloak around her shoulders.

The gentle sway of the soft material echoed the rhythm of her thoughts, each movement a step closer to the enigmatic surprise that awaited her. Amber's imagination wove intricate tapestries of possibilities, trying to decipher the purpose and significance of the forthcoming revelation.

She glanced sideways at Da'fydd and took a silent, deep breath as she tested their connection. *Are you seriously not going to tell me where we are going?*

No, Da'fydd playfully answered, a mischievous spark dancing in his eyes. *It's a surprise. Don't ask me again, little bird.* His gentle nudge punctuated his words as they continued their leisurely descent down the steps. Each step was taken with deliberate slowness.

Amber's gaze swept across the empty hallway, her steps faltering as she realized they had bypassed the bustling dining hall where the morning meal was being served. It wasn't a profound disappointment, for the quality of the meals had been lackluster in recent days. Still, the change did stir a flicker of surprise within her. Although, it shouldn't have. She had yet to witness Da'fydd consume anything. There was that 'peace offering' from the night before, but she hadn't witnessed him ingest them.

She pushed those thoughts out of her mind and focused on their steps. Seemed strange they weren't going to where Da'fydd wanted through a portal.

Some things are worth savoring. Da'fydd's silent words interrupted her pondering thoughts.

Of course they are. A gentle smile curved Amber's lips as she intertwined her fingers with Da'fydd's, a ripple of excitement coursing through her. Beyond the surprise that awaited her, something else piqued her curiosity.

It wasn't merely the allure of the impending revelation that tugged at her thoughts. It was the subtle shift in Da'fydd's attitude towards her that had caught her attention. There was a slight softening in him.

As they stepped beyond the castle's boundaries, Da'fydd guided Amber with a firm yet gentle grip, their intertwined hands forging an unbreakable connection. In front of them, a portal materialized, its ethereal shimmer beckoning them forward. With a shared glance filled with anticipation, they stepped into the enigmatic embrace of the shimmering opening.

Amber stood in a captivating entryway as the portal dissolved behind them. It was as if they had emerged into a hidden sanctuary of nature's splendor. Before her, stretched a breathtaking greenhouse, vibrant and alive with an array of flourishing plants. The leaves, touched by a magical essence, emitted a soft, luminescent shimmer that bathed the space in an otherworldly glow, to say nothing of the aroma that awakened all her senses.

Da'fydd gently released Amber's hand and, with a tenderness that touched her heart, took her cloak and hung it on a nearby hook in the alcove. The seemingly small gesture spoke volumes about his thoughtfulness and care for her comfort.

As Amber's gaze traced the contours of the greenhouse, she couldn't help but notice a subtle shift in Da'fydd's demeanor. There was an ease in his posture, a relaxed aura that surpassed any she had witnessed thus far in their brief time together. It was as if the world's weight had lifted from his shoulders, allowing him to fully immerse himself in this sanctuary of tranquility.

"Wait here." Da'fydd's voice carried a tinge of excitement and mystery.

Amber watched with a mix of curiosity and adoration as he stepped into the verdant expanse of the greenhouse. Her eyes followed his every move, captivated by how he seemed to navigate the space with familiarity and purpose.

The air within the greenhouse carried a delicate fragrance, a symphony of floral scents that enveloped Amber's senses. She stood at the entryway, her eyes alight with wonder, as Da'fydd disappeared among the vibrant foliage. The anticipation within her grew, her heart beating in synchrony with the enchanting surroundings.

Amber experienced a surge of gratitude for this moment, for the way Da'fydd had woven a tapestry of surprises to unveil before her. The hidden sanctuary they now stood within was a testament to the depths of his, she hesitated to say love, but with the lengths he had gone to bring this joy into her life, no better word came to her mind. Her heart constricted.

She pushed the uncomfortable emotions aside as she patiently waited, eager to witness the wonders that awaited her during this extraordinary moment together.

With gentle deliberation, Da'fydd moved amidst the lush foliage of the cave like greenhouse, his eyes darting between the vibrant fruits that hung from the thin branches of the bush like trees. However, his focus was not solely on the task at hand. Every so often, his gaze would involuntarily drift back to Amber, who stood at the entryway, a portrait of curiosity and anticipation.

A variety of emotions played across Amber's face as she observed him, a dance of expressions that intrigued Da'fydd. Her eyes were pools of contemplation, alternating between radiant smiles that illuminated her features and slight furrows that hinted at the depths of her musings.

Da'fydd couldn't help but wonder what occupied her thoughts at that moment. Were they fragments of their shared memories etching into her mind like intricate tapestries? Or were they visions of the possibilities that lay ahead, painted in hues of hope and curiosity? He didn't intrude telepathically into her mind, at least not entirely. Their connection grew in strength, and soon they would be wholly connected as one.

As he plucked two fruits, carefully selecting them with a gentle touch, Da'fydd found himself caught in a delicate balance between the task at hand and the enchantment of Amber's presence. The soft caress of the leaves against his skin seemed to mirror the gentle cadence of his heartbeat, each beat echoing his growing affection for the woman who had become the center of his world.

Their connection, a tapestry woven with threads of shared experiences like this one, continued evolving with each passing moment. As Da'fydd's fingers closed around the chosen fruits, he couldn't help but long to bridge the distance between them and unravel the secrets within Amber's captivating gaze and heart.

With a wistful smile lingering on his lips, Da'fydd returned to the entryway with his fruit selection in hand, captivated by the enigma of Amber. He approached her, stepping closer with an air of gentle anticipation, his heart echoing the rhythm of their shared journey.

At that moment, as their eyes met again, Da'fydd vowed to cherish every smile and every furrow etched upon Amber's face. Their connection was a dance of discovery, and he yearned to continue the intricate steps alongside her, revealing the depths of their intertwined souls as they navigated the path of love and the mysteries that lay ahead. Of course, he would not speak of the depth of his budding feelings to her.

Da'fydd rolled both pieces between his palms and then handed one to Amber. "As I mentioned yesterday, these are what sustains a Dia'Kharn."

"And why you don't eat? Because you can't digest the other food?"

Da'fydd gave a subtle shake of his head. "I can. I choose not to." Da'fydd laid a finger gently across her lips to silence the onslaught of questions he sensed in her mind.

Amber smiled and glanced down at the fruit he'd given her. The outside was spikey, and she wasn't sure how to eat it. She lifted her eyes to his just as he sunk his sharp incisors into the fruit, piercing its tough skin.

Juice trickled down the corners of Da'fydd's lips, yet his unwavering gaze remained locked with Amber's as he savored the juices. Despite the sweet distraction, he maintained a profound connection with her, his eyes speaking volumes, an array of emotions swirling within their depths.

Amber, determined to reciprocate the shared experience, brought the fruit to her lips. However, her incisors failed to pierce through the resilient skin, thwarting her attempts.

Frowning, Da'fydd instinctively reached out, using the tip of his finger to inspect her teeth, searching for any irregularities. "Strange," he murmured, a hint of concern lacing his tone.

Confused, Amber mirrored his actions, touching the same teeth with the tip of her finger, searching for any sign of an issue. The urgency in her tone couldn't hide the underlying fear that swirled within her. "What's wrong?" she asked, her words tinged with suspicion.

Da'fydd studied her, his eyes filled with caution and tenderness, before finding the words to explain. "When bonding occurs between a Dia'Kharn, blood is exchanged, making our genetics compatible," he said, his voice soft but laced with an unspoken weight.

Amber's gaze narrowed. Urgency pulsed through her, intertwining with growing fear. "Why do I sense there's more to it?" she pressed, her voice filled with apprehension.

A reassuring smile graced Da'fydd's lips as he gently cupped Amber's face in the palm of his hand. "There is nothing to fear, little bird," he murmured, his voice a soothing balm. "The exchange serves to solidify our connection, to deepen our bond."

Unsatisfied, Amber yearned for complete transparency. "But why do I sense there is more?" she insisted, her eyes locked with his, pleading for truth.

In response, Da'fydd tenderly kissed her forehead, a gesture of reassuring comfort. Taking the fruit from Amber's hand, he pierced it with his own elongated, sharp incisors, an aspect she had not entirely noticed before, at least not in the way she did at this moment.

Drawing her closer, their bodies pressed against each other in an intoxicating embrace, Da'fydd's hand gently cradled the back of Amber's head. The subtle taste of the fruit's juice lingered on her tongue, a tantalizing reminder of their shared connection. Time seemed to stand still in that charged moment, as if the world around them had faded into insignificance, leaving only the fiery passion that ignited between them.

A surge of electricity coursed through Amber's veins, setting her senses ablaze with desire. Her heart pounded within her chest like a wild creature, its rhythm echoing the fierce yearning that pulsed through her entire being. Da'fydd's touch, tender, yet filled with untamed passion, left her breathless, aching for more.

Da'fydd wiped away the juices that slipped down her chin with the pad of his thumb, followed by his tongue, capturing every bit. He gently coaxed her mouth open and squeezed more of the juice onto her tongue.

Amber closed her eyes as the surprisingly cool liquid slid down the back of her throat. The warm, humid air grew increasingly warmer. She sighed as the last of the spicy, sweet juice was squeezed into her mouth.

Their gazes locked, their eyes becoming windows to their souls, revealing the depth of their longing. In that shared glance, the air crackled with an unspoken intensity, a promise of the forbidden pleasures that awaited them.

Da'fydd discarded the remaining shells of the fruit and wrapped his arms around Amber. She melted into his embrace. In that heated moment, the world ceased to exist, and they were consumed by a maelstrom of desire. Their lips met in a fervent, hungered kiss, igniting a flame that burned hotter than any inferno. Their tongues danced in a passionate tango, intertwining, and exploring with ardent fervor. The lingering spicy sweet taste mixed with their burning desires.

Lost in the intoxication of their shared passion, they were swept away on the currents of desire, their bodies molded together as if they were created to fit perfectly in each other's embrace. Each touch and caress sent shivers down their spines, sparking a raw, primal hunger that demanded to be sated.

Amber and Da'fydd transcended the boundaries of time and space, surrendering to the consuming force of their love. Their bodies moved in a graceful symphony of desire, their souls entwined in a dance that defied logic and reason. It was a union forged by destiny, fated to ignite the heavens with their ardor.

As their hearts beat in unison, their breaths intermingled, a symphony of pleasure and passion resonating through the depths of their shared connection. In this realm of ecstasy, they discovered the true power of their budding affection. This force could shape their destinies and conquer any obstacle that stood in their way.

And so, in the throes of their embrace, Amber and Da'fydd surrendered to the fierce, unyielding flames of desire, lost in a world where love reigned supreme. The boundaries of their reality blurred into a tapestry of unbridled passion.

Caught off guard by the intensity of their heated embrace, Amber stumbled backward, her legs nearly giving way beneath her. Da'fydd's firm and steady grasp prevented her from falling in that perilous moment. His grip was a lifeline that kept her anchored to the world.

Breathless and flushed, their clothing clung to their bodies, a testament to the lingering desires that pulsed between them. The air crackled with unrequited passion as if the very fabric of their beings longed to be entwined in a dance of intimacy.

Their eyes locked, and the silence that enveloped them spoke volumes. Each other's longing gazes a silent plea for more. In that charged pause, the weight of their unfulfilled desires hung heavily, teasing them with the promise of sweet surrender.

Amber's chest rose and fell with the rhythm of her rapid breaths, her senses aflame with a heady mix of anticipation. Her body yearned to be enveloped by Da'fydd's touch, to feel his fingertips against her bare skin, igniting a fire that burned deep within her core.

Da'fydd, his own desire mirroring hers, held her gaze with an intensity that sent shivers cascading down her spine. His touch, though steady, conveyed an urgency, a hunger that matched her own. They were poised on the threshold of a precipitous fall, teetering on the edge of surrender.

As the world held its breath, Amber and Da'fydd stood on the precipice, their bodies magnetically drawn together, longing to indulge in the sweet surrender that would unlock a world of pleasure and ignite a love that transcended the boundaries of mere mortal existence.

Da'fydd's touch was gentle yet electrifying as he caressed the side of Amber's face, his fingers weaving through her dark hair's silky strands. A soft smile graced his lips as he gazed into her eyes, a tender intimacy passing between them. "What are your plans for today?" he inquired, genuine curiosity twinkling in his eyes.

Amber's brows furrowed, a medley of confusion and irritation etching itself onto her face. "Excuse me?" she responded, her voice edged with a nervous laugh. His question seemed incongruous after the passionate exchange they had shared moments before.

Da'fydd chuckled, his laughter carrying a hint of mischievousness. "You mentioned something last night about the state of my kitchens," he said, his words laced with playful humor. The memory of their conversation danced at the edges of their shared recollections.

Amber's frown deepened, her confusion mounting. "You can't be serious," she replied, nervous laughter escaping her again. The dissonance between their passionate encounter and the mundane topic of kitchen affairs bewildered her.

Da'fydd pressed a light kiss to her lips, a tender gesture that conveyed a promise of things to come. "I have some matters to attend to," he confessed, his voice low and filled with a trace of longing. "But don't worry. I'll have my way with you soon enough."

Amber shook her head, disbelief passing over her features. "You are unbelievable," she chided him, exasperation lacing her tone.

Taking her cloak from the hook where he had hung it earlier, Da'fydd draped it over her shoulders, securing it with gentle care. "I'll make it up to you later," he assured her, his words laden with a promise that sent a shiver down her spine and moisture pooling between her thighs.

Stepping through the swirling vortex of the portal, Da'fydd and Amber arrived at the grand entrance of the castle. For a fleeting moment, he allowed his eyes to adjust to the shift in scenery, taking in the familiar high walls and the towering

turrets that overshadowed the entryway. As they materialized, two guards snapped to attention. With an almost imperceptible nod, Da'fydd acknowledged their presence. The
gesture, subtle but imbued with an unspoken command. It
was an effortless exchange, one that spoke volumes about
Da'fydd's unchallenged authority within these walls.

Master of the castle, Amber teased.

Da'fydd glanced down at her, his eyes twinkling with mischief. *Always, little bird,* he responded, his voice tinged with
playfulness that negated any possible severity of his words.
You'd do well to remember that.

Amber merely smiled up at him in response.

Da'fydd raised an eyebrow at her. With his hand on the
small of her back he guided her towards their destination.

As they moved towards the kitchens, Da'fydd's commanding presence accompanied her, and the lingering shadows of
the two guards trailed in their wake. The mere sight of their
protective presence brought comfort and unease to Amber's
heart. After everything she had experienced, trust remained
a delicate matter for her.

Arriving in the bustling kitchen, Da'fydd addressed the staff,
his instructions clear and unwavering, emphasizing their cooperation with the changes Amber would make. The authority in

his voice carried an air of respect, a reflection of his commitment to supporting her endeavors.

Amidst the flurry of activity, Amber briefly thought of how she might navigate the realm of culinary creativity, her mind filled with vague visions of transformation. She found solace in the fact that Da'fydd had given her full authority, indicating his trust in her. Amber turned to thank him just as he opened a portal and disappeared. She shook her head at the empty space before focusing on the task in front of her.

Chapter Twenty

*A*mber!

What? Why are you yelling at me? Amber sensed Da'fydd take a mental pause.

After sampling the mixture presented to her, she nodded approvingly to the young kitchen girl. Tonight's evening meal promised to diverge substantially from the norm, hopefully for the better. Amber wasn't a culinary expert, but she knew what tasted good. The uproar that had followed her dismissal of the head cook and his subsequent replacement with a mere slip of a girl, barely out of her youth, still had the kitchen staff reeling. However, she believed she saw a spark in the girl that justified the gamble. The real challenge now was orchestrating a full-fledged meal for a sizable crowd in the limited time.

Return to my chambers!

Amber's expression shifted into a frown. *I am currently occupied with the task you assigned me,* she replied, a hint of frustration within her mind.

Da'fydd drew in a deep breath, his eyes closing as he attempted to compose himself. He stretched his neck, feeling the satisfying pop of tension releasing. *I don't have time to explain,* he began, his silent tone filled with urgency. *Please, obey my instructions.*

A firm resolve filled Amber's response. *No.* Her refusal resonated through their telepathic connection, its weight hanging as a steadfast declaration of her autonomy and unwillingness to comply.

Da'fydd created a portal, whisking Amber away from the bustling kitchen. She found herself standing in his chambers, surrounded by a force field that stung her fingertips when she reached out to touch the door.

This is going too far, Da'fydd! Amber lashed out, her frustration evident. *You can't just trap me here without any explanation or regard for my feelings. I thought we were building trust, but this... this is unacceptable.*

Amber let out a surprised squeal when Da'fydd materialized behind her without warning. She hadn't even felt the cold chill that usually preceded the opening of a portal before his hand was on her shoulder, spinning her around to face him. The suddenness of his arrival and the contact left her disoriented for a moment, her heart pounding in her chest.

Da'fydd's expression softened, although his features were etched with concern and urgency. "Amber, please understand," he pleaded, his voice conveying a genuine effort to remain patient with her. "There are forces beyond my control, and I have no time to explain."

Amber crossed her arms defiantly, her gaze unwavering. "Try."

"Not this time." Da'fydd turned and raised his hands.

Amber touched his arm to regain his attention. "Trust is a two-way street, Da'fydd."

The palpable tension between them thickened as her words lingered in the air. Da'fydd turned towards her, his eyes meeting hers. Reaching out, he gently cupped her cheek in the palm of his hand. "Please understand," he murmured softly, his touch conveying reassurance. "It is not about trust but your safety that drives me." He placed a chaste kiss on her forehead.

Amber's anger slowly ebbed away, replaced by affection while she remained confused. She recognized sincerity in Da'fydd's eyes, and his genuine desire to protect her at all costs. "I appreciate that you want to keep me safe, but I need answers. What has happened? Did Rory return?" She hated the need to speak that man's name aloud.

"No," Da'fydd's grip tightened on her arm, his voice firm. Sensing her apprehension, he exerted an effort to loosen his hold, his unwavering gaze locking with hers. "I promise, Amber. I will explain everything once I return," he assured her.

Amber's frown intensified, and she shook her head. Before she could say more, Da'fydd opened a portal and stepped back into it, leaving Amber alone and trapped within his chamber.

Not happy with you, Da'fydd.

He did not respond to Amber as he stepped out of his portal at the Gateway. His mind was a whirlwind of emotions, unquenchable curiosity, and gnawing concern. The memory of the Arkyn Lords' visit, an encounter etched in his mind from when he'd first arrived on Celtan, echoed within him. But now, with the resounding signal piercing his mind, a foreboding sensation gripped his heart. Something of great magnitude must have occurred.

Assuming a wide stance, Da'fydd clasped his hands behind his back, his eyes fixed upon the shimmering Gateway that signaled its activation. A surge of anticipation coursed through his veins as three imposing figures materialized before him. Clad in garments befitting their esteemed status as Lords, their simple yet regal attire harmonized with the vibrant hues of their distinct skin tones, radiating even within the depths of the forest where the Gateway resided. The lush environment seemed to bow in reverence to their presence. Da'fydd had seen them many times before, but the Lords' commanding presence never failed to garner his admiration.

With a warm smile gracing his face, Da'fydd extended his arm, offering a respectful greeting befitting warriors. His hand met the forearms of each Lord, their touch firm and resolute. A silent acknowledgment passed between them, a recognition of their shared camaraderie. Tight smiles adorned the faces of the Lords, mirroring Da'fydd's expression, a testament to the unspoken bond that united them.

Da'fydd stood amidst a convergence of worlds, his immortal essence entwined with the ageless power of the Arkyn Lords. As they stood together, surrounded by the backdrop of Celtan's embrace, he regretted not bringing Amber with him to greet the Lords.

Da'fydd's eyes widened for a brief moment when a human female emerged from the Gateway. Startled, he swiftly regained his composure and redirected his focus to Adryan, the figure who stood before him, and the Primary Lord of Arkyn.

"Da'fydd, our esteemed friend, it has been far too long," Adryan declared, assuming his role as the leader, taking the initiative to speak first. His eyes blazed with an intensity akin to flames, their vibrant red hue exuding an ethereal glow that seemed to push back the encroaching shadows.

"What brings you to Celtan?" Da'fydd inquired as he withdrew his arm from the previous greetings, their exchange of pleasantries coming to a close.

"We have come on a mission to assess whether the males of Celtan pose a threat to Arkyn," Adryan proclaimed, his voice laced with determination. The brilliance of his red eyes reflected the fiery resolve burning within him.

Da'fydd shook his head, his brow furrowing as curiosity and concern settled over his features. "What has occurred?" he asked, his tone tinged with an urgency that emphasized his genuine interest in understanding the situation.

"A fool, a cretin, dared to lay claim to my Primary," Adryan informed Da'fydd as his gaze briefly flickered toward the female figure who stood slightly to the side and behind him, nestled between the other two Lords.

Da'fydd's eyes darted to the female, his attention captured by her presence. Standing with an air of strength and resilience, she seemed to possess an aura that demanded respect. Crossing his arms over his chest, Da'fydd's voice carried a hint of defiance. "And he still draws breath?" he questioned, his words underscored by a subtle surprise.

"For now," Adryan responded, his tone acknowledging the precariousness of the situation.

The news weighed heavily on Da'fydd. Knowing the consequences that would surely follow, he couldn't fathom who would be foolish enough to challenge a Lord's claim; especially Adryan's.

With his unruly blue hair, Darius absentmindedly brushed it away from his eyes. In contrast, Khunrik's silver eyes glinting like moonlit snow stood with an air of discomfort. Both remained silent, as they often did, even after their initial greetings. Such reticence was their nature, at least in more formal settings.

Sensing the need for a more suitable environment, Da'fydd extended his arm in a welcoming manner. "Why don't we continue this conversation in a more appropriate location?" he proposed, his body half-turned, inviting them to return with him to his castle.

As Da'fydd opened a portal that would transport them, a tumultuous blend of anticipation and trepidation tightened his heart. Self-consciousness crept in, casting a shadow of doubt on how the Lords would perceive his ill-kept village. He keenly felt the inadequacy of his surroundings, acutely aware of how it reflected upon him.

Their friendship, nurtured by the seeds of admiration that had been steadfastly rooted in Da'fydd's heart long ago, held a sacred space within his soul. The memories of their shared experiences, the profound respect, and the camaraderie that had blossomed over countless centuries fueled his unwavering resolve to prove himself. Da'fydd was determined to rise above any doubts or insecurities that threatened to cast shadows upon the bond they had forged in the past when he still was a true Dia'Kharn.

With a resolute breath, Da'fydd cast aside his nagging un-certainties. In this crucial moment, he chose to embrace confidence, to trust in the strength of their connection. He finished opening the portal and inclined his head.

The Lords strode forward, taking the lead as they stepped into the shimmering opening. Da'fydd followed. His heart raced with anticipation as he observed their reactions. However, what he witnessed struck him with disappointment.

Their expressions contorted with silent disgust, their disappointment evident in their downturned features. Da'fydd winced, realizing that the impression he had feared was now a harsh reality. He gazed upon his village, seeing it through the same lens as the Lords.

A grim visage of decaying trees and roads covered in dirt and mud, snaking between the dilapidated homes and neglected gardens. Despite the delicate carved details that adorned its façade, Da'fydd's castle loomed over the dreary village, an unwelcome sight that marred the already somber surroundings.

"You should have accepted our offer to kill your father and avoid this wretched fate, confined to a world devoid of progress and forsaken by technology," Khunrik taunted, a wicked gleam in his silver eyes as he smirked at the desolate scenery.

Da'fydd locked eyes with Khunrik, his unwavering gaze conveying a profound insight into his deepest desires. "Probably," he admitted, his words capturing Khunrik's attention.

In response, a broad smile spread across the silver-eyed Lord's face. "We can correct that oversight," Khunrik replied, playfully slapping Da'fydd on the back.

Leading the Lords into the dining hall of his castle, Da'fydd's brows furrowed in annoyance. The bustling activity within the room seemed out of place, especially considering it was not yet time to gather for the evening repast.

Asserting his authority, "Out!" he commanded with a firm tone. In an instant, the villagers and servants scattered like frightened rats, dispersing into the shadows. The four men stood in solitude, the weight of their presence filling the vast expanse of the room.

The atmosphere in the room thickened, each inhalation tasting of the unspoken tension that filled the air. Da'fydd stood opposite the assembled Lords, his posture rigid with resolve. His expression bore the gravity of the moment, every line and contour of his face sculpted by the seriousness of his role. The Lords watched him, their collective gaze heavy with layers of expectation. Each one of them a friend, yet his association with Celtan cast an indelible mark upon these relationships. He felt the weight of their concerns settling on his shoulders, a complex burden of leadership and friendship, blending with the bitterness of his link to a place they all viewed with skepticism, if not outright distrust.

Da'fydd gestured for the Lords to take their seats at the nearest long table, his mind briefly shifting to Amber, knowing she would still harbor anger toward him. He reached out to her mind. *I'm going to portal you to the great room. Please behave yourself. We have important guests.*

I always behave myself, Amber retorted, her tone tinged with pent-up frustration.

Da'fydd had kept her confined to his chambers. While he anticipated a potential outburst from her, he hoped she would find a way to contain her anger at him until later, when they had privacy.

With a swift motion, Da'fydd effortlessly transported Amber through the portal, bringing her to the great room. He pulled her into his arms so her back rested against his chest. "May I present my mate?" He directed his words toward the three Lords. He sensed a subtle shift in Amber when her eyes landed on the Lords.

Mate?

We've talked about this already, little bird. It is what you are to me.

Amber let the matter drop and focused on the males before them.

"Amber," Da'fydd said, his voice carrying through the primarily empty great room, "This is Adryan, Khunrik, and Darius. They are the Lords of Arkyn." The words reverberated, the echoes filling the space as Amber adjusted to the presence of the powerful beings before her.

Da'fydd contained a frown as he sensed hostility within Amber towards the Lords.

What about the woman? Amber inquired, her curiosity piqued as she sought clarification from Da'fydd.

Da'fydd guided Amber to a seat beside him at the table. *She is Adryan's Primary. Do not engage with her without permission. She will do the same. These boundaries must be adhered to.* He infused his words with strong emotion to impress upon Amber to maintain this decorum with the three Lords.

Da'fydd sensed a shift in Amber's demeanor, a darkening of her countenance. Concerned, he probed further, asking, *What's wrong?*

Nothing, Amber curtly replied, her response laced with pent-up emotions. Da'fydd recognized that there was something more within her mind. He would wait until a more appropriate time to delve deeper.

Though Amber plastered a smile upon her face, it failed to reach her eyes. She offered a slight inclination of her head towards the three Lords, who acknowledged the gesture with a single nod.

Da'fydd breathed a silent sigh of relief that the Lords had not taken notice of Amber's chilly demeanor, hoping that the tension between them would subside as their encounter progressed.

Da'fydd settled into a seat across from the three Lords to better engage in the forthcoming conversation. The woman, Adryan's Primary, stood nearby, a subtle presence that did not escape Amber's notice. Da'fydd observed Amber's gaze as it lingered on the woman, her curiosity evident.

"What is it that you require of me?" Da'fydd's hands rested on the tabletop.

"We seek your assistance in locating the imbecile who tried to claim my Primary," Adryan stated, his words capturing Da'fydd's full attention.

"How did he attempt to claim your Primary?" Da'fydd inquired, his mind contemplating the situation.

Adryan cast a quick glance at Khunrik and Darius before refocusing his gaze on Da'fydd. A fierce frown marred his features. "The fool presented a stone, spouting nonsensical claims that it indicated she belonged to him."

Da'fydd's attention shifted towards Amber, his eyes locking with hers in a silent exchange of understanding. He retrieved something from his pocket, revealing Amber's lineage stone. "A stone like this one?" he asked, displaying the stone for Adryan to see.

Adryan's eyes narrowed as recognition flickered across his face. "Yes," he confirmed.

Da'fydd responded with a solemn nod. "Did this idiot give his name?"

"Heylyn." Darius provided the answer.

Da'fydd heaved a heavy sigh. He secured Amber's lineage stone in his pocket. "These are lineage stones for Druidesses sent away from Celtan long ago." His eyes darted to Amber, acknowledging the gravity of the situation. "Regrettably, we must involve the High Druidess in this matter." The weight of his words hung in the air. The last thing he wanted was to involve Kaily. It did appear that she had indeed sent others out after the lineages. A foolish move.

The Lords exchanged brief glances of puzzlement, their expressions reflecting their confusion. Da'fydd allowed a small smile to grace his lips. Understanding their preconceived notions, Da'fydd knew how the presence of a female leader might challenge their perceptions and force them to address her as an equal. It was an intriguing prospect, one that Da'fydd anticipated with interest. He knew that on Arkyn, females were protected treasures.

In a telepathic command, Da'fydd instructed the servants to prepare the rooms in the second tower for their esteemed guests. It was a communication style he rarely used, and the servants were always taken aback by the sound of his voice resonating within their minds. Da'fydd, albeit aware of the fear it instilled in them, couldn't help but find a hint of delight in their reactions.

"May I offer sustenance?" Da'fydd inquired, addressing the Lords with genuine hospitality.

No! Amber responded telepathically to his question.

Da'fydd's eyes darted to her as she also shook her head. *Why not?*

Because nothing is ready yet! My progress in the kitchen was interrupted.

A glimmer of amusement danced in Da'fydd's eyes as he nearly allowed a smile to grace his lips in response to her silent rebuke. It was a subtle and cunning display of her disapproval, veiled in passive-aggressiveness, which he relished correcting in private.

The Lords exchanged glances, and Adryan spoke on their behalf, graciously declining the offer. "No, thank you. We currently have no need for sustenance. Nonetheless, we appreciate your kind offer."

Da'fydd nodded. "For the best," his gaze shifted to Amber. "I have been made aware that the kitchen is not quite prepared for guests or the evening meal." He raised an eyebrow.

Amber glared at him before averting her gaze. However, a small smile played at the corners of her lips as she crossed her arms protectively over her chest.

Curiosity gleamed in Darius' eyes as he spoke, a hint of mischief coloring his words. "Your mate has spirit."

"Too much," Da'fydd responded. "Return to the kitchen." He told Amber. It was in her mind to refuse. *Don't!* Da'fydd rebuked her. *The evening meal will be expected in a few hours, and the Lords and I have much to discuss.*

As you wish! Amber replied.

Da'fydd chose to ignore the snideness in her silent tone.

"Kyara," Adryan called out, pausing to wait for his Primary to kneel beside him, his voice filled with a commanding yet tender tone. "Accompany Amber to the kitchens and lend your assistance in preparing the evening meal." He affectionately caressed the back of her head before bestowing a delicate kiss on the top of her head.

Kyara acknowledged each of the Lords with a nod before rising to her feet and redirecting her gaze towards Amber.

Sensing the unease in Amber's expression, Da'fydd subtly shook his head, urging her to comply.

Amber, heeding Da'fydd's gesture, mustered a small smile and motioned for Kyara to follow. "This way," she said, leading the woman towards the kitchens.

As they departed, Da'fydd's attention turned back to the Lords, curiosity lacing his words. "How are things faring on Arkyn?" he inquired, his interest piqued by their earlier mention of the world he once frequented in his youth.

Adryan's response held an underlying invitation. "You should come and see for yourself. It has been some time since you last set foot on Arkyn."

Da'fydd suppressed a sigh, fully aware of the significant passage of time since his last visit to any world beyond Celtan. Longing laced his tone as he responded, "Perhaps." His gaze briefly shifted towards the diligent servants, acknowledging their prompt response to his earlier command. "Your rooms have been prepared whenever you are ready to retire for the evening."

"Thank you, Da'fydd." Adryan expressed his gratitude with a nod.

Da'fydd returned the gesture, inclining his head in a nod of mutual respect. The conversation between them soon deepened, shifting from casual chatter to substantive dialogue. Tales and anecdotes were exchanged, laughter punctuating the air as they caught up on all that had transpired in Arkyn. For every story shared, a similar tale from Da'fydd's own preferred home world would flicker through his mind, each one accompanied by an ever-intensifying pang of bittersweet longing.

However, he allowed none of this internal struggle to surface. His features remained a masterful portrait of equanimity, adeptly concealing the roil of emotions beneath. This time spent among friends, even with its undertow of unfulfilled yearnings, was a gift. Each moment a reminder of bonds that, though tested by differing loyalties and worlds, remained unbroken.

Chapter Twenty-One

Amber found herself cocooned within a world painted in shades of pre-dawn twilight as the surprising sanctuary of her dreams gave way to reality. With a soft sigh, she gently pushed back the warm covers that had been her shield against the nocturnal chill. In the hushed silence, her eyes, diamonds of curiosity, traced the familiar patterns of Da'fydd's chamber as images of the previous evening and night danced through her mind.

Her gaze lingered on the window, a silent sentinel that bore witness to the passage of the days. It was usually a kaleidoscope of morning light hues, a daily spectacle of warmth. But at this moment, the canvas remained devoid of color, a testament to her early rising. The bite of the morning air prickled at her exposed skin, causing a parade of goosebumps to march across her bare legs.

The allure of the enveloping warmth of the bed and the rhythmic breathing of Da'fydd were tempting invitations to snuggle back into his magnetic energy. But Amber, imbued with a sense of purpose, resisted. There were tasks that required her attention and surprises to be prepared before the household stirred for the morning meal.

With a touch as light as a whisper, Amber leaned over Da'fydd. Her lips met his in a feathery caress, lingering just long enough to feel the ghost of a connection even as he slept. His face, usually so wrought with complexities, appeared serene in the landscape of his dreams. Seemingly untouched by her actions, he continued to breathe evenly, lost in a tranquil slumber that she was loath to disturb.

Taking great care, Amber began her delicate maneuvering to the edge of the bed, each movement calculated to preserve the harmony of the moment. She held her breath as she slipped into her clothes, the fabric whispering against her skin in quiet complicity. It was a dance of stillness, each step an act of reverence for the newfound quietude that had fallen over them like a veil of grace. The room seemed to hold its breath with her, and for those few minutes, their peaceful coexistence felt almost sacrosanct.

An accidental encounter with a chair sent an abrasive screech slicing through the stillness, and Amber's heart skipped a beat. She threw a concerned glance over her shoulder, fully expecting Da'fydd to be jarred awake. But, as her eyes fell on his serene expression, her heartbeat stilled, and a sigh of relief escaped her lips. Finishing the task of dressing with renewed care, she tiptoed her way towards the door, intent on leaving the sanctuary of Da'fydd's chamber and stepping into the realm of a new day.

A rumble of drowsy words wafted through the air, enveloping Amber in a familiar baritone. "And just where do you think you're sneaking off to?" Da'fydd's voice, thick with sleep, broke through the silence.

"Ensuring we're not reduced to stale bread and cold cheese for the morning meal," Amber playfully shot back, a lilt dancing in her voice. A smile spread across her face as she took in Da'fydd's struggle against the call of sleep. His eyes, heavy with the remnants of slumber, bore a glint of contentment he hadn't bothered to disguise, making her heart skip a beat. His hand moved to lazily rub his face, an unexpected picture of tranquility.

"Good luck," came Da'fydd's sleep-laden mumble, his attempts to stifle a yawn not entirely successful.

"Thanks," she replied. She paused at the door a moment, drinking in the charming spectacle of his morning disarray. With a soft click, she pushed the door open and stepped out of his bed chamber, leaving Da'fydd to rouse himself from the tendrils of sleep.

Amber's eyes flicked to the two guards who fell into step with her, their movements synchronized and unobtrusive. Her initial reaction to this protective detail had been a complex knot of emotions, combining discomfort with a vague sense of intrusion. Over time the familiarity had begun to dull the edges of her initial apprehension. They moved like shadows, echoing her steps without intruding upon her space.

She didn't speak to them, nor did they attempt to engage her. The silence was a protective shroud, allowing her the semblance of solitude she craved. At the back of her mind was a lingering reassurance that Da'fydd's influence was at work here, an invisible safeguard. It was enough to grant her a wary sense of security, even as she navigated through the still unfamiliar terrain of her new life.

Amber navigated through the corridors, her steps purposeful as she made her way to the kitchen. The servant girl she had recently promoted to the role of cook was there, ensnared in the peaceful embrace of sleep. Her breathing was even, her body relaxed, blissfully unaware of the day's impending responsibilities.

Gently, Amber nudged the girl's shoulder, awakening her without shock or alarm. As the girl's eyes fluttered open, Amber offered a reassuring smile. Their partnership was new, their understandings still forming. They hadn't yet discussed Amber's culinary preferences or the daily menu before Da'fydd's unanticipated intervention. The unexpected arrival of the three Arkyn Lords had led to her being quickly sequestered in Da'fydd's chambers, and then the rush to prepare an acceptable evening meal, had left behind loose threads of details that demanded to be tied.

Ironing out the hint of a scowl that had started to carve itself onto her face, Amber turned her attention to the young servant girl. "I require your assistance, Mia." She sank onto a single knee to bring herself eye level with the girl, her hands finding solace in the smooth texture of the stone floor for support.

Mia sat up and rubbed sleep from her eyes. "Wouldn't someone older be better suited for head cook, m'Lady?"

"No, Mia." Amber shook her head.

Mia's eyes met hers, but she said nothing, as if waiting for an explanation.

Amber's gaze softened, understanding filling her eyes. The young girl didn't seem to be accustomed to conversing with others, let alone being tasked with responsibilities. However, that was about to change. "Because, Mia, I see potential in you. A spark waiting to be kindled. Will you trust me?" As she urged the girl on, Amber held Mia's gaze, anchoring her with the sincerity in her eyes.

Mia seemed to ponder Amber's words, her gaze drifting momentarily to the stone floor beneath them. When she looked back up, her eyes carried a glint of something that hadn't been there before; perhaps the first fragile stirrings of self-belief.

Amber stood and waited for the girl to gather her courage.

Mia took a deep breath and pushed herself to a standing position. "What are we preparing?"

Amber clasped her hands, her fingers threading together. "You tell me, Mia. What can you whip up that's amazing?"

The answer was a flat, discouraged, "Nothing."

Undeterred, "Try again, Mia," Amber coaxed, her tone brimming with the kind of encouragement she wished someone, anyone, had given her when she was Mia's age.

There was no logical reason for her faith in Mia's cooking abilities. But there was something raw and earnest about Mia and her interactions with food that spoke volumes to Amber. She'd caught a glimpse of it the day before when Da'fydd first brought her to the kitchen.

She'd witnessed the girl's spirit drop from the scolding the old cook had given Mia for her 'creative' streak. The exchange had ignited a desire within Amber to guide this young girl, to help her blossom.

With a slight pause, Mia hesitantly ventured, "Hot herb rolls and porridge." Her words spoken as if she were sharing a secret. "It's not too difficult to make, and some have said it was delicious."

"Excellent." Amber headed towards the sink. Mia trailed behind her. As Amber washed her hands, her gaze roved across the kitchen. It was remarkably cleaner, the counters scrubbed, and the hearth not quite spotless but close. Turning to Mia, a question etched itself onto her features. "Mia, did you do a deeper cleaning after Kyara, and I departed last night?"

Mia, taken aback, managed a shy nod. "Aye, I thought it would be better to work in a cleaner kitchen," she admitted, a hint of hesitation lacing her words.

Amber's face broke into a warm, appreciative smile, her eyes sparkling with admiration. "You thought right. Let's get to it." She helped place items on the counter that Mia grabbed from different pantries. She attempted not to cringe after glancing into a couple of them.

Mia glanced at Amber with a touch of uncertainty. "After the morning meal, I'll finish cleaning," Mia quietly offered.

Amber acknowledged Mia's dedication with an approving nod. "We'll ensure you have assistance with the remaining cleanup," she assured her.

As the dawn broke, the other servants started to trickle in, their weary bodies trudging through their morning routine. Amber took the reins, reaffirming Mia's new role as head cook. Their responses were mostly indifferent.

With the morning meal preparation and the kitchen staff well within Mia's command, Amber was satisfied enough to turn her attention elsewhere.

What are you doing? She probed Da'fydd's mind, her mental touch as gentle as a feather. The telltale aura of his presence indicated he was in the dining hall.

Rearranging, Da'fydd's silent response echoed in Amber's mind, simple and focused yet carrying a light-hearted undertone from their earlier banter.

Why? Amber found herself intrigued, her curiosity piqued. Leaning nonchalantly against entrance, she observed from her secluded vantage point. Her eyes, bright with intrigue, took in the room's transformation.

With an innate sense of command, Da'fydd orchestrated the movements of the male servants. His instructions were clear and decisive, leaving no room for ambiguity. Yet, he was far from a distant overseer. Melding his physical actions with the subtler art of his abilities, he directed his powers to assist in moving the cumbersome, elongated wooden tables. His will made manifest, the energies responded, lightening the load as if the tables were as insubstantial as feathers.

The room buzzed with a kinetic energy, as servants and crafts-men darted about with purpose. At one end, the transformation on the raised platform was nearly complete. A long table, set parallel to the room's length, adorned its top. Matching tables on the main floor lay perpendicular to it, creating an organized contrast. Chairs populated the platform, each angled to face the room, inviting conversation rather than a one-sided proclamation. The setup hinted at openness, a departure from the traditional, imposing throne-like platform. Yet, despite this air of approachability, there was no mistaking for whom the platform was intended: the 'Master' of the castle.

Amber's eyes sparkled with a blend of amusement and newfound respect as she watched Da'fydd from across the room. The contrast between the stern, imposing figure who had first welcomed her to the castle and this more collaborative version was striking. The idea that he would lend not just orders but also his abilities to the room's setup came as a pleasant surprise. She could see a smile beginning to form at the corners of her mouth, almost as if it were a secret she couldn't help but share. Here was a Da'fydd she could genuinely appreciate, one whose actions spoke of a complexity she was eager to explore.

"Food and drink for the high table," Da'fydd instructed. Amber watched as the servant nodded, scurrying off to fulfill his orders.

You do know nothing is ready yet, right?

Da'fydd gave her a nonchalant shrug.

Amber shook her head at him. As she pivoted to return to the bustling kitchen, a firm hand clasped hers, halting her in her tracks. She swiveled back, her gaze colliding with Da'fydd's.

"What is it?" she asked, curiosity pricking at her.

Da'fydd's response was sincere, a rare softness lining his eyes. "You've already done more than enough. You do not belong in the kitchen."

Amber mulled over his words. When she had last left the kitchen, Mia seemed to have everything under control, her command over the situation steadily growing. After a moment of consideration, Amber relented. "Alright," she agreed, allowing herself to be led by Da'fydd, surrendering to his guiding hand as he steered her towards a quiet corner to sit and observe as the servants completed rearranging the dining hall. The warmth in his touch was a silent promise that no matter where she found herself in the castle, she was right where she belonged.

Time seemed to stretch out infinitely as Amber sat in companionable silence beside Da'fydd, their peaceful quiet interspersed with the muted chatter of people trickling in for the morning meal. Then, as if on cue, the grand doors of the dining hall swung open, announcing the arrival of the three Lords.

With fluid grace, Da'fydd rose to his feet, a silent salute to the Lords as they crossed the room and took their places at the table. A customary exchange of greetings was performed, their forearms clasping in a firm, comradely grip before they dropped onto their seats with an almost boisterous energy Amber had come to know as a characteristic of men.

Adryan took his place to Da'fydd's left, a position that seemed to signify some level of importance or closeness. Khunrik and Darius opted for chairs closer to Amber, filling in the spaces on her half of the table. The seating choices seemed strategic, and Amber sensed a subtle division, one that added another layer of complexity to the already intricate dynamics of their association with Da'fydd.

As Amber's eyes flitted around the room, her thoughts turned to Kyara. The absence of the enigmatic woman was conspicuous, especially considering her connection to the Arkyn Lords. A flicker of concern crossed Amber's mind. Had something happened to her? Or was there a reason Kyara had chosen to distance herself from this gathering? The questions added a ripple of unease to the already palpable tension within Amber towards the Lords.

As the room filled with the villagers and a steady hum of conversation ensued, Amber's quiet unease grew. Da'fydd subtly extended his hand under the table, capturing hers in a comforting squeeze. It was a silent yet powerful gesture, his warmth seeping into her through the intimate contact. *Breathe, little bird.*

Amber smiled up at Da'fydd. *Where's Adryan's Primary?* She asked Da'fydd within their private link.

It's not for us to pry, Da'fydd responded, softly defusing Amber's inquiry while maintaining a modicum of compassion.

Amber found herself a quiet observer, her gaze flitting across the villagers as they bustled about the dining hall. The platters of rolls were passed around, steaming bowls of porridge finding their way into eager hands. All the while, Da'fydd was engaged in a deep conversation with the Lords, his voice weaving into the hum of surrounding chatter.

Amber's body might have been present at the table, physically beside Da'fydd, but her mind was elsewhere. The conversation around her became mere background noise, blurring into a soft hum that barely touched her consciousness. Her thoughts kept drifting toward Kyara, wondering where she could be and whether she was alright.

Da'fydd's words from earlier replayed in her mind, subtle but laden with meaning. 'It's not for us to pry.' The message had been clear; certain topics were off-limits, and in Arkyn society, boundaries were more than just lines. They were walls, seldom crossed without consequence. She felt the weight of those words, recognizing that they were not only a guideline but also a warning to be heeded. But still, she couldn't shake the feeling that Kyara's absence meant something more.

Even as Amber acknowledged the need to respect cultural norms and unspoken rules, her natural concern for Kyara couldn't be easily quelled. Her eyes flitted to Da'fydd, who was engrossed in a fervent conversation with the Lords, his attention fully absorbed in the matters at hand. Observing his deep involvement gave her a momentary pause, a brief window of time to mull over her jumbled thoughts.

A whirlwind of questions and speculations swirled within her mind, each vying for her focus as she tried to make sense of her feelings and the enigmatic situation surrounding Kyara's absence. Her gaze returned to her own hands, folded neatly on the table, but her thoughts were far from settled. There was a disquiet within her, a subtle unrest that belied the lively atmosphere of the room. It was a paradox, the contrast between the exterior world and her interior monologue.

"This meal exceeds my expectations," Darius commented, his tone tinged with astonishment as he enthusiastically delved into his porridge. The action left small splatters on his chin, which he quickly dabbed away with a cloth.

Casting a quick, amused glance at Darius, Da'fydd redirected the conversation. "You should extend your gratitude to Amber," he said, subtly steering attention her way.

Caught momentarily off guard, Amber glanced up as her name was mentioned. She met Da'fydd's eyes, noting the glint of amusement there before turning her gaze towards Darius. His expression of delight over the simple meal warmed her, dispelling some of her earlier concerns about her role in the castle.

"Ah, then my compliments to you, m'Lady," Darius said, meeting her eyes with evident gratitude, the cloth still in his hand from wiping his chin.

"I'm glad you're enjoying it," Amber replied.

Darius spoke through his bites. "You've truly taken hold of this rustic place, and I'm intrigued to see what other transformations you bring." His smirk was infectious, drawing a scowl from Da'fydd that rapidly wiped the smile from Darius's face.

Amber's gaze flickered up at the sound from the entrance as Adryan's Primary entered the dining hall and marched with purpose towards the high table.

"You're almost late," Adryan mildly reproached Kyara, spooning the last of his porridge into his mouth with a final, slightly irksome clack of the spoon against his bowl.

"I apologize. I was dispensing a lesson in manners." Kyara retorted, her tone smooth as she settled into a squat beside Adryan.

Adryan's eyebrow arched in intrigue at her cryptic statement, "And what exactly does that entail?"

As if on cue, a man limped into the room, coming from the same direction as Kyara. Amber's breath hitched in the back of her throat and a cold fear snaked its way up her spine. She could feel Da'fydd's hands balling into fists next to her. Rory. Amber's own inner voice trembled at the recognition. Seeking confirmation from Da'fydd, she turned to him, only to find his gaze already hardened on the limping figure. His eyes mere slits, his face tight with a concealed fury.

Adryan, taking in the scene, nodded slowly. "I see," he said, a newfound understanding flickering in his eyes.

Adryan cast a quick glance at Darius and Khunrik, receiving curt nods in response. His gaze landed on Da'fydd. "Would you produce a few of the rudimentary weapons of this world for us?"

In response, Da'fydd's hand moved in an unfamiliar gesture, more intricate than when he conjured flames or opened portals. Suddenly, four broadswords materialized on the table, avoiding any disruption to the food and drinks. The Lords shifted their dishes aside and rose, each claiming a sword and evaluating its weight with a discerning gaze. The ease with which they handled the weapons hinted at their familiarity.

"These are satisfactory," Adryan concluded, his nod approving.

Da'fydd rose next, his hand closing around the worn leather hilt of the remaining sword, lifting it from the table. *What do you intend to do?* Amber inquired telepathically, curiosity tinged with dread.

No more than what should have been done in the first place.
Da'fydd's reply held a firm resolution that brokered no argument. He signaled to the three Lords.

Amber's attention snapped to Rory, who seemed to have become an ice sculpture in the doorway, possibly realizing his return to the castle was a dire error. Noticing Da'fydd and the others brandishing their swords, Rory hastily retreated from the dining hall, his injured leg impeding his escape, a trail of blood in his wake.

"You have indeed excelled in your self-defense training. You've proven a swift learner," Adryan praised his Primary, his voice warm. In response, she offered him a smile and leaned in to whisper something into his ear, her head bowed. His response was a tender kiss on the top of her head. "You may," he said, his voice gentle.

Kyara rose gracefully, repositioning herself to sit next to Amber in Darius's previously occupied seat. Reaching out, she selected a roll from a nearby plate that had cooled slightly. Almost seamlessly, a servant materialized to place a steaming bowl of fresh porridge before her as though forewarned of her desires.

As Amber wrestled with the enigma of the woman choosing to sit beside her, the quartet of men departed. Their pace was unhurried, but their strides were determined and prolonged, embodying an air of impending conflict as they held their swords in semi-ready positions. The castle's inhabitants noted the men's departure, but no discernible reaction rippled through them.

"They're heading out to kill him," Amber noted, watching the men vanish through the double doors and out of sight.

"It's their right," came the unexpected reply from Kyara, her matter-of-fact tone startling Amber. "The man should have kept his hands to himself." Her gaze, devoid of any semblance of pity, met Amber's. "I noticed the way you regarded him. That brute. You've had an unfortunate encounter with him, haven't you?" She continued to chew her food, casually tossing the remainder of the roll back onto the plate.

Amber's gaze fixed on the half-eaten roll. "You could say that," she murmured.

A heavy silence hung between the two women, a chasm that Amber wasn't quite sure how to bridge. She stopped herself from telepathically connecting with Da'fydd's mind, recoiling at the mere thought of vicariously witnessing death through his consciousness. With a faint shudder, she forced those haunting thoughts away, endeavoring to maintain her composure in the wake of looming violence.

Softening her gaze, Kyara quietly added, "It's not easy dealing with such encounters. It leaves a mark, even if it's not visible. Know that you're not alone, Amber. We've all had our battles and scars. But we grow stronger with each trial we face." She offered Amber a sympathetic smile, bridging their chasm of silence with a shared understanding.

With a silent nod, Amber accepted Kyara's words. She found herself instinctively drawn to the grand entrance of the room, fighting the urge to connect with Da'fydd's mind. Eventually, Amber sighed quietly and redirected her attention to Kyara. "How do you live alongside someone like Adryan?" she asked.

Kyara paused, swallowing her food, her gaze upon Amber thoughtful and slightly perplexed. "I respect all the Lords immensely," she responded.

Choosing to sidestep Kyara's response, Amber's gaze drifted back to the double doors. The castle's inhabitants seemed unfazed, going about their business as if nothing had transpired. She wondered how they could be so complacent towards violence.

Guilt and relief clashed within Amber as her mind circled back to Rory. The discord of her feelings unsettled her, creating a complex tapestry of emotions that she struggled to untangle.

Da'fydd had exiled Rory, yet he had found his way back. Now, he faced a death sentence by the swords of four men that he couldn't escape. A part of her recoiled at the thought of his impending demise; another part found solace. Rory had caused her immense pain; did he not deserve to face the consequences?

Amber's mind strayed to the other two men Da'fydd had banished, stirring up a whirlpool of emotions. She shook her head as if physically trying to clear her thoughts. The memory of Da'fydd's contradictory behavior surfaced. He was a formidable force, yet simultaneously tender and protective of her.

Perhaps this was his way of safeguarding her, Amber mused. Da'fydd was eliminating Rory to prevent him from harming her again, and Adryan was doing it to avenge Kyara. A slight wave of relief washed over Amber as she realized Rory would no longer pose a threat to any woman again. If only she could purge the guilt that gnawed at her, the guilt of bearing responsibility for his impending doom.

Chapter Twenty-Two

Surrounded by the towering stone monoliths, Da'fydd trod lightly, his worn boots brushing against the plush carpet of moss. As he navigated the cold, ancient stones, his eyes fluttered shut, releasing a sigh that seemed to echo the weight of a millennium. He'd summoned Kaily, yet the sting of her absence throbbed in the silence. Anxious questions began circulating in his mind, frustrations filling the void her tardiness had carved. His gaze shifted, searching for the telltale signs of an emerging portal.

Navigated by the ethereal twilight, neither dawn nor dusk, Da'fydd ventured deeper into the serene expanse of the meadow, his presence ghost-like in the hallowed grounds of antiquated power. A notable heft dwelled in his soft, well-worn leather pants pocket. It was Amber's lineage stone, inextricably bound to her destiny.

He retrieved the stone, its smooth texture brushing against his fingertips, a tangible symbol of its unimaginable significance. The peculiar object flared to life and hummed gently in his hands, an ancient melody meant only for him.

A stone basin at the center of the monolithic pillars, almost tucked away from mortal eyes, offered an oddly serene aura. This tranquility that might enchant many; stirred unease in Da'fydd. The basin's deceptive simplicity belied the potent energy it housed. A fleeting smile etched on his lips, memories flashing back to when Kaily revealed its existence to the Druid Council. Its purpose had been a revelation, a promise of the return of the Druidesses.

The clueless Council members were entirely oblivious to the profound implications that the return of the Druidesses would hold for Celtan. Yet, Da'fydd was acutely aware. After all, he alone bore knowledge of Ravenna and her 'sisters.' A fervent hope bloomed within him, a longing to bear witness when Ravenna unveiled her true self to the self-appointed High Druidess.

Exhaling sharply, Da'fydd allowed a sigh of impatience to escape his lips. The burden of waiting was an unpleasant chore that left a sour taste in his mouth. He crossed his arms over his chest, each passing moment stoking the flame of his frustration. His gaze was a steady glare, fixed unyieldingly on the space where she should be.

Beneath the unmoving gaze of the Stone Pillars, Da'fydd felt his impatience tighten around him like a noose. The old meadow seemed almost apathetic to his emotional turbulence. His breaths came in sharp intakes, nose flaring with each cycle of air, as he waited with diminishing patience.

Deep in a labyrinth of repetitive thoughts, Da'fydd found his instincts pulling him toward the notion of connecting with Amber. He caught himself just as swiftly, reining in the urge. While he had entrusted her safety to the three Arkyn Lords, a choice that bolstered his own confidence, he knew all too well that she neither welcomed nor concurred with his decision.

Navigating the complexities of interacting with Kaily came with its own set of challenges, not the least of which was the near-constant presence of Ethan. These days, the man seemed to orbit Kaily like a dutiful satellite, rarely out of her immediate sphere. Da'fydd found himself grappling with a visceral dislike of the idea of Amber crossing paths with Ethan, an emotion amplified tenfold when considering the Kahoali warrior, Kaily's bonded mate. The mere thought left an unpleasant taste in Da'fydd's mouth, stirring a deep-seated desire to keep Amber as far removed from such influences as possible.

Da'fydd's indifference toward Kaily's choice of a bonded mate was nearly absolute, just as the intricacies of Celtan's governance held minimal sway over his interests. What commanded his attention, what eclipsed all else, was keeping Amber at a safe distance from these potentially complicating factors. Under the rulership of Deykin, the increasingly unhinged, aging Druid, flying under the radar had been a relatively straightforward affair. But now, Da'fydd found himself standing on the edge of a delicate balance, contemplating the mask of diplomatic agreement he might have to don. It was a role he'd reluctantly consider playing, all for the sake of winning Kaily's cooperation concerning matters involving the Arkyn Lords.

Before he could tumble further into the abyss of his relentless ruminations, Kaily materialized beside the stone basin at the clearing's heart, Moto in tow. Da'fydd held his ground, maintaining a safe proximity from the basin, and greeted them with a subtle nod. Ethan's absence was a surprising relief, but the tension hung heavy between them all. Da'fydd had seldom prioritized establishing cordial relations, but he realized that the tide of their relationship had to turn, for now.

Kaily's eyes roved the meadow, her voice piercing the silence. "Where's Amber?"

"Where she belongs," Da'fydd retorted with an air of casual indifference, irked that Kaily's first concern was Amber instead of the grave matter that had prompted him to summon her.

Kaily's eyes, burning with intensity, bore into Da'fydd. "Summon her here."

A scowl briefly shadowed Da'fydd's features. "No."

"As the High Druidess, it is my right to ensure her safety," Kaily asserted, her eyes unyielding, locked on Da'fydd. Moto, her silent sentinel, stood slightly behind her, his steely silver webbed gaze unwavering from Da'fydd.

"No," Da'fydd refuted again, punctuating his refusal with a decisive shake of his head.

"I insist," Kaily retorted, her arms folded defiantly across her chest as Moto edged closer to her side. "Ethan is not a part of this. Look around. He isn't here," she added, gesturing with her outstretched arms, her body twisting slightly to emphasize her point.

With a hardened edge to his voice, Da'fydd finally capitulated. "Very well, Kaily," he said, pointedly using her name, devoid of any titles, to emphasize familiarity instead of respect. "I'll accede this time, for Amber's sake." His steely gaze underscored the reluctance that flavored his concession.

With an inward focus, Da'fydd mentally reached out to Amber. *I'm going to portal you to me.*

Why? Amber queried through the silent channels of thought.

You have been summoned by the High Druidess, he responded, his telepathic voice tinged with a hint of scorn.

Alright, Amber conceded without an argument, for which Da'fydd was briefly grateful.

Da'fydd began the intricate dance of his hands with skilled precision, forming the portal as near to him as was safely possible. The sudden drop in temperature, the telltale harbinger of a forming portal, sent a shiver down his spine, a sensation he chose to ignore. Amber materialized at his side almost as swiftly as he had opened the portal. He offered her a fleeting smile of reassurance before shifting his focus back to Kaily and Moto.

Da'fydd's initial reason for summoning Kaily, to discuss the appearance of the Arkyn Lords, had become secondary in the unfolding dialogue. An internal urgency nudged him to redirect the conversation to its original purpose. Yet Kaily's own agenda had monopolized the discussion, leaving him with scant opportunity to steer it back. What Da'fydd wanted to avoid at all costs was unexpectedly dragging Amber into these intricate affairs. So he waited, honing his patience, gauging the ideal moment to bring the focus back to the Arkyn Lords without compromising Amber's separation from the issue.

"Join me, please," Kaily entreated, gesturing for Amber and Da'fydd to approach the stone basin.

Da'fydd experienced the sight through Amber's fresh perspective as they moved closer. The large stone vessel, filled with waters pulsating with unseen power, commanded attention atop its tall pedestal. It was evident that the basin had been untouched for some time. The verdant surroundings were breathtaking to Amber, who was looking at it for the first time. Her gaze riveted to the basin with an intensity that hinted at a deep-seated fascination.

What is this place? Amber asked Da'fydd, her shoe stirring the ground beneath, leaving deeper impressions wherever she exerted more pressure.

This is a sanctuary of Celtan's potent energy, In that moment, Da'fydd found words insufficient to encapsulate the gravity of what he wished to convey. He sensed that as time unfolded, she would naturally grasp the profound implications and nuances that mere words could never capture.

Kaily seemed to maintain her patience as long as she could. "Amber, come here, please." She turned her gaze toward Da'fydd. "Hold out the stone, Da'fydd. I'm certain you have it with you."

Da'fydd drew the stone from his pocket with a dismissive shake of his head. As Amber drew nearer to him, a wave of anxiety crossed her features. *What's happening?* she inquired.

"I require both of you to simultaneously touch the stone," Kaily instructed, her voice ringing with authority.

We are being tested. Da'fydd tersely replied.

For what?

He offered no response, his attention steadfastly fixed on Kaily, a wave of displeasure washing over him due to her demand.

Da'fydd, with Amber, yielded to Kaily's command, albeit with reluctance. Da'fydd extended his hand towards Amber, the stone resting in his palm. She slowly raised her hand, her fingers brushing the stone's surface. Suddenly, the stone blazed into life, glowing with an intensity akin to a swarm of fireflies concentrated around them. Amber instinctively averted her gaze, but Da'fydd kept his eyes fixed on the brilliant spectacle until its radiance became unbearable, forcing him to squint and turn away. Amber withdrew her hand, and Da'fydd could feel an electric charge humming through both their bodies.

"What was that?" Amber asked. "What does this signify?"

Da'fydd's focus remained fixed on Kaily. "Satisfied?" Da'fydd tucked the stone back into his pocket, his tone laced with thinly veiled sarcasm. *I'll explain later.* Da'fydd telepathically advised Amber.

"Yes," Kaily affirmed.

Moto positioned himself behind Kaily, arms crossed, as she pursued her objective with a fiery determination in her eyes. "It's clear, you two are true mates. You both must undergo the bonding ritual soon. If not, the energy's call might overwhelm Amber, and she may be lost to it for eternity."

A gentle breeze swept across the meadow, causing the water within the basin to ripple. Amber's eyes fastened onto Da'fydd, myriad questions shimmering within her mind.

What is she talking about? What is this 'call of energy'? Amber's brows knitted together as she questioned Da'fydd.

Da'fydd's gaze briefly flickered over to Kaily and Moto, who seemed to be conversing mind-to-mind. He turned back to Amber, wrestling with the same questions that troubled her. He hadn't sensed her experiencing any energy from Celtan calling to her.

"Kaily, Amber hasn't experienced this 'calling,'" Da'fydd informed her.

Kaily turned to Amber for verification. "In truth?"

"I don't know what that means," Amber admitted with a shrug.

This unexpected admission seemed to perplex Kaily, as her face flushed with confusion. "How?" She exchanged another glance with Moto, her expression dancing with emotions, although no other words were uttered.

Da'fydd found this amusing, though it was also tiresome. Kaily might have been consulting Moto all along, and the Kahoali might not be as compliant as Da'fydd had initially assumed. Yet, the warrior was an enigma, his emotions hidden behind a stone-like countenance. Those were mere speculations since Da'fydd couldn't truly comprehend their silent discourse.

"Kaily, I have an urgent matter that requires your attention," Da'fydd interjected, stepping forward. "The Lords of Arkyn have arrived on Celtan and seek an audience with the High Druidess."

"Why?" Kaily shot Da'fydd an irritated yet concerned look.

"One of the Druids you dispatched off-world to procure a Druidess tried to abscond with one of their own," Da'fydd gestured towards Amber. "Did you really think bringing back the Druidesses would be so easy?"

You could be more polite, Da'fydd. He felt Amber's reproachful gaze on him.

"Which one?" Kaily asked.

With a hint of amusement creeping into his demeanor, Da'fydd noticed her selective attention to his words. "Does it matter?" he asked, shrugging dismissively.

"Yes." Kaily's eyes remained locked with Da'fydd's.

"Heylyn," Amber answered when Da'fydd remained silent.

Remain silent, little bird, if you wish to remain for the remainder of my conversation with Kaily. Da'fydd reprimanded.

Even without words, Da'fydd could sense the heat of Amber's unspoken displeasure emanating from her. It was as if her silence had its own language, a bristling energy that spoke volumes, even without their connection, alerting him to the undercurrents of her discontent.

"I agree to their request for an audience," Kaily declared, her gaze returning to Da'fydd. "Present them to me in the morning." She lifted her hand to dismiss Da'fydd and Amber yet paused in her motion. "Regardless of Amber's apparent insensitivity to the call of Celtan's energy, the two of you should be bound before too much time has passed. Be ready. The moment looms closer than you might wish."

Da'fydd nodded tersely, then retreated a few paces where he conjured a portal. Amber was the first to step through the shimmering void, and he followed her, her questions already echoing in the recesses of his mind. *Patience,* he telepathically assured her as they left the serene meadow and Kaily's stern warnings behind.

Stepping through the portal onto the neglected soil of the forest surrounding his castle, Da'fydd was immediately struck by the contrast to the lush meadow within the Stone Pillars. The disparity gnawed at him, a physical ache that paired poorly with the unsettling scents of decay and dampness pervading the air. As he composed himself, his eyes narrowed, catching sight of a silhouette partially obscured by the ragged outlines of withered trees. It was Ravenna, her presence there adding another layer of complexity to his already tangled thoughts.

Da'fydd's brow furrowed, a visible sign of his mounting irritation. Tension collected in his shoulders, and he rolled them in an attempt to dispel it. Just as he was succumbing to his inner turmoil, a light touch on his shoulder jolted him back to reality. It was Amber. He quelled the sigh rising in his chest and pivoted to face her, letting his annoyance dissolve. In that moment, he remembered that whatever vexations the world thrust upon him, they paled in comparison to the sanctuary he found in her presence.

"Don't concern yourself with her," Amber said, commanding Da'fydd's focus and diverting his attention from the Huntress. "Why did you bring us here?" Her question filled the space between them, breaking the tranquility.

Da'fydd silenced her spoken words, pressing a finger gently against her lips. *I require a private conversation with you.* His gaze shifted to the ground, the challenge of initiating this delicate subject weighing heavily on him.

What's the matter? You can confide in me. Amber's eyes, filled with affection, sought his, her hands tenderly clasping his.

Do you genuinely desire to bind your existence to mine? If your answer is no, I promise to let you go without a hint of resistance. Da'fydd held her gaze, losing himself in the depth of her eyes, watching them shift and change as she absorbed his question.

Although it would wound him, he wouldn't force her to stay. In his perfect world, she'd remain by his side, his companion through countless seasons as he led his domain into the future. He'd never wanted to discover his true mate, having believed such a life wasn't for him. Now, he was conflicted between a life with Amber and the life he once knew. Returning to his old ways would be simple, but was it what he genuinely wanted?

Da'fydd could sense the weight of his proposition bearing down on Amber. The full scope of choosing to stay and forever entwine her life with his was beyond her immediate comprehension. Gently, he probed her thoughts, glimpsing her internal struggles. Amber craved freedom yet found it difficult to picture her life devoid of his presence. Sensing his subtle invasion, she shielded her mind to the best of her ability.

Respecting her boundary, Da'fydd retracted his mental exploration.

I require some time to think about your question, Amber conveyed her thoughts to him. *Once I fully understand what's between us, I'll give you my answer. You have my word.* Her hand, resting on his cheek, radiated a warmth that offered him solace.

When she withdrew her touch, he found himself yearning for more. Her response, or the lack of one, didn't satisfy him. He gave her a curt nod, acknowledging her need for time.

Amber playfully nudged Da'fydd.

He smiled down at her. Gently, he took a loose curl of her hair and swept it back behind her ear. Taking her hand in his, he guided her towards his castle on foot, craving more alone time with her. He gazed across the desolate expanse of almost alive trees, noticing that the light of day would fade too soon. While he rarely experienced fatigued, the idea of a tranquil evening appealed to him more than partaking in the night's feast. To be fair, he rarely participated but his presence would be missed by their guests.

A mischievous grin spread across Amber's face as they approached the dog pens. Da'fydd already started shaking his head, discerning her intentions through their mental bond. But before he could voice a word of protest, Amber darted towards the dogs with a giggle. Sighing good-naturedly, Da'fydd trailed after her as she scooped up the female puppy she had a particular fondness for. He observed the glimmer of pure joy in her eyes as she gathered another jet-black pup from the litter into her arms.

"How are they faring?" Amber called out, expecting Bren, the usual caretaker, to be nearby.

Emerging from the back of the barn, Bren replied, "Seems like they've missed you, especially that one," he said, indicating the female puppy. "They're gradually becoming independent, eating solids and relying less on their mother." Shrugging, he added, "They've been outdoors all day. The pup would probably appreciate your company, m'Lady."

Da'fydd fixed Bren with a ferocious glare, emitting a menacing growl.

Bren lowered his gaze and scurried toward the barn's backroom.

"My goodness, they've grown so much," Amber cooed, picking up another eager puppy. "I wish I could take them all," she said, lavishing attention on the wagging-tailed furballs.

Despite his resistance, Da'fydd found himself holding a little beast that Amber thrust into his arms. Her incessant cheer bordered on unnerving. As she beamed at him, he advised, "You may not bring these beasts into our bedchamber."

Amber stifled a laugh at Da'fydd's awkward handling of the puppy held out at arm's length, who chose that moment to relieve itself, fortunately missing Da'fydd due to the distance he'd maintained.

"Be kind to the poor thing," Amber chided, caressing the puppy's head while cooing softly, seemingly smitten by the 'horrendous beasts' as Da'fydd mentally labeled them.

The creature would make a fine boot, Da'fydd grumbled inwardly.

I heard that, Amber retorted telepathically, sauntering towards the castle. Da'fydd hastened his steps to keep up with her, shifting the squirming beast in his arms to secure a better grip. As he trailed her, he shook his head in response to her playful actions, all the while admiring her retreating figure.

Chapter Twenty-Three

Da'fydd led Amber with an effortless grace, her hand lightly perched on his forearm. Together, they navigated through the intricately carved double doors of wood, stepping into the grand meeting room at the core of the newly unveiled City Center. This majestic arrangement of stone edifices had recently risen to prominence near Gregori's tower, capturing everyone's attention, except for Da'fydd's. When Kaily had briefed the Council about the City Center, he had tuned her out, finding other matters more pressing. Now, however, the significance of their surroundings was not lost on him, especially with Amber at his side. It served as yet another facet in the ever-changing tapestry of their complex world, a world he was increasingly sharing with her.

Da'fydd sensed the wonder that rippled through Amber's thoughts, her mental voice tinged with awe. *This place... it's magical*, she shared, the resonance of her thoughts bridging the space between them. Her eyes drank in the grandeur, a stark deviation from the simple elegance she had come to know. And in that moment, he couldn't help but appreciate the intricacies of the world anew, seen through her eyes, a blend of enchantment and revelation. It was as if her awe awakened a dormant layer of appreciation within him, a facet he seldom allowed himself to entertain.

Da'fydd's soft chuckle echoed in response, a warm, comforting sound. He glanced around in an attempt to see from Amber's eyes. *Do you like it better than mine?* He teased, his eyes gleaming with amusement.

No. Amber favored Da'fydd with a smile before continuing. *There's something;* she gave herself a mental shake as she attempted to find the right word.

Majikal. Da'fydd replied.

Amber's fingers tightened slightly on his arm as she glanced at him. *It is, but something more. It's all quite overwhelming in a way.* Her discomfort slipped into his mind through their shared connection. *I wish you would have let me wear the hunting outfit rather than this gown,* she confessed, her tone threaded with longing.

With a gentle, reassuring squeeze, Da'fydd offered his solace. *Next time, little bird. You are stunning in the gown.* His tone was a soothing melody of compulsion.

Amber gave him a slight shake of her head in disagreement. She glanced back at Adryan and Kyara, who were a few steps behind, mirroring their formal stance. Kyara's attire was far more extravagant than her own, radiating a royal grandeur that starkly contrasted Amber's simpler attire. Kyara's gown shimmered under the room's illuminating glow. It was as if the starlit night had been woven into the fabric of her dress.

Kyara's gown... it's breathtaking, Amber murmured to Da'fydd through their link, entranced by the woman trailing behind them. *I might find wearing a dress more appealing if –*

Da'fydd's mental voice unfurled like a low growl, arresting Amber's train of thought. His eyes met hers, a softened gaze that belied the gravity of his unspoken words. *Careful what you wish for, little bird,* he cautioned in the silent recesses of her mind. His words were as much a challenge as they were a comfort, a layered murmur that caressed her imagination and dared her to dig deeper, to question, yet also invited her to find solace in the complexity of their shared connection.

A delicate blush spread across Amber's cheeks, betraying her sudden self-consciousness. She looked away, her eyes finding an inconsequential point in the room as she suppressed a nervous laugh that bubbled at the edge of her lips. The complexity of Da'fydd's words, his caution mingled with an unspoken invitation, left her in a state of emotional intricacy she wasn't yet ready to unravel.

Da'fydd's gaze swept across the room. To his surprise, the gathering was far less populous than he had anticipated. At the very least, he would have expected the Druid Council to be present as was customary for significant occasions. Not that Celtan adhered to any sense of proper decorum since before his arrival. Still, he'd expected a certain level of etiquette for the Arkyn Lords. The seeming lack thereof was another reminder of Celtan's isolation and Kaily's ineptitude as a leader. Surely, dignitaries from other worlds deserved the utmost respect, particularly at a meeting hosted by the self-proclaimed High Druidess.

Guiding Amber further into the meeting room, Da'fydd's mouth tightened at the sight of Ethan and Heylyn. His posture remained upright, a pillar of self-assuredness as he advanced, Amber's hand delicately perched on his forearm. With a measured fluidity, he transitioned into the role of formal host, preparing to introduce the distinguished Lords to those assembled.

"I have the distinct honor of presenting the esteemed Lords of Arkyn." Da'fydd's voice filled the chamber, dignified and resounding. "Lord Adryan, whose wisdom has guided Arkyn through tumultuous times. Lord Khunrik, whose strength has never faltered in the face of adversity. And Lord Darius, whose cunning has secured many a victory for their world."

Da'fydd and Amber gracefully stepped to the side, allowing the room's focus to shift to these men of import.

Amber tightened her hand on Da'fydd's arm. *What about Kyara? It's rude not to introduce her.*

With a discreet movement, Da'fydd pulled her hand away from his arm and enveloped it in his larger hand. *The etiquette is different for the Lords, little bird. You already know this.* As Kaily stepped to the edge of the raised platform in front of an ornate throne, his eyes hardened, his shoulders tensing as Adryan took a deliberate step forward to meet her. Da'fydd was acutely aware of Amber's gaze lingering on Kyara, who had retreated closer to the other two Lords, almost merging with their looming shadows.

"I am told you are the ruler here. The High Druidess of Celtan." Adryan's voice dripped with an air of condescension, his tone a clear declaration of his less-than-flattering opinion of Kaily.

Amber's voice was a low murmur in Da'fydd's mind. *Is it me, or is Adryan displaying a surplus of insolence today?* Her gaze, sharp as an arrowhead, was fixed on Adryan's back.

No more than what's been directed towards him and the other Lords, Da'fydd replied. He continued to survey the room, a slight grumble rumbling in his chest. He wasn't certain what exactly was causing his unease. Maybe the lack of attendance. Maybe Ethan or maybe the fool, Heylyn.

Amber's eyes strayed to Kyara.

Da'fydd was keenly aware of Amber's discomfort with the apparent disregard for Kyara, her troubled thoughts almost palpable. With a gentle squeeze on her arm, he recaptured her attention.

Amber, stop fretting. Kyara is not a mere possession but respected and cherished by the Lords; if you'd only observe more closely, you will see this, Da'fydd counseled, keeping his telepathic tone calm while gently admonishing Amber before turning his attention back to Kaily and her ever-present shadow, her bonded mate.

Amber didn't respond. She harbored doubts about the Lords despite Da'fydd trying to assuage them. On her world, men like these didn't respect women in the slightest. Instead, they claimed them as possessions to be cast aside once their value had been exhausted. A sigh slipped past her lips as she grappled with the idea of her possible bonding with Da'fydd, potentially becoming another 'possession' if his indifference towards Kyara's situation was any indication.

You are not a possession, little bird. Da'fydd's tone was unexpectedly stern. *Females are scarce on the Lords' world, Arkyn, and many others.*

Amber let the topic drop. She was well aware of how scarce females were on some worlds. She blamed that scarcity for the woes of the females left behind on her own home world. Her gaze lingered on Kyara. The woman didn't appear to be unhappy; in fact, she seemed radiant.

Amber's attention was yanked toward the simmering confrontation unfolding before them.

Heylyn, hot-tempered, spat out, "She rightfully belongs to me!" His tone was harsh, grating even as his eyes darted toward Kyara.

Kyara's fiery blue gaze locked with his, a blazing stare that matched her fiery hair. Her chin raised high, her countenance one of pure defiance that spoke louder than words.

Da'fydd's mind became utterly still.

Amber, frowning, shifted her gaze to his countenance. *Is Heylyn always this hot-tempered?* Amber asked, exchanging a glance with Da'fydd, who was slowly disengaging her grasp on him. *What's the matter?*

Adryan, his voice steady but his stance rigid, "You should watch your words, fool," he warned. His quiet intensity unnerved Amber. She could sense an impending storm if Heylyn failed to rein in his audacity.

Heylyn merely smirked, puffing himself up to his full height. "She is mine," he sneered, glaring past Adryan.

The retort was instant, Kyara's voice cutting through the tension. "I belong to no one!" Her fists clenched, her cheeks flushed with indignation.

A torrent of words, steeped in hardly controlled fury, erupted from Adryan. His outburst was so vehement, so potent, it left Amber flabbergasted. Her eyes widened as she registered the depth of his rage.

Da'fydd uttered a few choice words, drawing Amber's attention. Da'fydd's cold stare remained fixated on Heylyn.

Heylyn stumbled back, retreating under Adryan's fiery onslaught and Da'fydd's fierce glare.

Amber's gaze drifted toward the Primary Lord.

Adryan drew in a deep breath. His gaze was ice-cold fiery steel that flicked to Kyara as he slowly turned his back on Kaily and those assembled on the raised platform as if they no longer mattered.

Unsure of the escalating tension, Amber sidled closer to Da'fydd. *What's happening?* Her silent query was infused with urgency as she attempted to make sense of the scene before her.

Da'fydd exhaled sharply through his nostrils, his irritation evident. *Kyara has publicly denounced the Lords' claim over her. It's a gross insult and a monumental embarrassment.*

A low growl emanated from the Lords, immediately extinguishing the room's background murmur. Silence enveloped the assembly, their collective focus now sharply attuned to the palpable tension in the air.

With all eyes on her, Kyara sunk to her knees, pressing her forehead to the cool stone floor in a desperate plea. "Please, Lords, forgive me. I did not mean the implication of my careless words spoken," she implored, her voice tremulous with unshed tears.

Adryan's response was mercilessly stern, his simmering anger palpable in his rebuke. "Stand! You forfeited your right to kneel before us."

With a casual flick of his hand, Adryan signaled to Darius and Khunrik. They stepped forward, lifting Kyara and draping a fur-lined wrap over her slender shoulders. Pulling the hood up, they guided her towards the double doors, maintaining a firm grip on her arms.

Whispers rippled through the gathered crowd, punctuating the silence.

Almost instinctively, Amber's gaze pursued Kyara, her head swiveling unbidden to maintain a line of sight as Kyara was guided away. Tears streamed down Kyara's face, but she didn't appear to be in pain. Driven by instinct, Amber took a few steps toward the departing Lords but was swiftly halted. She spun around to see Da'fydd's stern gaze, his shake of the head a clear warning not to interfere.

"Declare your intentions towards that woman!" Kaily demanded, her jaw set in a stubborn line.

Adryan, his patience obviously worn thin, shifted his gaze to Moto. "It behooves you to instill some manners in your woman." A hint of mockery lurking in his tone. Moto held Adryan's gaze, his own face a mask of stoicism. With a disdainful nod and an audible huff, Adryan dismissed him. His frosty stare lingered on Kaily. "We are done here." His gaze darted towards Moto. "Unlike Celtan, we do not neuter our males on Arkyn."

Moto cast an intense scowl towards Adryan for his insult. It was the kind of look that could turn blood to ice in one's veins. Despite his visible anger, he remained rooted by Kaily's side. The aura of tension radiating off them both was tangible to Amber.

Her gaze shifted to Moto's open palms. A small frown marred her features as Kaily laid a calming hand on his arm. Before she could ask Da'fydd about it, Adryan's voice echoed in the silence.

"Deadly force will be administered to protect what is ours should any other Celtan male attempt to take what belongs to Arkyn." Again, Adryan turned his back on the those on the raised platform as he strode from the meeting room, ignoring Kaily's retort.

"Come," Da'fydd urged, taking Amber by the arm, and guiding her towards the exit with his hand at the small of her back.

Amber complied, albeit reluctantly. If only there was something she could do to dissipate the storm brewing. Quietly, she let Da'fydd guide her from the meeting room, resisting the urge to glance back or remain. Her concern focused solely on Kyara. She needed to see to her safety if she could.

Da'fydd guided Amber away from the structure they had just left, drawing her attention toward Adryan, the other Lords, and Kyara. A frown of concern etched into her features as she took in the sight as they neared the group. Amber detected a tangible despair in Kyara's lowered gaze. An occurrence which ignited a whirlwind of unanswered queries in the recesses of Amber's mind.

Without uttering a word, not even a silent one, Da'fydd stilled Amber's inquiries. With no other recourse, Amber was relegated to the role of the observer as they carefully maneuvered their approach toward the Lords.

"What do you require of me?" Da'fydd directed his question to Adryan, who ignored him.

Amber's gaze shifted between Da'fydd and Adryan. She spared a glance towards the other two Lords. There was much she wanted to say, but she held her tongue for fear of making things worse for Kyara.

Adryan kept his attention focused on his Primary. "Do you wish for your release?" His words were harsh in Amber's ears as she listened to the exchange.

"No!" Kyara adamantly replied. Tears streamed down her face. Amber's heart broke.

Don't interfere, little bird.

Amber's gaze darted to Da'fydd. *Something needs to be done!*

Not by us. Please trust me on this.

Amber didn't answer. She didn't trust what she couldn't understand. Still, she had little choice in the matter.

It will be alright, Amber.

You can't know that. Look at her!

Da'fydd wrapped a protective arm around Amber's waist and pulled her close to his side. *I am, little bird. Kyara will survive this.*

Amber shot Da'fydd a quick, scathing glare before her rapt attention was irresistibly drawn back to Kyara and Adryan.

"Are you prepared to face the repercussions of your reckless words?" Adryan demanded, his tone biting and his eyes gleaming with a dangerous challenge.

"Yes," Kyara affirmed, striving to steady her ragged breathing.

Adryan shifted his stance, distancing himself as though deep in contemplation of his next move. He pivoted back towards Kyara, retrieving a corded rope from a pouch attached to his belt. "Present your hands."

Obediently, Kyara lifted her hands, her inner wrists touching, ready for the binding. Adryan gripped the rope taut, skillfully winding it around her hands in a binding pattern that left no room for struggle. He turned to Da'fydd. "Can you strip her senses?"

Da'fydd nodded; his reluctance was palpable in the subtle tension of his stance. Amber's instinctive move to protest was met with a gentle mental touch from Da'fydd. The telepathic equivalent of a soothing voice in her mind, his unspoken message stilled her. She halted, a ripple of reassurance from Da'fydd lacing through her thoughts, though her heart continued to thunder in her chest. The enormity of what Kyara was bracing herself to endure was unfathomable, stirring a surge of profound empathy within Amber that echoed painful memories of her past on her home world, Sethre.

"Causing trouble, lordlings?" A woman's voice pierced the air, her form materializing from the surrounding shadows. All attention immediately converged on her.

"I see you continue to grace us with your presence, Honored One," Adryan greeted, his head dipped in a respectful bow. The other Lords echoed his deference.

A frown marred Da'fydd's face, leaving Amber with a gnawing sense of unease. *What's going on?*

I'm unsure. Da'fydd's mental voice echoed within Amber's mind, both ensnared in the spectacle of the approaching woman. *It's my father's mate, Elina,* he continued, his silent voice resonating with a mental equivalent of a shaken head. *I had no knowledge of any association between the Lords and her.*

Could they have met when last the Lords were on Celtan?

Da'fydd shook his head.

Elina moved to Kyara's side, the Lord's firm grip still on the bound wrists of the young woman. A poignant melancholy shimmered in from the depths of Kyara's eyes, a silent testament to her sorrow.

Elina turned her attention to Adryan. "She did not recite the ritual words of separation."

"I'm aware, but as you know, we adhere to our ways, even the implied ones," Adryan retorted, a hint of smug satisfaction tainting his otherwise dismissive words.

Amber found his attitude jarring. His initial bow had signaled respect, indicating Elina's high standing, yet his words dripped with audacity, a blatant contradiction that left Amber unsettled. *Are you following any of this?*

I haven't been able to follow since becoming aware the Lords knew Elina.

"I will confer with Kyara in private," Elina declared, her gaze unwaveringly set on Adryan. His reply was silent, his arm muscles tightening under the weight of her gaze. Unfazed, Elina squared herself before him, asserting her will. "You will grant her permission to converse with me in private." Her words bore the tone of a decree, leaving no space for dissent.

Adryan inclined his head in a profound bow, acquiescing, "As you command, Honored One." As he lifted himself back to his full stature, his eyes locked onto Kyara's. "You have my permission for a private discourse."

Amber watched Elina gently lead Kyara away, her mind teeming with uncertainties. Amber found herself clinging to hope that this enigmatic woman was here as a savior for Kyara.

As time stretched on, punctuating the unseen discourse between Kyara and Elina, Amber noticed a movement from the corner of her eye. She turned, discovering Kaily, Moto, and several others stepping out from the meeting building. A prickling curiosity seized her as she pondered what had occurred in that meeting room after she and Da'fydd departed.

Elina reappeared, Kyara accompanying her, the pallor of her countenance evident, but her tears had subsided. As Kyara took her place beside Adryan, he acknowledged her with a nod. A veil of silence fell over them, none revealing the content of the private conversation nor hinting at what would transpire next. Amber's heart sank in the face of such uncertainty.

Elina inclined her head toward the three Lords before turning to intercept the group headed their way.

Feeling the undercurrents of tension, Da'fydd distanced himself from the Lords by a few strides and gestured to create a portal. His intention to guide the group away and prevent further confrontation in the central region of Celtan was evident.

Halting beside Da'fydd on his way to the portal, Adryan spoke tersely. "Proceed."

Da'fydd met his eyes and gave a solemn nod. Then, with a discreet gesture, he muted Kyara's senses.

With a nod that conveyed a silent weight of gratitude and urgency, Adryan guided Kyara toward the shimmering portal. Trailing a step behind, Khunrik and Darius exchanged a quick glance before also stepping into the shimmering vortex.

Amber cast a backward glance to witness Elina placing a calming hand on Kaily's shoulder, her words drifting to Amber's ears, "Let them go. This is their way." Sensing the gravity of the situation, Da'fydd intertwined his fingers with Amber's. *Come, little bird. This is not over.*

Chapter Twenty-Four

"What are we doing here?" Amber demanded, shortly after stepping out of the portal, her voice filled with frustration. She yanked her hand from Da'fydd's grasp. "Why didn't you take us to where Kyara is?"

Da'fydd, recognizing Amber's distress, placed his hands on her shoulders, ensuring she remained facing him and held her gaze locked with his. He flooded her mind with soothing tones, trying to calm her racing thoughts. "I must help the Lords, and you must remain here."

Amber shook her head adamantly, her determination evident. "You can't leave me here!" Her eyes darted around the underground greenhouse where Da'fydd had previously brought her. "Kyara is not safe. We need to help her!"

Da'fydd gave Amber a gentle shake, his voice filled with earnestness. "Kyara is safe! You have to let go of this animosity you have toward the Lords. It's not helping the situation." *Please, Amber, you must trust me.* His heartfelt plea echoed within Amber's mind.

"Stay out of my head," Amber snapped, pulling against Da'fydd's firm grip.

Da'fydd released his hold on Amber's shoulders, allowing her to step back from him. Although every fiber of his being urged him to pull her closer and shake some sense into her, he resisted. "I have known the Lords my entire life. They will not harm Kyara."

Amber shook her head in disbelief. "You don't know them. They are just like the ones on my world, Da'fydd."

The mention of Arkyns on her world caught Da'fydd's attention. He searched Amber's eyes for confirmation. "Are you saying Arkyns reside on your world?" It had been a long time since he'd visited Arkyn, but not so long as to believe that the Lords would allow their populace to spread out to other worlds when they were struggling against their own extinction.

"They don't call themselves that. The three clans have their own names for their kind, but they are essentially the same. I knew it the moment I laid eyes on them. They are cruel and unforgiving. Any male from one of the three clans would instantly kill any female who embarrassed them," Amber's voice was tinged with fear and anger.

Da'fydd took a deep breath. "Amber, they are not the same. Kyara is safe with the Lords."

Amber turned her back on Da'fydd. She crossed her arms and rubbed her hands up and down them. "She is not."

Da'fydd was torn between his responsibility and his concern for Amber's well-being. He forced her to face him once again. "Kyara is safe, Amber." He drew in an exasperated breath as his eyes darted to the entrance nestled in the alcove of his sanctuary. His mind shifted elsewhere. He refocused his attention on Amber. "We will continue this conversation when I return. Can I trust you to remain here? Or do I need to put up a force field?"

Amber glared at him, her defiance evident.

Da'fydd held her at arm's length, his eyes filled with determination. "I don't want to put up a force field, little bird. I really don't." He embraced her and gently smoothed down her hair, trying to offer some comfort. "But I will if I have to."

Hesitantly, she gave him a single nod of her head. "I don't like being forced into compliance," Amber admitted, her voice tinged with defiance, as she locked eyes with him.

Da'fydd's hold tightened, his voice filled with authority. "And I don't like being disobeyed. Your word, Amber, that you will remain here."

With a determined expression, Amber grudgingly gave Da'fydd a solitary nod, tacitly agreeing to his wishes, at least for the time being.

Da'fydd studied her for a moment, gauging her resolve before finally releasing her. "You should know the door does not lead out of here."

Amber narrowed her eyes, suspicion evident in her gaze. "So, I am trapped like a prisoner."

Da'fydd shook his head, his voice laced with reassurance. "No, little bird."

"It certainly feels that way," Amber retorted, her arms crossed tightly over her chest. Despite her defiance, a sense of isolation began to settle in.

"We will talk when I return," Da'fydd promised.

Amber unfolded her arms, sensing Da'fydd's frustration and urgency. "Go," she said, waving him off. "I'll be here when you get back."

Da'fydd inclined his head, acknowledging her words, before opening a portal and disappearing from sight.

Left alone in the underground greenhouse, Amber closed her eyes. She rubbed her temples in an attempt to ease the pain growing in her head. When she opened her eyes, they landed on the ethereal glow of the luminescent plants and the spiky fruits that surrounded her. The vibrant hues and intoxicating scent in the room were unlike anything Amber had ever experienced, a stark reminder of the extraordinary world Da'fydd must have come from. A world she knew precious little about.

Amber's initial defiance began to wane as time passed, and the weight of her isolation settled heavily upon her. She wandered aimlessly through the rows of luminescent plants, their gentle glow offering little solace to her restless mind.

With each passing moment, Amber's weariness grew physically and emotionally. She settled into a state of resigned waiting, feeling trapped within the confines of Da'fydd's underground sanctuary. The greenhouse walls seemed to close in on her, their leafy inhabitants becoming a silent audience to her isolated predicament.

Just as Amber's frustration threatened to boil over, a sudden change in the atmosphere captured her attention. A veil of stillness settled upon the greenhouse, and an electric anticipation filled the air. In that charged moment, a voice reverberated within her mind, commanding and powerful.

Hear me and heed my words, Da'fydd's voice resounded telepathically. Amber's heart skipped a beat, and her senses heightened. She didn't know how she knew, but he had reached every mind within his village and elegant fortress. *Clear the castle and return to your homes. Do not return until commanded otherwise, not even for mealtimes.* Da'fydd's words echoed within her mind.

Amber froze, her eyes widening as she heard the universal command reverberate through her mind. The weight of the words settled heavily upon her. Why had he cleared the castle? She could think of one reason which did not sit well with her. She hesitated to reach out to Da'fydd, afraid of what she might find within his mind.

Following Da'fydd's telepathic proclamation, a sense of urgency radiated from Amber, pervading the air within the greenhouse. She battled to stabilize her thundering heartbeat and sealed her eyes shut. The challenge for her was to extend her consciousness beyond the greenhouse, to perceive the exterior world without touching Da'fydd's mind. Navigating unfamiliar waters, she envisioned herself suspended high above the village, relying on her mental vision to recreate the unfolding scene.

Initially, there was only an abyss of black. Gradually visuals materialized beneath her, hinting that she might be genuinely perceiving the current events.

Down below, the villagers moved in a flurry, their actions powered by fear and determination. Amber's mental gaze was swept along the swift tide of activity, driven onward by the sheer magnitude of the predicament.

With a determined focus, she concentrated on the castle. She forced her mind down the twisting corridors and interconnected chambers, flowing against the collective exodus. As the villagers dispersed, she could almost make out their footsteps echoing against the stone floor.

Anxiety pulsed within her, mingled with a flicker of hope that she was seeing what was happening in her mind and not simply imagining it. Amber's thoughts whirled with anticipation. She continued down the corridor in her mind, which would lead to the three Lords' chambers.

Just as Amber was on the precipice of accessing the chamber within her mind, a sudden reverberation echoed, forcefully sealing her mental probing from the events taking place. Like a hot lance, a searing pain pierced her mind, striking a concordant rhythm with an overpowering wave of nausea that began in the pit of her stomach. The discomfort swelled and crested, surging upward through her body, causing her insides to roil as if tossed by a turbulent sea. As she blinked to refocus her eyes on her surroundings, awash in the radiant glow of the greenhouse, seemed to tilt and undulate, exacerbating her distress. She tasted the bitter tang of bile, and each breath became a struggle for equilibrium. Succumbing to her mounting frustration and physical despair, Amber emitted a piercing scream, tortured by her inability to discern Kyara's fate amidst the storm of pain and nausea.

Amber briefly considered seeking Ravenna's assistance, despite the potential chaos it might trigger. But the bitter reality was that she couldn't afford to gamble on uncertainties when the stakes were so high. Gathering her strength, she clenched her teeth against the pulsating pain in her head and the churning sickness within her. She had to push through her discomfort and mounting fear and try again, for Kyara's sake.

Tentatively, Amber closed her eyes again, steadying her shaky breaths and attempting to clear the fog of pain and nausea clouding her focus. Her mind, doused with determination, reached out once more in search of the elusive chamber that held the answers she desperately sought.

Chapter Twenty-Five

From a concealed corner of the greenhouse, Da'fydd observed Amber with a blend of admiration and concern. His decision to block her telepathic venture had been a painful one. It was an act of self-preservation as well as a desperate attempt to protect her. The raw fear in her scream was seared into his memory, a poignant reminder of the fragile balance between them.

Da'fydd watched Amber as she battled her own physical distress while remaining determined to help Kyara. Da'fydd grappled with the gravity of his actions, suspecting that the consequences could be twofold. On the one hand, he had saved Amber from potential mental trauma, sparing her from witnessing events for which she was unprepared. On the other hand, he had inadvertently unveiled the true depth of his powers, revealing a facet of himself he had hoped to keep hidden for a while longer. He disliked revealing just how powerful a Druid he truly was, even to Amber, or perhaps especially to her.

That's enough, Amber! Da'fydd shut her mind down, his hands balled into fists at his side.

Amber's eyes snapped open, and the faintly illuminated greenhouse assaulted her vision. The gentle glow emanating from the plants pricked at her eyes, causing them to water from the stinging sensation. "Show yourself!" she called out, her voice filled with trepidation. She could sense Da'fydd's presence in the room but could not visually pinpoint his location.

Da'fydd emerged from his shadowed corner, stepping into her field of sight.

"Is this your doing?" Amber's voice rang with heavy accusation. Her eyes glistened, brimming with unshed tears.

Da'fydd paused, taking in the sight of Amber. Her face, pale in the dim light, wore an expression of defiance. Her accusation hung between them, a charged question demanding an answer.

"Yes." Da'fydd's voice was a mere murmur in the verdant quiet of the greenhouse. He would not lie to her, even if his actions cost him her trust.

His confession did nothing to temper the storm in Amber's eyes. "Why?" Her voice wavered, betraying a note of vulnerability. "Why would you do this?"

"I did it to protect you, little bird," Da'fydd held her gaze. "I didn't want you to see something you're not ready to witness. And...," he trailed off, searching for the right words to articulate the complex reasons behind his actions.

Anger flared in Amber's eyes, transforming her touch of vulnerability into a force to be reckoned with. "And who are you to decide what I'm ready for, Da'fydd?" Her voice carried a steel-hard resolve that resonated through the quiet greenhouse.

Stung by the force of her words, Da'fydd fell momentarily silent. Anger kindled in his gaze as he met her accusing stare. His jaw set in defiance against her vehemence, and he glared back. "I am your bonded mate," Da'fydd finally said, his voice echoing with a hardness that mirrored his steely stance. "It is my responsibility to keep you safe, even from yourself!"

Amber's eyes flared with a defiant light. "Being my bonded mate doesn't mean you get to control me, Da'fydd," she snapped back, her voice slicing through the tense air of the greenhouse. "I am not some weak, helpless creature that needs protecting from herself!"

Amber's retort shook him, but he refused to accept his actions as a mistake. Da'fydd was determined to protect and help her, even if that meant shielding her from harsh realities. His help would not come in the form of standing idly by while she confronted dangers she was not equipped to handle, whether she agreed with him or not.

Amber took a step closer, her anger radiating off of her. "Your duty as my mate is to support me, not make decisions for me. And most certainly not to lock me out of my own abilities!"

Her words hung heavily in the silence that followed, an emphatic reminder that their bond, strong as it seemed, was still very fragile and new for them both.

Da'fydd absorbed Amber's words, his glare softening somewhat even as his stance remained rigid. "I am not trying to lock you out of your abilities, Amber," he defended, his voice losing some of its previous hardness. "Nor do I see you as weak or helpless." *Not entirely.* The last part inadvertently slipped from his mind.

Not entirely?

Da'fydd took a step toward Amber, matching her intensity with his own. "Even the strongest warrior requires protection at times."

"From themselves?"

"Especially from themselves!" The steely resolve in Da'fydd's gaze returned. "As your mate, my duty is to protect you, even when you don't think you need it and even when you hate me." His words were a promise and a declaration in the face of her indignation.

A flash of frustration crossed Amber's features at Da'fydd's stubborn persistence. "And who will protect me from you, Da'fydd?" she shot back. Her voice trembled with anger and hurt. "Who will protect me from your decisions, from your control?"

Amber advanced another step, bringing them toe-to-toe. "You don't get it, do you? It's not about hating you. It's about trust!" Her words pierced the tense air between them, each syllable echoing her plea for understanding.

Da'fydd's hardened stare remained locked with hers, his response a shroud of silence.

"You need to trust me, Da'fydd." Amber gestured with her hands for emphasis. "Trust that I can handle my abilities, whatever they may be, my decisions, and my life. Our bond isn't a chain of control; it's a link of trust, respect, and equality." Her voice softened, the fire in her eyes dimming to a smoldering ember. "You need to learn to respect who I am."

Da'fydd's stern gaze never left Amber's face, but beneath the hardened exterior, her words resonated to a point. They too closely mirrored his own arguments with his father when he was first brought to Celtan. He remained silent for a moment longer, the tension palpable. "Kyara is safe, by the way," he finally broke the silence, his voice softening a fraction.

One of Amber's eyebrows arched. "You're monitoring them, then?"

"No." Da'fydd gave a slight shake of his head.

"Then how do you know?"

Da'fydd's gaze softened as he took in Amber's expectant look. Sensing the necessity for more than just words, he reached out to her. Gently, he pulled her arms away from her body, bringing her hands to rest against his chest.

"Kyara will be alright," Da'fydd reassured Amber, the depth of his conviction resonating in his voice. "She made the choice to align herself with the Lords. To be Adryan's Primary. Believe me when I say that she was aware of the implications that choice entailed." Da'fydd's words echoed in the space between them, offering comfort amidst the chaos of their confrontation.

Amber locked her gaze with Da'fydd's, seeking confirmation of his truth. He appeared earnest in his beliefs in the Lords, but doubt gnawed at her. If the Lords were anything like the three clans' males on her world, then she didn't believe Kyara fully comprehended her precarious situation.

A part of her yearned to probe Da'fydd further on the matter. Amber couldn't shake the nagging suspicion that he was not entirely convinced by his own admonition. She sensed that Da'fydd was not being altogether forthcoming or open with her about aspects of the situation between the Lords and Kyara.

Da'fydd glanced at the greenhouse door as he reached out his senses. He needed to return to the Lords to keep apprised of the situation. Yet, the thought of leaving Amber again, especially amidst such uncertainty, filled him with apprehension.

His gaze shifted back to Amber, her expression a complex tapestry of worry, defiance, and doubt. Leaving her behind didn't seem like a good idea after everything that had unfolded. But he was equally unsure about bringing her with him.

He rubbed a hand over his face, struggling with the decision. "Amber," he began, his voice heavy with the weight of his dilemma. "I need to return to the Lords. But I don't want to leave you here, not again."

His gaze bore into hers, searching for something to help him decide what to do with her. "Yet, I'm not certain it's wise to bring you with me. Your animosity toward the Lords could make this situation unpredictably difficult." The words hung between them, an unsolved puzzle seeking a solution.

Amber's gaze remained locked with Da'fydd's, a fiery resolve igniting her features. "I won't be left behind this time, Da'fydd!" Her voice remained unwavering. "My animosity towards the Lords notwithstanding, I refuse to be kept in the dark any longer."

Da'fydd's eyes narrowed as he studied her. *Do not do anything to worsen the situation!*

Amber didn't respond.

Da'fydd turned and opened a portal.

The moment they stepped from the portal into the dining hall, Da'fydd's demeanor noticeably shifted. Da'fydd's stance became rigid, his energy sparking a silent alarm within Amber. Her gaze scanned the room.

Darius and Khunrik were seated at one of the long tables. They looked up, their faces etched with pensiveness. Da'fydd locked eyes with them, his expression hardening. Amber's eyes narrowed to mere slits for a brief moment.

"Why aren't you with Adryan?" Da'fydd's voice cut through the thick tension hanging in the room.

"Too brutal, even for us." Darius's response carried a dark undertone.

Kyara is fine? Isn't that what you told me?

Not now, Amber! He shot her a pointed look before refocusing on the two Lords present.

Amber's countenance darkened, but she remained silent.

"You have to stop him!" Da'fydd retorted, his voice filled with concern.

Darius shrugged nonchalantly. "You want to come between Adryan and his Primary, be our guest. It's your funeral."

Da'fydd's gaze tightened into slits, and his jaw clenched. *Wait here, Amber,* he commanded. He spun on his heels and made a beeline for the staircase without waiting for her acknowledgment that she would obey him. As he sprinted away, Darius and Khunrik stood, seemingly compelled to follow him for some obscure reason.

Da'fydd bounded up the stairs two at a time. A portal would have been faster, but also unpredictable, given the circumstances. The sound of Darius and Khunrik's heavy footfalls against the stone floor resonated behind him, affirming they were indeed trailing close. Yet their pursuit was the least of his concerns, and he cared little to understand their motivations.

His focus was on Kyara and preventing an atrocity from happening unnecessarily. He knew Kyara's misstep necessitated repercussions, but there was a boundary he wouldn't permit to be breached. It spoke volumes if what was happening was too much for Darius and Khunrik to witness. Anger boiled up at their lack of concern or desire to stop whatever drove them from the chamber.

Da'fydd didn't hesitate or bother with formalities such as knocking when he reached the guest chambers he'd previously prepared upon the three Lords' arrival. He retracted his hand, palm aimed at the door, and propelled it forward. With a force that echoed through the hallway, the door blasted open and collided against the stone wall with a resounding crash. Shards of the splintered latch scattered across the room.

The sight that unfolded before his eyes left Da'fydd stunned and unable to take immediate action.

Adryan's hand tangled in Kyara's hair, pulling at her scalp, while the tip of a sharp knife pressed against the rhythmic beating of her pulse in her neck. With each frightened heartbeat, the blade quivered in tune as he held her head tilted back and to the side.

Amidst this tense and deadly stand-off, neither Adryan nor Kyara flinched or reacted to Da'fydd's explosive entrance. Their attention remained fixated on one another, their gazes locked in a silent and intense exchange.

Da'fydd shook off his momentary shock and took a decisive step further into the chamber.

"DO IT!" Kyara shouted. Her eyes glowed with a challenge, daring Adryan to carry out his deadly threat.

"SAY THE WORDS!" Adryan tightened his grip in her hair, rage burning in his fiery eyes.

"NO!" Kyara yelled. "You want me released? Then kill me! I will not say them!" Kyara held Adryan's gaze unflinchingly, her spirit robust in a silent battle of wills.

Da'fydd found himself nearly admiring her courageous determination, even in the face of impending doom. Yet, he held back any semblance of a smile. Provoking the Lords was always a risky venture. Despite this, he knew he couldn't stand idly by.

"Adryan!" Da'fydd cautiously approached the couple with his hands extended outward from his sides.

"Stay out of this, Da'fydd." Adryan tightened his grip on the knife and pushed the tip into Kyara's skin just enough to draw a trickle of bright red blood.

Da'fydd's heart sank as he fully comprehended the excruciating torment Kyara must be enduring. Astonishingly, not a single wince escaped her lips, leading him to believe she had surpassed the pain perception threshold. Her resilience was truly remarkable, defying the constraints that held her upright. He suspected she possessed an unyielding determination that would keep her standing even without the bindings. However, given her audacious defiance of Adryan's authority over her, her lucidity remained uncertain.

A startled gasp behind Da'fydd caused him to grimace. Annoyance filtered through his mind. Without shifting his gaze from the distressing scene, "Go back downstairs, Amber," he commanded. He'd intended to shield her from this situation.

"You call this fine?" Amber demanded, her chest heaving with indignant fury. She jabbed her finger toward the grim spectacle unfolding within the confines of the room.

"Darius, please escort my wayward mate back downstairs," Da'fydd's tone was frigid as he issued the command. He was cornered into a course of action he'd rather avoid. He couldn't permit her to get ensnared in this perilous situation.

"No! Get your hands off me!" Amber yelled.

Da'fydd's gaze flickered to Amber. "Without causing her harm."

Amber's movements were wild and uncoordinated as she resisted, making it challenging for Darius to hold her securely. "Your mate is not exactly cooperating," he grumbled through gritted teeth.

Exasperation clouded Da'fydd's eyes. "She's stubborn," he admitted begrudgingly. *Cease your struggles, Amber!* He silently commanded. *Don't make me put you to sleep.*

You wouldn't dare! Amber's eyes burned with fire as her glare locked with his.

Da'fydd's eyes narrowed. *Keep disobeying me, and you'll soon find out!*

"We've got, Amber," Khunrik said, stepping forward to aid Darius. His gaze briefly swept over Adryan and Kyara before meeting Da'fydd's. "You attend to them." His tone held an unspoken gravity, highlighting the urgency of the situation.

Go with them, little bird. I cannot help Kyara if my attention is focused on you. Da'fydd gave Amber an encouraging nod as he reeled in his rising temper. He could see the impact of his words in her eyes, despite not meaning to hurt her. Nonetheless, they held a necessary truth. To fully concentrate on resolving the dangerous predicament, he needed her away from the chaos, secure, and out of harm's way.

"Fine! I'll go." Amber snapped, her glare piercing Darius, who was still gripping her arms.

Acknowledging her concession, Da'fydd signaled Darius with a discreet nod.

In response, Darius relinquished his hold, stepping back to create a path for Amber to exit. The cool stone floor echoed with the fall of Amber's boots as she seethed, shooting Da'fydd a final venomous glance before storming out of the room.

Darius returned Da'fydd's nod, following the trail of Amber's fury as he exited the chamber.

Khunrik, his gaze lingering on Kyara, moved closer to Da'fydd. His hand found its place on Da'fydd's shoulder while his eyes, filled with unspoken concern, remained on Kyara. He leaned in, his whisper almost audible, "Do whatever it takes, even if it means healing her."

"You know the cost," Da'fydd warned, his voice low and resonating with the gravity of the situation.

"We do," Khunrik assured, his eyes pleading. "Just help her, please."

Da'fydd reciprocated with a solemn nod. He watched Khunrik follow the others out of the room, leaving the tension thick and tangible. With a slow, steadying breath, Da'fydd shifted his focus back to the coupled locked in a contest of wills. "Adryan, I implore you to stop. Kyara has endured enough." His tone held a steely firmness.

Adryan glared at Da'fydd. Before he could speak, Kyara put her weight, as much as her bindings would allow, against the knife, driving it deeper into the pulsing vein the tip rested against. Blood flowed down her neck and between her breasts, soaking the delicate fabric of her gown. The flow rapidly made its way toward her abdomen.

The chamber filled with harsh words as Da'fydd and Adryan unleashed a barrage of expletives, each in their distinct languages.

With a swift movement, Da'fydd lunged forward just as Adryan, in a panic, dropped the knife that had pierced Kyara's artery.

A gush of crimson surged, even as Da'fydd's hands fought to stymie the flow. He could feel her growing limp under his grasp, her eyes fluttering shut in an ominous surrender to the encroaching unconsciousness.

"Save her!" Adryan's desperate plea cut through the tension. He retrieved the fallen blade. With swift, focused cuts, he severed the bindings holding Kyara aloft. He swept her up in his arms, his eyes pleading with Da'fydd.

"You know the price," Da'fydd retorted, his words sharp as steel.

"Yes!" Adryan uttered a few choice explicative insults directed at Da'fydd. "Save her!" Adryan seethed, clutching a dying Kyara to him.

"Do you agree to the price?" Da'fydd's words dripped with a dark glower aimed squarely at Adryan. He knew that healing Kyara the Dia'Kharn way would exact a heavy toll, not only on her but on himself as well. He deliberately pushed aside any thoughts of its potential consequences on Amber, focusing solely on the immediate task at hand.

Adryan swiftly moved to the bed as Da'fydd applied pressure to stem the torrent of blood, his palm pressed tight against the wound. As Adryan gently settled Kyara onto the mattress, Da'fydd's grip faltered, causing a fresh spurt of blood to escape.

"Yes! You're wasting time!" Adryan cursed.

With firm pressure on the wound, Da'fydd channeled the potent energies of Celtan through his hands, desperately attempting to curb the crimson tide spilling from Kyara. Despite his efforts, the severity of her blood loss was painfully evident. Her face had taken on a haunting pallor, and her lips bore the chilling hue of icy blue, harrowing signs that the specter of death was closing in on her.

"Will you save her or not?" Adryan demanded, adding more choice insults.

Da'fydd shot back a steely glare. "Your barbs aren't aiding her survival." With that, he redirected his focus back to the gravely injured Kyara, deliberately tuning out any further remarks that Adryan might have thrown his way.

Just as it had been with Amber, the act of healing was a deeply intimate affair. Every sensation he'd experienced with Amber echoed within him now, forging a chasm of apprehension at the implications of his action. Yet, he was left with no other option; without utilizing his unique Dia'Kharn abilities, Kyara would succumb to her injuries. His healing powers seemed more a curse than a blessing in that instant.

Da'fydd detached himself from Kyara's body when he had done all he could. He closed the puncture marks on his wrist. The pallor had receded from her skin, and her pulse was once more robust. He glanced briefly at Adryan as he dressed, who had averted his gaze during the entire process.

Adryan, refusing to meet Da'fydd's gaze, hurried to Kyara's side. Without any further exchange of words, Da'fydd exited the room, leaving Kyara in the care of the Primary Lord. He paused in the stairwell, a heavy reluctance gripping him at the prospect of facing Amber. Not only was she undoubtedly aware of the steep toll exacted by the healing process, but their burgeoning connection also meant she had been in his mind, witnessing everything.

Chapter Twenty-Six

Amber's irritation reached a tipping point. Her foot slammed against the stone floor of the main landing as she spun to face Darius. "Stop following me!" Her voice lashed out, her eyes aflame with unyielding ire.

Darius didn't respond right away. He followed Amber to the dining hall, matching every step including her fretful steps as she paced aimlessly between the long tables. "What is your problem with us?" His voice tinged with genuine concern. "I have been racking my brain to figure out what we did to cause such animosity towards us. We have been polite for Da'fydd's sake."

Amber paused, her agitated movements coming to a halt as she locked eyes with Darius. Her face betrayed a turbulent array of emotions. She took a deep breath, attempting to find the right words to express her inner turmoil. "Don't take it personally, Darius. It's all of you, the constant reminder of what you are," she replied, her voice laced with a hint of weariness encompassed by overwhelming anger.

Darius furrowed his brows. His confusion was evident. "I don't understand. We have done nothing to you. Why does our presence bother you?"

Amber's eyes flickered with a touch of sadness as she spoke. "Because of what you are." She shook her head. "The mighty Lords of Arkyn!" Her tone dripped with sarcasm.

Darius took a step closer, his concern deepening. "Amber, I don't understand this anger towards us."

"Stay back!" Amber skirted around a table to place the object between them.

As Khunrik stepped into the dining hall, his brows furrowed in confusion, causing him to slow his pace. His gaze widened imperceptibly, and a flicker of concern danced in his silver eyes.

Amber clenched her fists. Her knuckles turned white with tension. The flush of frustration and resentment on her face accentuated the growing storm. Her jaw tightened, and each breath became rapid and forced, mirroring her inner turmoil. Unable to contain the anger and energy building inside her, she began pacing back and forth.

"Amber, please, just calm down for a moment," Darius implored, trying to keep up with her agitated pacing while staying on the other side of the long table. "I don't understand why you're so upset with us. We haven't done anything to warrant this animosity."

Amber abruptly halted, her face flushed. She turned, her eyes welling up with tears. She locked an intense gaze with Darius, and her eyes narrowed, radiating an unyielding determination. Her body subtly leaned forward, poised and ready for the inevitable confrontation.

"Sethre! Does that ring any bells?" Her voice trembled with unshed emotions.

Darius and Khunrik exchange confused glances.

Amber's whole body tensed with anguish and trembled with anger. She slowly turned to face Darius and Khunrik, her gaze piercing their bewildered eyes. The world around them seemed to fade into the background as Amber's emotions hyper-focused on the two Lords.

Her eyes continued to swell with tears, shimmering with unspoken pain. She stubbornly held them back. Her words hung heavy in the air as she choked them out, her voice trembling with a raw vulnerability. Her words were a desperate plea to make sense of a shattered truth.

"Sethre!" she exclaimed, her voice cracking with emotion. The single word carried a myriad of emotions, from betrayal to confusion, without a glimmer of hope.

Darius and Khunrik, their expressions mirroring the overwhelming flood of questions echoing in their minds. They were caught off guard by the intensity of Amber's revelation, unaware of the significance of Sethre to her.

Amber's gaze shifted between Darius and Khunrik, her eyes pleading for understanding. She yearned for a response, a hint of recognition, anything that could shed light on the why that haunted her existence.

Darius and Khunrik exchanged another glance, their confusion deepening as they attempted to make sense of the gravity of Amber's words. Sethre was a world within their solar system they hadn't thought about in ages.

Amber's tears streamed down her face, her voice trembling. She refused to let the overwhelming emotions consume her. Taking a deep breath, she steadied herself and continued, her voice laced with a newfound resolve.

"The three clan males sent to Sethre," Amber began, her voice quivering but resolute. "Do you two honestly have no idea what I'm talking about? Was it all part of a grand scheme to decimate the indigenous populace? Did your history seriously abandon an entire world, forget all about us, without a second thought?" She angrily swiped at her tears. "You can call yourselves Arkyns, but it doesn't change what you are!" Her words hung in the air, heavy with accusation and pain. They may not have been the ones that caused the catastrophe on her world, but they were the leaders of the world that had.

Darius and Khunrik stood in stunned silence, grappling with the weight of Amber's revelation. The truth she spoke of shattered their preconceived notions, leaving them at a crossroads of uncertainty and revelation.

Finally, Darius found his voice, his tone infused with no small measure of regret and guilt. "Amber, we... we had no idea."

A fierce frown marred Khunrik's features, yet he remained silent.

Amber's words hung in the air. Before she could say more, a sudden pain gripped her chest. She clutched her heart as she collapsed to her knees. A strangled cry escaped her lips. "No!" The single word carried the weight of a shattered reality.

Darius instinctively moved closer, his intention to offer comfort clear in his eyes.

Amber's blazing gaze turned towards him. She held up her trembling hand. Her voice strained. "Stay back!"

Darius froze in his tracks.

Amber, her tears streaming anew, struggled to her feet. Her pain was not physical but an internal battle, a storm of emotions raging within her.

"Don't follow me!" Without a backward glance, she blindly ran toward the exit, her steps heavy with the weight of her broken heart. The world around her blurred as tears clouded her vision.

Chapter Twenty-Seven

*L*ittle bird? Da'fydd uncurled from his stance against the wall, his mind slipping his query into the recesses of Amber's mind. Her distress was a palpable force, a vice threatening to squeeze the life from him. He had been helpless in her turmoil, his attentions dedicated solely to healing Kyara. But now that he had finished his healing task, he could not escape the piercing echoes of Amber's soul-wrenching pain.

GO AWAY!

Amber's words were a razor-edged expulsion within his being. Da'fydd let out a weary sigh as he began his journey downwards, treading the well-worn steps to the first floor. He traversed the expanse of the dining hall. He gave Darius and Khunrik a dismissive wave, ensuring they kept their distance. He had no mental reserves left to spare them a moment.

He was mildly surprised when they moved off with an inclination of their heads. He hadn't been fully aware of what had transpired between Amber and the two Lords when they removed her from the chamber. The demanding nature of the Dia'Kharn's healing process was such that it required his absolute concentration, an engrossing experience that left no room for any other focus, demanding every fiber of his being: mind, body, and soul.

Don't shut me out, little bird. Da'fydd crossed the threshold of the grand double doors and paused at the cool stone entrance. The rough, aged texture of the stone under his boots contrasted sharply with the crispness of the air that swept in with the dwindling daylight.

His eyes slowly adjusted to the subtle shift in light as the vibrant hues of the day surrendered to the muted grays of the encroaching evening. The waning light painted long shadows across the expansive courtyard, morphing familiar surroundings into shifting illusions of their daytime selves. A silvery glint of the impending night sky, just becoming visible, hinted at the nocturnal chaotic symphony soon to commence. He was taken aback by how much time had eluded him this day.

Da'fydd let his eyes flutter shut, turning his perception inward. His consciousness homed in on his prey, piercing the veil of thoughts like an arrow. Amber's absence of response didn't surprise him. He could practically sense her stifled breaths, the palpable tension as she wondered if he would discern her whereabouts. Naturally, he would.

Amber could run and seek the sanctuary of solitude, but she could never truly escape him. Their destinies were intricately woven together in a tapestry of time and existence. No distance was too vast, no hiding place too obscure to disrupt the tether that bound them. Her essence was a beacon that his senses could trace with unerring accuracy.

Their connection was not a mere happenstance but a cosmic design as perpetual and enduring as the Universe itself. She was forever intertwined with him, their souls irrevocably linked in a dance that transcended the mortal realm. She was his for all of eternity, her presence an undying echo within the chambers of his soul.

Da'fydd's eyes snapped open, the quiet concentration breaking like shattered glass as he detected her unmistakable presence. It emanated from the sprawling garden to his right, a pulsating beacon of familiarity. Her essence was an intoxicating blend of strength and vulnerability, a poignant melody that stirred the hunter within him.

His lips curled upwards, slowly unfurling into a predatory grin. The thrill of the hunt, the intoxication of the chase, and the certainty of an impending encounter added a sharp edge to his smile. His eyes shimmered with a glint of anticipation, mirroring the starlight that now held court in the evening sky.

We need to talk, little bird. Da'fydd took his time descending the steps.

No.

A smile tugged at his lips, kindled by the rebellion radiating from her lone uttered word.

Would you begrudge Kyara healing? Da'fydd sensed the vibration of Amber's exasperated sigh ripple through their bond.

That's not fair, Da'fydd.

His boots connected with the hard-packed ground, each step a deliberate echo in the quiet evening. Wheeling around, he set his sights on the garden, the barren oasis where his wayward mate sought sanctuary. He began his pursuit with resolute strides, drawn by the invisible thread that tethered them together.

And your angry silence towards me is fair, Amber?

The garden, bathed in the ethereal glow of twilight, awaited their inevitable rendezvous. It was too bad the ancient trees and blooming flowers had died off ages ago.

No words for me, little bird?

I have a word for you. Amber's fury poured into his mind, as palpable as the unspoken word that hung between them. The word was far from complimentary.

A smirk played at the corner of Da'fydd's lips. *Amber. Even in your silent fury, your choice of unspoken words remains as eloquent as ever.*

Sarcasm?

Da'fydd tsked at her in his mind as he wove his way through the garden paths, guided by the rustling sounds of the sparse foliage. His steps slowed as he approached his destination at the heart of this dilapidated sanctuary.

He avoided this garden, the village, and everything outside his castle as much as possible. They were nothing like what he left behind on the Dia'Kharn home world. He much preferred the sanctuary of his greenhouse. The only piece of home he could bring with him.

Under the sparse canopy of the garden's oldest tree, he found his Amber. Her silhouette was carved out by the gentle glow of the starlight. She sat nestled against the sturdy trunk. It was the largest tree left standing in the garden, a silent sentinel bearing the scars and victories of countless neglected seasons.

Amber's back was turned towards him, her posture radiating an air of resolute solitude. Yet, he could sense the whirlwind of emotions beneath her composed exterior just as she sensed his approaching presence.

"Running away, little bird?" Da'fydd's voice cut through the serene silence of the garden, carrying with it a cocktail of amusement and fondness. His shadow fell across her, the night casting a long, soft veil over them.

Amber didn't turn, but he could see her shoulders tense at his words. A sigh, more of resignation than frustration, filtered through the silence. "I'm not running, Da'fydd. I just needed space."

"Space," Da'fydd echoed, the term suspended like an unresolved chord in the crisp night air. His instincts clamored to pull her up, to make her eyes meet his in confrontation. But he resisted the primitive urge, choosing instead to slide down next to her against the gnarled trunk of the aged tree.

"Space is the last thing we need, Amber." His voice held firmness with a gentle undertone. The events of the day, especially the healing ritual, had drained him. What he wanted more than anything was to carry Amber to his chamber and hold her secure in his arms for the remainder of the night.

"We need to talk about what happened," he continued, his gaze fixed on the stars above. The truth in his words hung between them, a silent plea for understanding. The path they were treading was tumultuous but necessary. If they were to navigate the intricacies of their irrevocable bond, they would need more than space. They would need open hearts, candid words, and, most of all, an unflinching resolve to face whatever the Universe threw at them together.

Carefully, Da'fydd shifted his position, his hands moving to gently cradle Amber's face. His thumbs tenderly swept over her cheeks, brushing away the lingering dampness from her tear-streaked skin. *I apologize for the pain I've caused you, little bird,* he murmured within her mind.

Amber attempted to pull away from his touch. But he held her firm, an unyielding yet gentle anchor. "You asked me to aid Kyara," he reminded her, his voice firm.

"I know." Amber's voice was thick with emotion. She shook her head, lost in a sea of feelings, "I..."

He preempted her, shaking his head, "Don't claim ignorance. The healing I bestowed upon Kyara was no different than what I provided to you." Which wasn't precisely accurate. He gave Amber far more than he had Kyara, but that information would keep for another day's discussion.

"I don't recall any of it," Amber protested.

A trace of a smile graced Da'fydd's lips. "Perhaps not in detail, but its essence resides within you. Your heart understood what was necessary, even when your mind faltered. I'll ask again, do you begrudge Kyara the healing she received?"

Amber shook her head, her eyes betraying her inner turmoil.

"Then cast aside your anger and pain." His tone a compilation of controlled fury. "I am weary, and we both require rest, little bird."

Amber turned to fully face him, her eyes a storm of untamed fury. "Do you know why I am angry, Da'fydd?" Her voice was laced with a rising wrath as she pivoted to her knees, position-ing herself to confront him.

He remained silent, his gaze steadfast on her.

"It's because if you had taken my warnings about the Lords seriously, she wouldn't have needed healing in the first place."

"Amber..." Da'fydd started, only to be cut off.

"No! I don't want to hear it," Amber retorted, pushing herself to her feet in a display of defiant anger. "I need space, whether it's good for us or not."

Da'fydd rose to his feet as she spoke, his posture echoing her defiance. He stamped down his own rising anger.

"You'll need to find a different place to sleep tonight," she fired back before storming off, leaving him in the garden's silence.

He was left watching her retreating figure, an onslaught of unsettling emotions churning within him. He could insist she stay, even portal her to his chamber, and force her to his will.

Yet, he lingered in indecision, his gaze tracing her departure. He knew she did not need space, but perhaps it was time to teach her this lesson. He tore his heated gaze from the direction Amber had disappeared. He took a deep breath as he summoned a portal to his sanctuary, a secluded greenhouse that radiated remnants of his preferred home world would help ease his own weariness.

He'd deal with his rebellious mate in the morning. For now, the solitude of his sanctuary promised to give her the solace she so desperately wanted. She would learn the error of her desires soon enough.

Chapter Twenty-Eight

I n the deafening silence of Da'fydd's chamber, Amber lay wide awake, stroking the two slumbering pups nestled by her side. Each tear trickled from her eyes was a bitter testament to her sleepless night, her fitful rest punctuated with moments of raw sobbing. The vulnerability of her tears felt like a wound left open, an uncomfortable weakness that gnawed at her pride.

Her resentment was inflamed by Da'fydd's surprising inaction. He hadn't attempted to penetrate her protective field. It's not like pushing through would have been that difficult for him. She was only beginning to experiment with her own abilities she sensed bubbling to the surface. He didn't even attempt to break down the door. Not that it would have been necessary. He could have easily portaled into the chamber.

A profound hurt lodged in Amber's heart, borne of Da'fydd's seeming indifference. He had made no attempt to bridge their divide using the telepathic bond they shared, which had recently become a source of comfort and connection. She had half-expected him to reach out to her, coax her into opening the door, and seek solace in their shared mindscape. Yet, his silence echoed in her mind, making her feel more alone than ever.

Instead, he had chosen to give her the solitude she had requested, respecting her wishes even though she had secretly yearned for him to break through, to show that he cared. His compliance was like a slap to her face, only intensifying her feelings of abandonment. The harsh reality of their situation was far from what she had imagined, and the disappointment was a bitter pill to swallow.

Hot tears welled up in her eyes, a stark reminder of the tumultuous storm of emotions she battled. She tried to hide them, to present a facade of strength and resilience, but they betrayed her, stubbornly streaking down her cheeks. They were a weakness she fought against, showing even in solitude. How was she to control her overwhelming emotions in public if she couldn't control them in private?

With a surge of anger, she wiped them away fiercely, berating herself for the show of weakness. But as much as she hated them, the tears wouldn't stop. They were her silent scream into the void, a testament to the turmoil which raged within her.

Her mind was a battlefield, thoughts of the shocking incident between the Lords and Kyara replaying relentlessly. The experience of Da'fydd healing Kyara was a smear on her mind that she couldn't wipe away. She had begun to remember her own healing session with him, an intimacy that she hadn't fully understood until now. During the healing, she had sensed a stirring of desire in Kyara for Da'fydd, which prompted a sickening question she could not stop from surfacing. Was her own attraction to Da'fydd merely a byproduct of his healing?

Exhaling deeply, Amber propped herself up into a sitting position, pushing the cozy warmth of the covers aside. The shift in her demeanor ignited a spark of enthusiasm in the puppies. Sensing the change, they sprang off the bed with youthful agility, their infectious energy instantly filling the room.

The blanket carelessly pulled off the bed in their eager departure became their arena, the weave of fabric the canvas of their play. They tumbled and danced, their bodies intertwining and separating in a whirl of exuberant puppy antics. Their mock battles were punctuated by shrill growls and yips, their playfulness as uncontainable as their frenzied motion.

Amber watched, her gaze softening as she observed their innocent display of joy. It was a captivating spectacle that offered a temporary respite from the weight of her thoughts. Their carefree frolicking starkly contrasted the complexity of the issues she grappled with. She found herself lost in their playful choreography, the sheer joy they radiated offering a fleeting moment of distraction.

Their shenanigans allowed her mind to wander, the soothing repetition of their play-acting as a balm to her troubled thoughts. As she watched them, her mind drifted. Thoughts and memories swirled, twirling around each other much like the puppies in their playful dance. Each contemplation was a thread, weaving into the complex tapestry of her situation.

The soft growls of the puppies formed a backdrop to her introspection, their playfulness juxtaposed against the heaviness of her thoughts. And yet, as she watched them, a flicker of hope sparked within her. Their unwavering energy, their ability to find joy in the simplest of things, reminded her of the strength within her, giving her a sense of purpose amid the turmoil.

She rose from the bed, splashing cold water on her face from the porcelain bowl and pitcher, attempting to wash away the weariness. As the droplets rolled down her face, she reminded herself to confront Da'fydd about his outdated bathing facilities. How he managed to stay fresh without a proper bath was beyond her, although she was not quite as unkempt as she had feared. Her brows furrowed. She'd have to ask Da'fydd about that later, after she gave him a piece of her mind about his blatant disregard for her.

She slipped into her clothes, the familiar texture a comforting touch against her skin. Turning her attention to her hair, she began to smooth the tangles with her fingers. To her surprise, her fingers sailed effortlessly through her long locks, not encountering the usual resistance of knotted strands.

The newfound manageability of her hair was puzzling, another mystery that Da'fydd would have to answer. With a rueful shake of her head, she realized how much their lives were intertwined, how much she had yet to understand about the world she was now part of. The thought filled her with a strange sense of frustration and anticipation, the latter a testament to her burgeoning curiosity.

She inhaled deeply, her gaze falling on the romping puppies. A pang of responsibility hit her; they needed sustenance and to be let outside before bodily functions resulted in an indoor disaster. Her eyes strayed to the rug before the hearth, showing their inability to wait until they were taken outside. The sight, however, did not provoke annoyance. Instead, a tender smile began to bloom on her face. She should have thought to take them out earlier.

"Alright, my tiny troublemakers," she cooed, ruffling the soft fur atop their heads with affectionate hands. The simple action seemed to still their energetic bustle, drawing their attention to her.

"It's time to face the day." She continued, her voice filled with warmth. She pushed the door open and guided the puppies with a gentle sweep of her hand.

Amber made her way down the grand staircase with the playful puppies tailing on her heels. Their little feet scampered excitedly behind her, eager to follow wherever she led. The soft padding of their paws against the stone floor was a comforting rhythm as they navigated their way into the dining hall.

Upon entering, she found Da'fydd seated at the high table, lost in his own world of deep contemplation. An unsettling emptiness filled the grand space, an echo of the castle's usual bustle that was conspicuously absent. The villagers had been barred from entry, Da'fydd's orders leaving the castle strangely devoid of its normal life and warmth.

Da'fydd's decision had unsettled Amber. The castle was more than just a stronghold. It was a lifeline for the villagers who relied on it for their daily sustenance. Seeing it in such a desolate state stirred a knot of guilt within her. She knew the hardship his command imposed on the innocent inhabitants. This guilt continued to jab at her conscience, gnawing at her peace with each passing moment.

Managing to push her troubling thoughts aside for the time being, Amber's gaze swept over the empty room before landing on Da'fydd.

Noticing her presence, Da'fydd seemed to physically shake off his pensiveness. His posture straightened, and he attempted a smile that didn't quite reach his eyes. *Morning, little bird,* he greeted, his silent tone cautious in the tension between them.

Her reply was a curt nod. A wave of reluctance washed over her as she considered joining Da'fydd. The distant echo of heavy footsteps descending the castle stairs persuaded her to swallow her resentment and take her seat next to Da'fydd. She couldn't afford to stir up drama in front of the others, especially Kyara, not after what the woman's been through.

How are you?

Amber glared at him. *Fine.* She turned her attention to the group entering the great hall. She lifted the puppies onto the platform; one at a time. She blatantly ignored the brief scowl that crossed Da'fydd's features, although he remained silent as she settled in the chair next to his. The pups settled at her feet.

The somber procession entered the room with Kyara at the lead, her face obscured beneath her hood, followed by the Lords, their expressions grim. Adryan's hand rested on the small of Kyara's back. The sight tugged at Amber's heartstrings, but her sympathy for Kyara was soon eclipsed by the hot rush of resentment towards the Lords.

Once the group stood before Da'fydd, Adryan announced, "We are ready to depart." Da'fydd rose from his seat, glancing at Amber, *I'll return shortly,* he advised.

No, she shot back, her mind filled with determination. *I'm going with you.*

Taken aback, Da'fydd stared at her before giving a reluctant nod.

Amber was momentarily taken back when the puppies disappeared.

Peace, little bird. I portaled the beasts back to the barn where they can be cared for.

Amber gave a slight nod of her head. Bren would make sure they were fed.

Stepping off the platform, he unveiled a portal, leading the Lords and Kyara into the ethereal passage before Amber and himself. At the Gateway, he traced the runes for Arkyn, bidding the three Lords farewell with a curt, "Safe journey."

Adryan gave Da'fydd a curt nod in return before he guided Kyara gently into the iridescent shimmer of the Gateway. Darius and Khunrik trailed after them, exuding a palpable air of solemnity.

A wave of protective instinct washed over Amber as she watched them enter the center of the stone circle. She wished she could intervene to remove Kyara from their influence and guide her away from the uncertainty that loomed ahead.

Once the Lords had vanished into the Gateway, a weighty sigh escaped Amber that held the echoes of her inner turmoil, she allowed her eyes to slide shut, surrendering to the helplessness that tugged at her. A deafening silence blanketed the area, leaving Amber alone with the echoes of her thoughts.

Amber opened her eyes and glanced at the forest the Gateway stood within as she attempted to quiet her mind. She briskly rubbed her arms, trying to fend off the creeping chill. The action did little to warm her. She berated herself for her lack of foresight. Her impulsive decision to accompany them caused her to leave her cloak behind. Her frustration simmered, kindled by her lack of understanding of her abilities.

Beside Da'fydd, who wielded his abilities with innate ease, Amber felt like a fledgling navigating an intricate maze blindfolded. Her nascent powers clung to her awkwardly, a jarring counterpoint to his effortless mastery.

Once Da'fydd closed the Gateway, he turned to face Amber. His face was lined with weariness, but his silence fueled her anger.

"How could you let her go with them?" Amber's emotions boiled and seethed. Every aspect of the situation seemed to fan the flames: the high-handed arrogance of the Lords, the upheaval they had thrust upon her and Da'fydd's budding connection, the scars they had etched into Kyara's life, and Da'fydd's apparent disregard for it all. It was a storm of indignation, a maelstrom of rage that threatened to consume her.

"Kyara belongs to the Lords." Da'fydd tone lacked any hint of regret over his acquiescence.

"And that justifies their treatment of her?" Amber demanded. Her arms fell to her sides before she crossed them defensively. Her gaze, filled with resolve, remained locked on his. "Let's not even imagine the atrocities they might subject her to once they return to Arkyn!" She gestured angrily toward the Gateway.

Da'fydd's hand instinctively moved to rub the back of his neck, a physical manifestation of his growing temper. His gaze never wavered from Amber's. "What do you suppose would have happened had we tried to wrestle Kyara away from the Lords?" he asked.

"So preserving peace takes precedence over the woman's safety?" Amber challenged, her voice strident.

Something dangerous sparked in Da'fydd's eyes at her accusation. "Do you really believe Kyara would thank you for your interference?" He countered with a derisive scoff.

Amber averted her heated gaze from him, her anger replaced by uncertainty. She didn't possess a ready answer to his probing question. In her heart, Amber hoped Kyara would appreciate someone stepping in to protect her. Yet, she couldn't assert this with absolute certainty.

Da'fydd assessed Amber with a pensive gaze as the silence stretched between them. The muscles in his jaw clenched for a moment before he exhaled slowly, his eyes softening despite the tension that hung in the air. He stepped forward, reducing the distance between them.

"Amber," he began, his voice a gentle contrast to the charged atmosphere, "You're viewing Kyara's situation through the lens of your own past experiences. It's obscuring your perception of the unique bond the four of them share."

The words hung in the air, a stark truth she didn't want to acknowledge. She was still tethered to her past, a prisoner to old fears and grievances that clouded her judgment. The implication struck a nerve, and she stiffened, her defiant gaze flicking back to him.

As if sensing her discomfort, Da'fydd tried to pull her towards him. His anger was palpable, yet it was tempered by an inherent protective instinct, a desire to shield her from pain. "Amber, you need to let go of the past to navigate the present," he urged, reaching for her.

"Ravenna!" The name exploded from Amber's lips, slicing through the cold, quiet air. It was a summons, a defiance that echoed off the surrounding forest, reverberating through the trees with startling clarity.

Almost instantly, Ravenna appeared, materializing out of thin air as if she had been lurking just beyond the periphery. A spectral presence, ready to intervene at Amber's call.

Spinning back towards Da'fydd, Amber's body was taut with defiance. The flames of her anger reflected in her eyes, churning with a chilly resolve. "I will never bond with you," she declared, her words as hard and unyielding as the steel in her gaze.

Da'fydd was rendered motionless by her declaration. He could only watch as Amber moved away, striding purposefully toward Ravenna. Together, they vanished, their forms dissolving into the ether with the same startling abruptness as Ravenna's appearance.

The impotence of the moment sparked a hot, raging growl from deep within Da'fydd. His fists clenched, knuckles white, as he processed the sting of Amber's words and her swift departure. His actions, it seemed, had done nothing but drive a wedge further between them. This moment marked a crossing of lines, a leap over the precipice.

Her readiness to leave with Ravenna, to abandon what they had built together, was tantamount to a betrayal. Fury simmered within Da'fydd, replacing the cold emptiness of her departure with a raging fire. "Oh no, little bird. You are quite mistaken."

Chapter Twenty-Nine

Stepping out of the portal, Amber stood in a captivating cavern that seemed more akin to a setting of the imagination rather than the real world. She was rooted to the spot, her senses taken over by the surreal beauty of her surroundings. The sudden halt almost caused a minor collision with Ravenna, who had been following on her heels.

"Where are we?" Amber asked, her voice quiet as her gaze roamed the cavern, filled with wonder and awe.

"We are in a labyrinth of caverns in the Llosgfynydd region," Ravenna replied, the gentle pressure of her hand on Amber's shoulder grounding the younger woman amidst the overwhelming spectacle.

As Amber moved aside to give Ravenna space, her eyes were drawn to a focal point within the cavern. In its center was a small, fluorescent pool encased by a ring of smooth, grey stones. The luminescent light emitted from the pool painted the stones in their own spectral colors, reflecting off the surrounding stony walls and amplifying the cavern's natural charm. The soft, otherworldly glow imbued the cavern with an atmosphere of tranquility and enchantment unlike anything Amber had ever experienced.

Mesmerized, Amber slowly walked closer to the pool, drawn in by the soothing pulse of the phosphorescent water. The cavern's magical aura and the quiet hum of hidden life below its surface entranced her, making her feel like she had stepped into an entirely different world.

The rustling sound of clothes being shed captured Amber's attention. Glancing over, she noticed Ravenna disrobing, her body fading into a blur as Amber's gaze darted shyly away. Her blush deepened when Ravenna slipped into the pool, her form causing ripples that danced across the water's surface, reaching out to the edges of the stone basin.

"Come," she held out her hand in invitation. "Join me," Ravenna beckoned softly, her tone relaxed and inviting.

Summoning the courage to look at Ravenna again, Amber was relieved to find her submerged up to her neck in the pool, her features distorted by the water's surface. Uncertainty crossed Amber's face as she shook her head, her arms instinctively crossing over her chest. Yet, Ravenna's calming smile and inviting gaze chipped away at her hesitations.

"I... umm," Amber stammered, wrapping her arms around herself defensively as a modest smile played on her lips.

In return, Ravenna offered a soft, reassuring smile, her eyes inviting Amber into the luminescent water. "Trust me, it's an exceptional experience. I don't bite; much."

Amber chuckled nervously, her eyes briefly clouding with uncertainty. It wasn't that she harbored any qualms about nudity per se. The prospect of exposing herself in the presence of another caused her trepidation.

Ravenna gave her a reassuring smile. "Don't worry, Amber," she said gently as if sensing Amber's discomfort. "This is a place of tranquility, of acceptance. There is no judgment here, only peace. Take your time and do what feels right for you." Her voice resonated with understanding.

A spark of resolve replaced Amber's initial apprehension, a subtle smirk forming at the corner of her mouth at her own ridiculousness. Despite the discomfort of baring herself in another's presence, they were alone in this secluded haven, which afforded some measure of privacy. There was an undeniable allure to Ravenna, an enigmatic quality that captivated her while remaining elusive to Amber's comprehension.

"Alright," Amber finally acquiesced, the hint of a smirk growing. Peeling off her clothing, Amber stepped into the warm, bubbling pool, the effervescent water instantly soothing her anxieties and immersing her in a blanket of tranquility.

Amber released a weary sigh, allowing herself to sink beneath the water's surface. The warm liquid enveloped her, providing a momentary respite from the turmoil of her thoughts. As she emerged, her eyes met Ravenna's.

"Better?" Ravenna inquired, her voice carrying a hint of amusement.

Amber nodded, her expression tinged with a sadness that weighed heavily upon her. The burden she carried seemed insurmountable, leaving her uncertain about where to start unraveling the tangled mess of her life.

"I'm a good listener," Ravenna gently encouraged, her voice infused with empathy and compassion.

Amber shook her head, the depths of her eyes brimming with frustration and helplessness. "I don't even know where to begin," she admitted, her voice laced with an emotional rawness she loathed.

Ravenna offered a sympathetic nod, acknowledging the challenge Amber faced. "Sometimes, it helps to start by sharing what you're feeling," she suggested softly.

Amber emitted a sarcastic laugh, a bitter note underscoring her response. She shook her head again, the complexity of her emotions causing her distress. "It's complicated," she muttered, grappling with the intricacy of her inner turmoil.

"Tell me why you're angry at Kyara," Ravenna coaxed gently, her gaze never wavering from Amber's.

A frown tugged at the corners of Amber's lips as she shook her head in denial. "My anger is not directed at Kyara. It's Da'fydd I'm furious with," she said, her voice laced with an undercurrent of frustration. "I can't comprehend how he could stand by and let the Lords do what they did without any resistance." The last few words came out as a bitter sigh as she replayed the scene in her mind, her frown deepening.

Ravenna arched a single, curious eyebrow. "So, you harbor no resentment towards Kyara for allowing herself to be mistreated by the Lords?" she queried, her tone neutral yet probing.

The question made Amber shift uncomfortably in the water, creating soft ripples that sparkled under the cavern's ethereal light. "No," she replied curtly, putting some distance between her and Ravenna.

Her reaction seemed to amuse Ravenna, who pressed on. "Really, not even a hint of blame?"

Amber spun around, her eyes flashing with indignation. "Why didn't you intervene? You claim to be aware when a Druidess sets foot on Celtan. Why didn't you act in Kyara's favor?"

A ripple of amusement danced in Ravenna's eyes. "Your assumption that we did nothing simply because you didn't witness us act is rather naive, Amber. But your diversion doesn't alter the fact that you're still evading your unaddressed resentment towards Kyara."

Amber parted her lips to rebut, but Ravenna raised her hand, forestalling her. "We've been observing the Lords and Kyara since they entered Celtan, Amber."

Amber's face registered surprise. "Why haven't I seen you?"

Ravenna's smile softened. "You are young, Amber, with many facets of your innate abilities yet to be explored."

"But no one guides me or explains what these abilities mean!" Amber burst out, a tinge of exasperation in her voice.

Ravenna laughed, a hearty, echoing sound that bounced around the cavern walls. "A Druidess's abilities are not learned, Amber. They are inherent. Acceptance of who you truly are will unlock this knowledge."

"But how?" Amber's brows creased with confusion.

Ravenna's smile was gentle yet cryptic. "A Druidess is not trained. She is born. The answers you seek are present in the energy that surrounds us. It is akin to... testing the waters. Moreover, you're linked to Da'fydd, the most powerful Druid on Celtan. Your bond grants you access to his mind."

Amber's frown deepened, her mind trying to untangle the thread of wisdom that Ravenna had just spun. She felt like she was on the verge of an important discovery, but the connection was just out of reach.

"I don't hate, Kyara," Amber confessed after a pause, her gaze fixed on the luminescent water of the pool.

Ravenna's response was swift and sure. "I never said you did, Amber. I said you were angry at her. Now, tell me why?"

Amber's gaze slipped away at that, evading Ravenna's penetrating gaze. She drew in a deep, shaky breath as if gathering the strength to voice her thoughts. "She's... she's accepting a life of misery." Amber's words were weighed down by a deep, unsaid anguish.

Ravenna studied Amber for a moment, the silence between them thickening. Finally, she took a deep breath and moved closer, invading Amber's personal space. Their eyes locked.

"She has the power to free herself," Amber added, the strain in her voice apparent.

Ravenna's reply was simple yet held a sharp truth. "But you couldn't," she observed, her words cutting through the air like a cold blade.

Amber was briefly silent, her eyes welling up with unshed tears. "Not... not for a long time," she admitted, her voice choked with emotions. The mere acknowledgment of her own entrapment brought forth a wave of sorrow that had long been suppressed, brimming in her eyes like a silent plea for understanding.

Ravenna shifted her position within the pool, leaning comfortably against the edge. She gently guided Amber, encouraging her to relax against her so that Amber's back was cradled against Ravenna's front.

A fleeting surge of discomfort prompted Amber to pull away, but Ravenna pacified her. "Be calm, Amber," she gently reprimanded, her voice resonating with a soothing tranquility that seemed to permeate the air around them.

At her words, the resistance within Amber gradually ebbed away, replaced with a tentative acceptance as she gingerly leaned back against Ravenna. The unfamiliarity of the situation was still present, but Amber found herself slowly surrendering to the serenity offered.

"I had a conversation with Kyara," Ravenna revealed, her words seeming to float around them, carried by the ethereal glow of the pool.

"You did?" The surprise was evident in Amber's voice, her body tensing momentarily against Ravenna's.

"Aye," Ravenna confirmed, her voice steady. "It was when the Lords returned with her from their audience with Kaily."

"Before Da'fydd and I arrived?" Amber asked, her words punctuated with a hint of confusion.

"Before you returned," Ravenna countered, her simple response echoing within the tranquil silence of the cavern.

"Da'fydd was aware of your conversation with Kyara?" Amber questioned, her tone laced with a hint of accusation.

Ravenna responded with a gentle, almost teasing, laugh. "Don't harbor resentment against him, dear. Da'fydd and I share a fragile peace. Generally, I wouldn't dare to intrude on his sanctuary without him being conscious of it." She emphasized the word 'usually' with an impish undercurrent in her tone.

"Like you did for me?" Amber ventured with a lopsided smile, a soft giggle escaping her.

"Exactly," Ravenna replied warmly. She smoothed her hand across Amber's forehead, persuading her to lean back onto her shoulder.

After a moment of companionable silence, a question slipped from Amber's lips. "Why didn't you prevent Adryan's actions?" Her voice wavered, revealing the layers of unresolved emotions beneath.

Ravenna's response was delayed as she seemed to carefully consider her answer. "It wasn't Adryan who drove the knife deep; it was Kyara."

"I don't accept that," Amber responded abruptly, disentangling herself from Ravenna's comforting embrace and spinning around to face her, the anger evident in her heated gaze.

"But it is the truth." Ravenna held her ground, her voice steady as she met Amber's challenging stare.

"Why would Kyara willingly harm herself?" Amber demanded, her face wrinkled with confusion and disbelief.

Ravenna offered a noncommittal shrug in response, her calm demeanor starkly contrasting Amber's mounting frustration.

Observing Amber's distress, Ravenna gently took hold of her hands and drew her closer, establishing an intimate proximity between them. "I don't understand." Amber shook her head in a desperate attempt to make sense of it all.

"Kyara is exactly where she desires to be." Ravenna lifted Amber's face by her chin to ensure their eyes met. The sternness in her gaze compelled Amber to listen intently. "Often, it's challenging to make sense of a scenario when viewing it from the outside." Ravenna added, her voice laced with an undertone of empathy. A soft chuckle escaped her lips before she continued, "Kyara possesses a fiery spirit. I assure you, she wouldn't endure any situation without her consent."

"So, that makes it right." Amber's words bristled with heat, her eyes glowing like twin sparks in the cavern's soft luminescence.

"No, it doesn't make it right, per se," Ravenna replied, her voice steady and soothing as she brushed back the damp strands of Amber's hair. "It just makes it acceptable under certain circumstances."

Her words hung in the air, the undercurrent of her wisdom apparent. Ravenna had lived for countless ages, had seen civilizations rise and fall, and had been part of changes Amber could hardly fathom. Time had a way of shifting one's perspective, dulling the edges of harsh truths, and imparting the wisdom to discern the difference between what was easy and necessary.

A frown furrowed her brows as Amber's eyes wandered beyond Ravenna, roaming over the stony, light-kissed cavern walls. The enormity of Ravenna's worldview was a daunting panorama to comprehend. Her heart echoed with the raw realities of her own limited experience, struggling to reconcile her personal convictions with Ravenna's seasoned perspective.

"Consider this," Ravenna began, her voice echoing through the silent cavern. "You are but a young sprout in the forest of life, seeing only the trees closest to you. Over time, as you grow and rise above the undergrowth, your vision broadens. You begin to see the forest for what it truly is: a vast, interconnected web of life, where every action, no matter how small, has consequences."

"Time," Ravenna continued with a faraway look in her eyes, "gives you the gift of perspective. With each passing moment, every incident that once seemed significant fades into the backdrop of a much larger tapestry. What you perceive as right or wrong now may evolve with the wisdom of experience. That's the way of life."

Amber took a moment, absorbing the profound truth in Ravenna's words. Her mind swirled with new thoughts, perceptions, and questions. She was on the precipice of understanding, the fog of her thoughts beginning to dissipate, giving way to a new dawn of comprehension.

"Enough about Kyara," Ravenna said gently, her hand still holding Amber's. "You need to look inward and understand what lies in your heart."

Amber took a shaky breath, nodding as she did. The pool water seemed to murmur in unison, creating an ambiance of introspection.

"What do you truly desire, Amber, for your own life?" Ravenna prompted. Her voice was a soft echo in the cavernous silence.

The words took a moment to sink in. Amber frowned, deep in thought. After a long silence, she muttered, "Da'fydd."

Ravenna smiled knowingly. "And what's holding you back?"

The heated blaze returned to Amber's gaze, a tempest brewing in her verdant eyes. "He's insufferable, conceited, and..." her voice faltered. Amber's overwhelming emotions surged and caused her body to quake subtly with contained anger.

Ravenna chuckled lightly. "The princeling has his failings."

Amber's brows furrowed at the peculiar nickname. "Why do you call him 'the princeling'?" she inquired, her curiosity piqued.

Ravenna merely shook her head, a small smile playing at the corners of her lips. "That," she said, "is a tale for him to weave." As Amber drew in a breath, ready to fire another question, Ravenna raised a hand, effectively halting her. "When he chooses to unveil his history to you, you'll comprehend the reasons behind my words."

The uncertainty in Amber's voice was clear as she huffed out, "If he decides to share."

Ravenna was quick to correct her, her fingers gently guiding Amber's face back to meet her gaze. "Nay, Amber," she reassured, her voice steady and certain, "When he tells you, not if."

Amber's gaze locked with Ravenna, her eyes filled with uncertainty. "I..." She shook her head. A heavy sigh escaped her.

Ravenna met her gaze with a reassuring smile. "Go to him, Amber. Make things better between the two of you."

"But...," Amber hesitated, "what if he...?" Her last words spoken to him wafted through her mind. She'd hurt him. The moment the words left her lips, she knew they would hurt him deep down, and she uttered them anyway.

"Stand your ground," Ravenna interrupted. "You've both been through a lot, and he needs to understand your perspective as well. Da'fydd has been indulging his sorrow for too long. Quiet your doubts."

Amber mulled over Ravenna's words. "I told him I won't bond with him."

"I heard," a soft hum escaped Ravenna, her response veiled in enigmatic subtlety. "Leaving a bonded mate is not as easy as carelessly uttered words," she said, alluding to something deeper.

"But we haven't even bonded," Amber objected, trying to decipher Ravenna's meaning.

Ravenna offered a mysterious smile, leaving her words hanging in the air. She responded to Amber's puzzled expression, "Some pairs form a deep connection, a bond, without the ritual ceremony being conducted."

Taken aback, Amber stammered, "Are you implying we are one such couple?"

A gentle shrug was Ravenna's only reply. "What do you think, Amber?"

Amber's immediate instinct was to negate the thought, yet her denial wouldn't fully materialize. She started to shake her head but stopped, her refusal stuck in her throat.

"Find Da'fydd and mend the rift between you," Ravenna counseled. "Remember, you're his partner, his companion in this journey. His responsibility extends beyond mere leadership and encompasses more than the protection and wellbeing of those he governs. They also include you in so many ways than you are capable of comprehending right now."

Ravenna smoothly lifted herself from the pool's iridescent water, droplets cascading down her body in rivulets. With an effortless elegance, she began dressing in her attire, the clothes clinging to her figure as she laced them up.

Amber, although caught up in her swirling thoughts, followed Ravenna's actions. She cautiously emerged from the pool, her skin prickled with goosebumps from the contrast between the warm water and the cooler cave air. She picked up her garments from where they lay discarded earlier, methodically dressing herself while her mind replayed the cryptic conversation.

Ravenna finished dressing first and turned towards Amber. Her face held a comforting expression. "You're not isolated in this world, Amber," she assured her gently, her words echoing in the cavern. "You're not alone on this path, either."

Before Amber could ask more questions or seek further clarification, Ravenna initiated the portal. The mystic, swirling shimmer to another place hummed into existence, its energy filling the cave. And before Amber could utter a word or cast one final glance in Ravenna's direction, she was propelled into the portal, leaving the cavern and Ravenna behind.

Chapter Thirty

S tumbling out of the portal, Amber found herself back in the castle, the once bustling halls now silent and deserted. The echoes of her own footsteps served as a harsh reminder of the desolation inflicted by Da'fydd's command. But Amber was more determined than ever. She was ready to face Da'fydd and whatever came with it.

As she walked towards Da'fydd's chamber, her mind was full of thoughts about their heated conversation, contemplating Ravenna's words, and plans to confront Da'fydd. She needed him to see her for who she was, not his to be ordered around and someone to be protected. Not that she didn't appreciate his desire to protect her. She did, but not at the expense of her own will to decide what was best for herself.

Her eyes landed on Da'fydd as she pushed open the chamber door. He stood by the window, his back turned towards her. The tension in his shoulders was palpable even from this distance. He seemed lost in thought, perhaps regretting his earlier decisions or missing her. At least, she hoped he missed her.

"Da'fydd," Amber's voice was a soft murmur in the silence.

His shoulders tightened, his body reacting before his mind had a chance to. He pivoted to face her, surprise flashing across his features before being replaced by a guarded mask.

Taking a deep, fortifying breath, Amber drew upon the courage she had found in the tranquil depths of the cavern. "We need to talk," she announced, her voice holding a steadiness that belied the turmoil within her.

She moved towards Da'fydd with measured steps, their gaze interlocking in a silent dance of concealed emotions. As she closed the gap, Amber lifted her hand and placed it gently against his chest. His silence and the intensity of his stare sent a flicker of hesitation through her, but she pushed it aside. "Talk to me, Da'fydd."

"Do you know how worried I've been? What were you thinking?" Da'fydd's voice reverberated through the room, laced with frustration. "I couldn't sense you, couldn't locate you, couldn't mind speak to you at all." His gaze drilled into her, demanding an answer.

Amber's shoulders sagged, the weight of his words pressing down on her. The time she had spent with Ravenna had been a precious respite, a pause from the constant tension. But the peace was short-lived, and now it seemed they had another issue to fight over. Amber was weary of the battles. She craved conversation, not conflict. She moved to the bed with heavy steps and sank onto its edge.

Her gaze met his, steady despite the turmoil she felt inside. Clearing her throat, she asked in a quiet voice, "What do you mean you couldn't sense me?" Amber hadn't noticed his silence, but then again, she hadn't been seeking communication with him either.

Da'fydd's lip curled in a grimace. "A shield was put up against me. Why?"

"I don't know," Amber admitted, her voice subdued. "Perhaps Ravenna did it without me knowing."

A soft whimper sliced through their tension-filled dialogue. Amber's eyes involuntarily strayed toward the source. There, nestled together on a makeshift bed, were the two puppies. A large bone, gnawed to a fraction of its original size, lay discarded beside them.

Her eyebrows knitted together in a frown. Amber forced her focus back to Da'fydd. "She did help me." Amber's heart raced as she struggled to keep the rising tension at bay.

"How is running away helpful? You knew Ravenna would come and take you away if you called." Da'fydd massaged his forehead, frustration etched on his face. He jerked his arm, pointing accusingly at Amber. "You ran from me, saying you didn't want to be my mate."

"Da'fydd..." Amber began, her voice low. She swallowed around the lump forming in the back of her throat.

"No," he interrupted, "that's what you said. You don't get to take it back." With a swift move, he turned his back to her, his heavy breathing the only sound breaking the silence.

Slowly, Amber rose from the bed and cautiously placed her hand on his rigid shoulder. "I needed time to think. Please understand," she pleaded.

He shrugged her hand off with a jerk. "I'll never understand. I'm the one you should have turned to."

"How was I supposed to turn to you when you wouldn't listen to me, Da'fydd?" Amber's calm demeanor cracked. Heat rushed to her face as her patience evaporated. "What did you expect me to do? Stay and put up with your need to control me? You don't talk to me. You order me around and then scold me like I'm a child when I don't fall into line."

"You certainly ran away like one, Amber." His words were barbed, causing her to flinch.

"I'm sorry!" Amber's voice echoed through the room, louder than she had intended.

Da'fydd froze, his mouth closing abruptly. He stepped back, his tense features gradually softening, the crimson anger in his face fading to a softer pink. He appeared almost defeated, but in a way that suggested a reluctant acknowledgment of the complexity of their connection.

Amber exhaled a long, measured breath. "I'm sorry." Her gaze flickered towards the pups, then back to Da'fydd. "Thank you for looking after them."

Da'fydd waved off her thanks with a nonchalant roll of his shoulders. He treated the acknowledgment as though it were no remarkable feat, downplaying the significance of his actions. "I guess the little beasts can stay." A hint of a smirk played at the corners of his mouth.

Compelled by the warmth in his words, Amber stepped forward, weaving her arms around his body in a firm embrace. "I didn't mean to worry you. I had no idea about the shield." She felt Da'fydd's hands slowly rise to rest on her lower back.

Pulling back after a moment, Amber held his gaze. "But I need to be clear about what I can and cannot accept in how I'm treated." Her eyes bore into Da'fydd's. "If we do this bonding thing, it's as equal partners or not at all. I won't be subservient to you or any man. I've been through too much to allow that. Now, I have options I didn't have before. I choose you only if you want me and can live with these terms." Amber held her head high, her stance radiating resolve. She hoped he understood her seriousness.

"I agree to your terms, little bird." Da'fydd's face softened before hardening. "But know this: I am not an easy man to live with. You will heed me if your safety is at risk, subservient or not."

"If my safety is a concern, then we must at least communicate about it." Amber's gaze softened, the harsh lines of her resolve giving way to affection.

Da'fydd's eyes narrowed at her, yet a teasing smirk danced on his lips. "We'll see," he challenged.

A loud yawn escaped from Amber. "It's been a long day," she mumbled through a chuckle, her fingers ruffling through her hair in a weary gesture. Shivers rippled through Amber's body as the adrenaline of their tension faded. She'd forgotten about being pushed through the portal with wet hair and clothes clinging to her.

Da'fydd's eyes softened. "You're freezing," he murmured, pulling her closer. His warm hands gently brushed against the soaked fabric of her clothes. *My drenched little bird.* His silent words teased the edges of Amber's mind.

Amber met his gaze, her eyes filled with quiet determination. *As long as I'm not your caged little bird.* She countered and reached out, her fingertips brushing against the rough stubble on his cheek in a brief but tender touch.

Without a word, Da'fydd began undressing Amber, his movements careful to avoid causing her any more discomfort. Once she was down to her underclothes, he paused, his gaze meeting hers as if asking for silent permission.

She gave a slight nod, her teeth chattering. In response, Da'fydd extended his hands towards her, fingers slightly spread. A faint, warm glow emanated from his palms, a soft light that seemed to absorb the wetness from her skin and hair. It was a soothing sensation, like standing in the first rays of the morning light. Within moments, the shivers ceased, replaced by a comfortable warmth that enveloped her. *Well, that answers my cleanliness question.* Fully dry now, Amber gave him a weak smile of gratitude.

Da'fydd chuckled. "Does it?" The glow from his hands faded.

"Yes." A frown formed between her eyes. "I think so."

Da'fydd smoothed the crease of her brow with the pad of his thumb. "Better?"

Amber nodded, wrapping her arms around herself as she settled into the dry warmth that Da'fydd's magic had provided.

Without warning, Da'fydd enveloped her in a firm embrace. His steady, rhythmic breath brushed over her head as he rested his chin on it. *Don't scare me like that again, little bird.*

Amber melted into Da'fydd. *I am genuinely sorry. I didn't know.*

Da'fydd tenderly threaded his fingers through her long, silky tresses, a soothing motion that echoed their deepening connection. *You do now.* He placed a chaste kiss on the top of her head.

Amber's eyes fluttered shut. A sigh of contentment escaped her. "I could fall asleep right here," she murmured between yawns.

"I think the bed would be a more comfortable choice," Da'fydd chuckled as he guided her towards the edge of the bed and released Amber from his hold.

Under the blanket's warmth, Amber slid closer to the other side, her body a silhouette against the fire's soft glow. The inviting coziness of the room, fueled by the fire's radiance, made it impossible for her to resist burrowing further under the covers.

Da'fydd shrugged off his clothes and slipped under the blanket with his customary grace, joining her in the invitingly warm bed.

Once settled, Amber rotated towards him, her body naturally seeking his warmth. She snuggled into his side, her body curving to match his like two puzzle pieces. The contact was instantly comforting, a soothing balm to her senses.

The pups, invigorated by the room's tranquility, hopped onto the bed as the room sunk into soft shadows, leaving only the flickering firelight to dance against the walls and furniture. Despite Da'fydd's mild grumbling at the pups' intrusion, the moment was imbued with pure tranquility. A tangible warmth rippled through the room, anchoring them within its enchantment.

As one of the furry critters wriggled between their bodies, Da'fydd gently lifted it and settled the puppy on the other side of Amber, where its sibling had already snuggled against her back.

"Nothing is coming between me and my bonded mate." Da'fydd's voice rumbled low in the quiet room, a solemn oath that hung in the air between them.

Amber's lips curved into a soft smile, her fingers tracing an absent-minded pattern over Da'fydd's bare chest. "Nothing?" she echoed, her tone feather-light but with an undercurrent of steel. Her eyes sparkled with mischief and a hint of a challenge.

Da'fydd arched a brow at her, the faintest of smirks playing on his lips. By now, he was used to her tenacity, the gentle pushback that always followed his assertions. It was one of the things he admired about her on the rare occasion it didn't irritate him.

Amber's smile widened as her fingers traced a teasing path along the edge of Da'fydd's waistband. "Nothing?" she echoed, her voice a playful murmur in the quiet room. As her eyelids fluttered up, the flickering firelight captured the intensity of her gaze.

Da'fydd could hardly resist her teasing challenge. "You have a point, little bird," he conceded, the corner of his mouth quirking upward. With a swift movement, he turned her in his arms, pressing her back against the mattress. He playfully nipped the curve of Amber's neck.

She giggled in response and caressed his cheek with her fingertips.

The pups jumped from the bed and toddled over to their soft makeshift bed in front of the hearth. They curled up together, their bodies radiating warmth as they settled for sleep, their soft snores quietly audible.

A sense of contentment infused the very air around them, softening the edges of the day's earlier conflicts. As Da'fydd wrapped his arms more securely around Amber, their bodies molded together. The tranquility of the room was punctuated only by the crackling fire and the rhythmic beat of their hearts.

In that quiet moment, all the pieces fell into place. The room, bathed in the soft, flickering glow of the dwindling fire, seemed to shrink around them, their shared world encompassed within these four walls. Amber's eyes slowly drifted shut, surrendering to the rhythm of Da'fydd's gentle touches, his fingers stirring embers into flame, the smoldering heat of their bond bursting into a passionate blaze.

The last strains of tension ebbed from her body, replaced by a rising warmth that unfurled within her, stoked by Da'fydd's ministrations. His hands moved with purposeful intent, tracing paths of fire along her skin, each touch sparking the kindling of their bond into roaring life. His uttered promises in her ear were the sweetest of lullabies, luring her further into their shared desire and love.

The potency of their connection, the richness of their bond, sketched a vivid tableau across the early evening sky. In that instant, no obstacle seemed insurmountable. Their room became a sanctuary bathed in the waning sunlight, a sacred space where the smoldering embers of their mutual yearning softly ignited into a blaze.

As their bodies intertwined, each ebb and flow a testament to their unity, the flame of their bond danced, casting long, flickering shadows against the walls. It was a dance as old as time, of two souls entwined, sharing their love as freely as they shared their breaths. And as Amber finally surrendered to the rising tide of passion, she knew in the marrow of her bones that nothing would ever come between them in their bond. They were and always would be, eternally intertwined.

Chapter Thirty-One

A mber's tongue darted out to catch the tantalizing liquid as it slid down her chin, a flavor so exotic and rich it was like nothing she had ever tasted. She laughed, the joyful sound echoing through the greenhouse. Her newly sharpened incisors had grown sharp enough to pierce the skin of the spikey fruit cupped in her hands. Yet, mastering this new skill was proving to be a delightful challenge. Every time she tried, a drop or two escaped, trailing down her chin.

Unlike Da'fydd.

He seemed to have mastered this odd way of eating, his every move precise and elegant as he pierced and emptied the fruit of its delectable, life-giving liquid. The ease of his actions was a stark contrast to her fumbling attempts.

Amber's laugh, a melodious sound that resonated with genuine delight, caught Da'fydd's attention. His eyes sparkled with a playful glint, reflecting his amusement at her struggle. Yet, behind the humor, his gaze held a hint of tenderness that spoke volumes. Amber was adapting, embracing the new and unfamiliar with an enthusiasm that was uniquely her own. And he loved that about her. In her laughter and struggle, he saw the essence of who she was: a creature full of life, unafraid to learn, and determined to grow, despite the hardships of her past.

Here, let me show you. Da'fydd's silent tone was gentle, his words layered with patience. Reaching over, he guided Amber's hand with a firm touch that was simultaneously tender. He demonstrated the perfect angle to hold the fruit, where to pierce, and how to control the flow of the liquid. Every motion was an intimate dance, his fingers intertwined with hers, his closeness a constant reminder of their bond.

Like this? Amber's mind quivered with excitement and apprehension, her eyes wide with concentration. Under Da'fydd's watchful guidance, she bit again, this time more gracefully. The fruit yielded its succulent essence without spillage, and she savored the moment's victory.

That's it, my little bird, Da'fydd praised, his mind filled with warmth and pride. He leaned back, his eyes locking with hers, a proud smile playing on his lips. His nickname for her had always been endearing, but it took on a deeper meaning in this shared moment. Contentment radiated from him, reflecting his joy in these simple, shared experiences.

Amber realized how strongly they were growing as a couple, learning from one another, and finding joy in the mundane. It was a connection that went beyond mere companionship. It was a connection that extended far beyond sheer pleasure and the intimacy of this lesson. It was in the soft glances they exchanged, their shared laughter melodies, and their touch's natural grace. They were laying the foundations of a shared history, creating memories interwoven with love and trust. Their bond was not static; it was a living thing, dynamic and evolving, woven into the very fabric of their beings.

Da'fydd gazed affectionately as Amber made a second attempt at consuming the fruit that was marked with the confidence of growth. Though not quite perfect, it was a demonstration of her adaptability. A small drop of the liquid escaped her control, trailing down her chin, a playful defiance against her newfound skill. But her eyes sparkled with triumph. She had caught most of it this time.

Da'fydd's warm laughter filled the space between them as he watched her. His eyes twinkled with proud amusement, reflecting her triumph as his own. *Almost there, little bird. I have no doubt you'll have it perfected soon,* he assured her, his silent tone rich with belief in her. He gently wiped the stray droplets from her chin with the pad of his thumb. The motion unfolded gracefully in this enchanting tapestry of moments, and an intimate aura enveloped it. His touch lingered for a fleeting breath beyond necessity, a tender acknowledgment of their burgeoning closeness, a delicate testament to the depth of their connection.

Amber's cheeks flushed a delightful pink at Da'fydd's teasing. Still, her eyes sparkled with a playful challenge, her inner voice holding a teasing lilt. *I'm a quick study, especially when I have an adequately skilled teacher.*

Da'fydd's eyes playfully narrowed at Amber, his eyebrows arching. *Adequately skilled, huh?* His mind held a hint of mock offense as he reached out and snagged her arms, making her drop her fruit. He pulled her close to him. The mischief in his eyes was replaced with something more intense. *Shall I show you just how skilled a teacher I am?* His breath danced across the curve of her neck, sending shivers down her spine.

Amber laughed, a sound rich with genuine mirth, and struggled to pull out of his firm grasp. *No, no. I stand corrected.* Her laughter harmonized with the sparkling radiance dancing within her eyes.

Da'fydd's lips found the curve of her neck. He kissed it softly before nipping the soft skin with his incisors, leaving a red mark as a playful reminder of their interaction.

Amber shook her head, a soft chuckle escaping her lips as she cast a playful glance at him. A hint of mirth danced within her eyes, mirroring the twinkle of distant stars. Stepping back gracefully after his gentle release, she observed the deliberate motion of his hand swiftly plucking another fruit from a nearby bush. The fluidity of his actions held a mesmerizing cadence, an intricate dance that never failed to amaze her.

The interplay of their laughter wove an additional strand into the tapestry of their connection. This ephemeral yet profound layer united intimacy and lightheartedness. These instances etched their story onto the parchment of destiny, crafting the foundation of trust and affection that anchored their bond. Amidst the weave of their journey, Amber nurtured a hope, a quiet wish that these moments, like fragrant petals, would unfold more frequently between them.

Amber's thoughts meandered back to the resonating call of the High Druidess. This ethereal summons held a grave purpose. Though Da'fydd's sanctuary provided a respite, the ache lingered like a subtle echo, faint yet laden with significance. The summoning wasn't merely a straightforward beckon, but a nexus of responsibilities intertwined with duty and loyalty. As threads of destiny wove them into the fabric of Celtan, the weight of these intertwined expectations stood as a testament to their place in this enchanting world.

Da'fydd's brow furrowed as he glanced at Amber. His eyes, usually warm and inviting, were clouded with contemplation. Finally, he broke the silence, his baritone voice reverberating within the greenhouse filled with the sweet, spicy scent of fruits yet to bloom. "Our duty right now is to each other. The Stone

Pillars and Kaily can wait. I want to have you to myself for a bit longer."

His words were meant to reassure her, but a chill traveled down Amber's spine despite the warmth of the greenhouse. The summons was not something to be taken lightly, and the weight of beckoning hung heavily between them.

"Kaily won't like us ignoring her," Amber responded, her voice tinged with reluctance. Her eyes, studying Da'fydd's face, betrayed her concern. Yet, her hand reached for his, fingers entwined with a desperate need to remain in that moment and forget the outside world existed.

Da'fydd shrugged, his expression carefree but his eyes betraying a hint of defiance. *Just enjoy this moment with me a while longer, little bird.*

Amber's eyes narrowed, her intuition telling her there was more to his reluctance than he let on. Yet she trusted him, knew that he would not lead them into too much trouble with the High Druidess. Still, she had much to learn of this world, especially since it was now her home. With a soft sigh, she nodded.

Da'fydd slipped a strand of her hair behind her ear, his fingers lingering on her skin for a heartbeat. *That's my...*

...partner, Amber finished for him, eyes narrowing slightly. She knew that wasn't the word he was about to say, and a playful spark danced in her eyes.

Da'fydd's laughter reverberated in the space between them, rich and warm, but his eyes held a hidden question. "Oh, partner is a safer word?" he teased, though his smile didn't fully reach his eyes. He could sense Amber's reluctance to ignore the summons. She had questions, and he didn't possess the patience to provide answers. Not when those answers would spoil this moment between them.

Amber's brows furrowed in confusion, her fingers tightening around Da'fydd's hand, concern replacing the earlier playfulness. "What I don't understand is why summon us for a bonding ceremony in the first place. We are already bonded. Aren't we?" Her voice wavered on the last words, the question taking on a weight that extended beyond mere ceremony.

Da'fydd's eyes darkened, a flash of anger passing through them, his jaw tightening. "Because she thinks it's her place to meddle in matters that are not her concern," he said through clenched teeth. "She believes that by bonding in the energy, we'll be stronger, more connected to the ancient forces." His hand gestured vaguely, frustration evident in his movements.

Amber's heart pounded in her chest as she processed his words. "And you disagree?" Uncertainty crept into her tone, her eyes searching his for reassurance.

"I think," Da'fydd paused, his gaze fixed on Amber's eyes, choosing his words with care, "that our bond is perfect as is. We don't need ceremonies or rituals to tell us what we already know. Our connection is beyond that."

Amber's eyes softened, a sigh of relief escaping her lips, reassured by his conviction. "Then we'll ignore the summons. We'll stay hidden in our sanctuary and enjoy what we have." Her voice was filled with a quiet determination, a resolve to protect what was dear to her.

A smile tugged at Da'fydd's lips as he pulled Amber closer, the warmth of their bodies a comfort against unseen threats. "Exactly, little bird. Until we can't ignore it any longer." His voice was gentle, but his words carried a weight of inevitability that lingered in the air between them.

Amber leaned into Da'fydd's embrace, her head resting against his chest, feeling the steady beat of his heart. "Until we can't." Her voice was tinged with love and a hint of sadness. "But for now, let's make the most of our time. We'll face whatever comes as one."

Da'fydd grinned, his eyes sparkling with excitement and something deeper, something that spoke of their unique connection. "Sentiments of a true partner." He smoothed down her long, dark tresses as he cupped the back of her head, drawing her close, his touch gentle but firm. "We'll show them that our bond is ours to define, not theirs."

They stood in the glowing warmth of the greenhouse, their bodies entwined, faces alight with shared determination. The exotic scents of flowers surrounded them, but all that mattered was their presence in each other's lives.

Amber glanced up at Da'fydd, her eyes reflecting their shared resolve. They were no longer merely following the paths set out for them by others. They were forging their own way, guided by love and mutual respect.

Da'fydd's smile widened, echoing Amber's. His tender and intimate touch spoke of a comfort between them that went beyond mere words. In the greenhouse's soft glow, they were at peace with each other, a quiet haven from the Celtan's demands.

Amber's smile eventually subsided, and her eyes found Da'fydd's again. "You feel it's an imposition on us, don't you?"

He nodded, his eyes serious. "Our bond is ours, little bird. It's something we have nurtured, something unique and sacred. To have it summoned, commanded, feels intrusive."

"I understand," Amber replied softly, her hand reaching up to cup his face. "But we must respond. You know that, don't you?"

"I know." Da'fydd's sigh was one of resignation. "We will do as they ask, but we'll do it our way. We'll make it ours, as we have everything else."

Amber's smile returned, a warm, knowing smile. Her eyes shone with conviction as she reached up to touch his face. "Together. That's how we'll face everything."

Da'fydd's eyes twinkled with a playful glint, and his lips curved into a teasing smile. "And with a partner who obeys me."

Amber playfully swatted his chest, her laughter mingling with his. "Don't push your luck."

He laughed, pulling her close, his eyes filled with love and a hint of mischief. "Of course not." His breath was warm against her ear, his embrace protectively gentle.

Amber gave him a playful glare, her heart swelling with affection. Being Da'fydd's partner and reminding him that she was a partner would be a challenge, but one she would savor. At that moment, surrounded by the warmth of the greenhouse and the strength of his arms, she knew it was a challenge they would face, come what may.

Eventually, though, the pain of the summons grew, a persistent throb that was impossible to ignore. They both felt it, a demand pulling at their very essence.

Amber glanced up at Da'fydd. *It's time, isn't it?*

Da'fydd's eyes met hers. *Yes, my little bird. We can't ignore it any longer.* He kissed the top of her head, his voice soft. "We'll face it on our terms. I promise."

Chapter Thirty-Two

D a'fydd and Amber emerged from the shimmering portal, stepping into the mystical clearing of the Stone Pillars. The towering ancient stones, standing as sentinels, bore witness to countless generations of rituals and ceremonies. Here, they were now faced with the stern gaze of the High Druidess, her eyes as unyielding as the stones themselves. The unexpected presence of Gregori and Elina added to a tension that hung in the air like a storm ready to break.

He might not have come if Da'fydd had known of his father's presence. Uneasy stirrings of the past rose, but his focus remained firmly on Amber, whose strength and resolve comforted him.

Do we stay or go? Amber's mental query came through, laced with uncertainty. Her fingers interlaced with Da'fydd's, a tangible connection that fortified them both.

He sensed her anxiety but also her trust. Giving her hand a reassuring squeeze, he gazed into her eyes, his own reflecting determination. *Stay. While I disagree with Kaily about the necessity of this bonding ceremony, I'm curious about all the concerns.*

I'm not, but I'll follow your lead, Amber responded, her mental voice resonating with the loyalty that was the cornerstone of their relationship.

Da'fydd couldn't help but arch an eyebrow at her. *Really? Following me now?*

Amber's glare was almost playful, a spark in her eyes challenging him. She couldn't stop the corners of her lips from turning up, a hint of a smile that spoke volumes.

Their connection was interrupted by a sharp voice cutting through the charged atmosphere. "Where have you been?" demanded Kaily.

Da'fydd's head snapped towards her, eyes narrowing, a protective fire igniting within him. His voice was as cold and firm as the ancient stones encircling them. "Be happy we responded at all, Kaily."

The silence that followed was as profound as the mysteries held within the clearing. The Stone Pillars seemed to lean in, eager to hear what would unfold next in this ancient place where destinies were either claimed or rejected.

"High Druidess," Moto corrected, his voice carrying a note of reprimand.

Da'fydd raised an eyebrow at him, Kaily's constant shadow, but didn't respond, a hint of disdain in his silence. With a dismissive glance, his attention reverted back to Kaily, his voice tense with suspicion. "What is he doing here?" His eyes cut to Gregori for a brief, challenging moment before returning to the self-proclaimed High Druidess.

"Gregori is an intricate part of the bonding ceremony," Kaily replied, her voice steady. Still, her eyes betrayed a hint of irritation.

Da'fydd's eyes remained locked with hers, a battle of wills quietly playing out. His gaze darted to Gregori, who stood arms crossed, exuding arrogance as he waited for a response. Da'fydd denied him the satisfaction of one, returning his attention to Kaily, his voice laced with impatience. "Shall we get on with it then?" He experienced a fleeting satisfaction from the slight narrowing of Kaily and Moto's eyes and their furtive glances. The undercurrents were clear, but he chose to rise above them, his mind on the purpose of their presence.

The sooner they started this ceremony, the sooner he could return to his castle with Amber. Da'fydd's thoughts were consumed by a longing for privacy and peace, away from prying eyes and hidden agendas. The castle, with its towering walls and mystical charm, was their sanctuary, a place where they could be themselves without judgment or interference. Or will be in time.

In the clearing, where the ritual was about to begin, Da'fydd tempered his impatience with his love for Amber. Though wrapped in tradition and formalities, the bonding ceremony was a mere formality for what they already shared. Their connection was deeper, a union of souls that transcended ceremonies and outdated rituals. For Amber, he would endure this ridiculousness.

"You and Amber will stand here," Gregori interjected before Kaily could respond, his voice authoritative. He pointed to a spot near the center of the clearing, where the stone basin stood squarely at the heart of the mystical formation.

Da'fydd, with Amber's hand in his, moved to the spot indicated, his posture displaying a begrudging compliance. The connection with Amber remained strong, a grounding force amidst the mounting tension.

"Face each other," Gregori instructed, his voice now softer, almost reverent, as the ritualistic aspect of the ceremony took precedence.

Da'fydd and Amber complied, their eyes meeting, the world around them fading away. The Stone Pillars, witnesses to their love and the impending bonding ceremony hummed with ancient energy, ready to partake in a moment that transcended mere tradition.

As the energy of Celtan rose up to embrace the couple, doubts and suspicions were forgotten, replaced by a connection that went beyond the corporal. They were about to enter into a sacred bond beyond their comprehension, and nothing else would matter before all was completed.

As Gregori began to chant, the ancient words weaving a spell that resonated with the very core of the world, Da'fydd's eyes locked with Amber's. They held a promise, a commitment that went beyond the words being spoken around them. The power of the Stone Pillars, Celtan's pulse beneath his feet, and the stirrings of old majiks were palpable. Yet, they paled compared to the profound connection he shared with Amber.

In her eyes, he found his home, destiny, and future. A life filled with love and adventure awaited them, and he knew that no matter what came their way, they would face it together. Though soon to be over, the ceremony marked just the beginning of their journey.

Together, they stood on the precipice of a new beginning, bound by a love that was as unbreakable as the ancient stones surrounding them. The Stone Pillars bore witness to a union that was eternally timeless, forging a path for Da'fydd and Amber to walk hand in hand.

Da'fydd turned so he faced Amber, their hands remaining clasped as a tangible connection between them. Out of the corner of his eyes, he noticed Kaily and Moto stepping up to their sides, their movements synchronized and purposeful. Simultaneously, he sensed Elina and Gregori moving into position behind them, their presence like a looming shadow. He kept from cringing from sheer will, focusing on the task at hand.

"We welcome the second Druidess to Celtan," Kaily intoned, placing a hand on Amber's shoulder and one on Da'fydd's. Her voice carried a note of reverence. Her eyes held something undecipherable.

Second? What about Ravenna and the others? Amber asked, her mental voice tinged with confusion as she frowned.

Da'fydd allowed a slight smirk to spread across his lips, his eyes focused on Amber's, relishing in the secret they shared. *Not even my all-knowing father knows about the presence of the Druidesses.*

Why not? Amber's curiosity was piqued.

Da'fydd gave her a silent shrug within her mind, a flicker of amusement in his eyes. *It's for Ravenna and the others to reveal their presence. Personally, I don't care why no one knows about them.*

Amber's eyes twinkled with amusement, her connection with Da'fydd growing more profound with every shared thought. *But you take pleasure in their ignorance.*

A wide smile spread across Da'fydd's features, his happiness evident. *Of course,* he confirmed a playful edge to his silent tone.

The solemnity of the ceremony was interrupted by Gregori and Elina placing their hands on Da'fydd and Amber's necks, the contact almost jarring.

Amber sensed Da'fydd bristling. She remained silent. She knew the relationship, or lack thereof, between Da'fydd and his father was beyond complicated. Honestly, after all this was over, they both intended to remain apart from the brewing politics of Celtan. She and Da'fydd had their hands full with getting his region into better shape than it was.

That's quite the project you have in mind, little bird.

It was Amber's turn to give him a silent shrug. *I'm not spending my eternity in the dilapidated mess that your village has become.*

Our village. Da'fydd corrected her.

Lailoken region should be a shining gem of all of Celtan.

Da'fydd narrowed his eyes at Amber. *Careful, little bird. You might draw too much attention to our region.*

Can we charge a tax for that? Amber teasingly asked.

Da'fydd gave her a slight shake of his head. *You do know there isn't a monetary system on Celtan, right?*

Not yet.

Da'fydd gave her a slight shake of his head.

Amber's eyes darted to Kaily and Moto before landing on Gregori at Da'fydd's back as melodious words continued to flow from him. The ancient language, incomprehensible to most, held a beauty that reached into her very soul. She closed her eyes briefly, tears gathering at the back of her eyes, a response to the deep resonance of the words.

Da'fydd frowned in confusion, sensing her emotional shift. *Why the sadness, my little bird?*

Amber's eyes jumped to his, wide with surprise. *The words are so beautiful.*

Do you understand them? Da'fydd's curiosity was piqued.

Amber gave a slight nod, her face reflecting her wonder. *I do. I don't know what language Gregori is speaking.* She refrained from calling the man his father, recognizing their distance and lack of familial connection.

You astound me, Amber, Da'fydd's mind held a note of awe.

A frown and smile warred on Amber's features, her heart swelling with the praise from her bonded mate. She didn't know how to respond, caught between joy and humility.

As Gregori's words ceased, Amber wiped the tears from her eyes, her emotions lingering.

"You will need to exchange blood," Gregori said, his voice taking on a more clinical tone. "To honor the Dia'Kharn in you, Da'fydd." He finished, his words tinged with underlying meaning.

Amber admired the restraint within Da'fydd's mind, feeling the way Gregori's words about his preferred heritage rankled him. His ability to maintain control was a testament to his strength.

The ceremony continued, but for Amber and Da'fydd, it was a profoundly personal and intimate moment. They were not just following tradition but solidifying a bond that would transcend all barriers. Their love was not merely a romantic connection but a merging of souls, understanding, and shared secrets.

Da'fydd brought his wrist to his mouth, intending to puncture his vein for Amber, his face betraying no reaction to Gregori's barbed words. His eyes, however, were locked on Amber's, the connection between them a constant, reassuring presence.

I can do that. Amber advised, her voice soft yet filled with conviction.

Da'fydd's eyes sparkled with understanding. *As you wish, little bird.* He offered her his wrist while bringing hers to his mouth. With a practiced ease and an unspoken trust, both pierced the other's veins, each taking enough lifeblood to constitute a significant exchange. The life-giving liquid not only bonded them but altered Amber's essence to match Da'fydd's.

After the exchange was completed, their movements were mirrored, each sealing the puncture wounds, their healing touch as tender as their connection.

"It is done." Gregori's voice rang out, filled with a formal finality that resonated with the very essence of the ritual.

The moment his words were uttered, Da'fydd and Amber sensed the world dropping away. Their vision clouded, the presence of the others disappearing from their shared awareness, replaced by a floating sensation that enveloped them like a mystical fog.

Amber was vaguely aware of Da'fydd pulling her closer to him, enveloping her in his arms and energy. Their connection transcended the physical as she blended and melted into him. Boundaries vanished, and she could no longer discern where she left off, and he began, either physically or mentally.

Celtan itself seemed to open up for them, enclosing them in its embrace. The heartbeat of the world echoed within them, resonating in time with their own shared heartbeat, an ancient symphony that bound them to the world and to each other.

Do you feel that? Amber spoke into Da'fydd's mind, her voice tinged with wonder.

I do. Da'fydd's mind was filled with an awe that matched Amber's; his emotions laid bare before her. *I honestly didn't think our bond could be strengthened.*

If you had, would it have made a difference, Da'fydd? Amber sensed an amused smirk within Da'fydd, her own amusement reflecting back at him.

I might not have given Kaily such a hard time ignoring her summons, he confessed, a mischievous glint in his mental voice.

Amber laughed, a joyous sound that danced within their shared consciousness. She couldn't argue there. She might have been more persistent about answering said summons. Her sigh of contentment mirrored his, a harmonious reflection of their shared satisfaction and love.

The bond was sealed, not only through tradition and ceremony but through the profound connection that had grown between them. They were now truly one in mind, body, and soul. The world of Celtan had borne witness, and now their journey together was sanctioned and blessed.

Neither knew how long they remained suspended within the energy of Celtan and each other. Time became an abstract concept. Neither could pinpoint the exact moment their bodies and souls joined, truly joined as one. Or when the ritual words were etched into their core beings. The threads that bound them would forever be intertwined and never to be broken.

Both were consumed by an all-encompassing flame that spoke of passion and commitment, of a love that would never wane. Then, they were doused within a cooling wave that saturated their centers, a soothing embrace that tempered the fire, forging an ardent and gentle connection. Their shared release completed the final steps of their bonding, a culmination of a journey that had only just begun.

Awareness slowly drifted to the surface as they rose and settled on the shore of the underground pool, clothed only in their cloaks provided by Celtan itself. The garments were more than mere fabric; they were a gift from the world, a symbol of their newfound unity.

Neither spoke, reluctant to break the tranquil silence surrounding them like a gentle caress. They lifted their cloaks, examining the deep black-crimson cloth with bright red and gold threads splashed throughout. The colors seemed to dance and shimmer like the emotions flickered between them.

Da'fydd brushed back Amber's hair from her face and lifted her chin, forcing her eyes to meet his. A frown marred his smooth forehead as he stared into her glowing, dark hazel eyes. He saw a depth and warmth in them that he had never seen before, a change that went beyond mere appearance.

He saw through Amber's eyes that his eye coloring had also changed, a subtle alteration that spoke of their transformation. They had become something more, something deeper. They were no longer two separate entities, but a singular force bound by love and destiny.

What has happened to us? Amber's mind was filled with wonder and a touch of uncertainty.

We have become one, Da'fydd answered, his silent tone tender and filled with conviction. *Truly one, in every way beyond what I thought possible.*

Amber reached up, her fingers gentle and understanding, and smoothed the frown lines from Da'fydd's forehead. *You're troubled.* Her voice held knowing, her words more of a statement than a question.

Yes. Da'fydd's tone was soft as he stood, bringing Amber to her feet. He twirled her around, inspecting her at every angle, his eyes wide with wonder as they took in the faint golden aura surrounding her.

Amber loved the way he viewed her, an image filled with adoration and awe, and she happily embraced his vision.

Although, I'm not as troubled as you are. Da'fydd drew her close to his heart, their bodies melding together in a warm embrace.

What does this all mean? Amber asked.

Da'fydd shook his head, his eyes searching hers, looking for answers they lacked. *I don't know.*

Amber's eyes wandered, traveling over the almost dark cavern as swirling luminescent hues danced on the walls and the pool's water. "Beautiful," she whispered in astonishment, captivated by the magical surroundings. *I've never witnessed anything so beautiful in my life.*

I have, Da'fydd replied, his eyes shining with love and adoration as he stared at her.

Blushing at his words, warmth spread through Amber, knowing the compliment was meant for her and her alone. She was his beautiful world, and she relished the feeling.

Ready? Da'fydd asked, his silent tone gentle.

Amber shook her head, her eyes still mesmerized by the sights around them. The cavern held a peace she had not known before, a tranquility that beckoned her.

Da'fydd's gaze followed hers, absorbing the beauty that had captivated his 'little bird.' The cavern's mystique reminded him of places dear to him, drawing him in with a magnetic pull. Yet, he sensed something more, an underlying call that resonated with them.

We must return to the Stone Pillars before we lose ourselves here, he said firmly, yet tenderly, shifting Amber's gaze to meet his. The urgency in his voice was tempered with understanding that had previously illuded him when Kaily exhibited such concern at the possibility of Amber being lost to the energy before the ceremony was completed.

I know you're right, Amber sighed, her voice tinged with regret and fear. *Something happened here that frightens me.*

Da'fydd smiled at her, his eyes soft and reassuring. *I feel it, too.* His words were a promise, an acknowledgment that whatever they faced, they would face together. Their bond was strong, their love unwavering, and nothing could stand in their way.

"What is it?" Amber's voice broke the silence, her eyes searching Da'fydd's for answers, probing the depths of their connection.

Da'fydd shook his head, his eyes reflecting the uncertainty that lingered between them. "We won't figure it out here." His words were firm but gentle, acknowledging the mystery without yielding to fear or confusion.

Amber's gaze drifted to the cavern floor, her mind lost in thought, grappling with the enigma that now enveloped them. Da'fydd remained silent, patient, and understanding, giving her the space to puzzle through her emotions.

After a time, Amber nodded, her eyes lifting to meet his once more, filled with a determination and clarity that deepened their connection. "I don't think Kaily will have the answers either."

"She won't," Da'fydd agreed, his voice steady and reassuring.

"What about Gregori?" Amber's voice wavered slightly as she asked the question, the complexity of their relationship with Gregori added another layer to their situation.

Da'fydd shook his head, his eyes darkening with frustration and intuition. "I sense this knowledge will come to us from another source."

"Is that sense tainted by your complicated relationship with him?" Amber's voice was soft, yet her words were pointed. She hated asking the question, but she needed to know.

"No." Da'fydd's response was immediate and sincere. "There's something..." He shook his head again, the words escaping him, unable to understand what he sensed. The uncertainty in his voice mirrored the ambiguity of their situation.

"How do we get back?" Amber's question was practical but tinged with longing, the magical cavern still calling to her even as they prepared to depart.

"Hold on to me." Da'fydd's voice was filled with confidence as he tucked Amber into the material of his cloak and closed his eyes. His mind reached out, connecting with the energy of Celtan, envisioning the clearing at the Stone Pillars. He knew, with a certainty beyond mere belief, that the ancient land would carry them there, opening a portal only Celtan could create.

At that moment, they were aware of something greater than themselves. This connection went beyond mere love or destiny. It was a bond that transcended time and space, linking them to the very heart of Celtan.

Chapter Thirty-Three

D a'fydd and Amber materialized in the clearing; their feet seemed to hover just above the ground before they gently settled on the mossy carpeted covering. His arms clasped her tightly against him, her form cocooned within the shadowy folds of his cloak. As they arrived, the golden aura that haloed Amber seemed to pulsate, glowing brighter against the lush backdrop. The Stone Pillars surrounding them resonated, emitting a mystical hum that rose and fell in cadence as if the stones sang an age-old tune.

No sooner had they adjusted to the clearing's energies than Da'fydd noticed who was and wasn't present, and a sense of relief washed over him. He was grateful that Gregori and Elina had left. For him, it was more so Gregori's absence that he desired. Elina was inconsequential, although her interaction with Adryan and the other two Lords had sparked his curiosity. He'd always thought of her as Gregori's mate and nothing more. Now, he had to reconsider his previous perception.

His eyes flicked to where Kaily and Moto stood near the center of the clearing. Their faces were etched with varying degrees of confusion and awe. But it was the sudden appearance of Ravenna and her entourage of mysterious women at the edge of the Pillars that demanded his immediate attention.

Why is Ravenna here? Who are all these other women? Amber's silent query interrupted his musings.

I don't know why Ravenna's here. You know who the other women are. Da'fydd brushed a kiss on the top of Amber's head while locking eyes with Ravenna. He paid no attention to Kaily or Moto. Neither mattered in this situation. He'd known there were other Druidesses on Celtan that had not left when Morgana sent the Druidesses away, but he had no idea there had been so many.

Have you noticed Kaily's reaction? Or Moto's? Amber's mind was filled with amusement laced with trepidation. She didn't like surprises. While she liked Ravenna, the Huntress was imposing enough the new arrivals escalated that sense of intimidation tenfold.

Kaily's out of her depth here, as is Moto. Da'fydd answered. He kept Amber and himself planted in place, waiting for Ravenna to reveal her purpose for being at the Stone Pillars. His gaze slid to Kaily for a brief moment. He almost barked out a laugh at the comical confusion on her features as she spun in a circle. The High Druidess's eyes darted from one woman to the other in between, casting a furtive glance at Moto.

Da'fydd couldn't help but wonder about the silent exchange between Kaily and Moto. He sensed an undercurrent of frantic telepathy between them, like buzzing bees. Although eavesdropping on bonded couples was beyond even his abilities, he felt a fleeting itch of curiosity. He'd managed to penetrate the thoughts of fellow Dia'Kharns in the past. Still, he had never really tested those boundaries on Celtan. Telepathy was rare here, and to be honest, few things on this world had ever piqued his interest enough to even try.

What is Ravenna waiting for? Amber asked.

Da'fydd gave her a mental shrug. *Maybe for Kaily to find her voice. Or perhaps for us to say something.*

Kaily, with Moto close beside her, stepped towards Da'fydd and Amber. "Who are these women?" Her eyes slid to his before returning to Ravenna, who had stepped closer to the center. The other woman remained where they had first appeared.

Da'fydd's eyes locked with Kaily's. A smirk played at the corners of his mouth. "Druidesses," he finally replied.

"What?" Kaily exclaimed. Moto wrapped his arms around Kaily and pulled her closer to him. "How?"

Da'fydd couldn't help the sparkle in his eyes. *Stay put, little bird.* He told Amber as she made to pull out of his arms. He could see within her mind that she intended to walk to Ravenna and help defuse the situation.

You're enjoying Kaily's discomfort far too much, my love. Amber countered, but she relaxed back against Da'fydd's bare chest. She was not happy that they were only garbed in a cloak. She had no idea what had happened to their clothing, only that they'd emerged from the energy pool with only the cloaks wrapped securely around them.

Kaily's eyes slid back to Da'fydd. She opened her mouth as if to say something and then closed it abruptly. A frown creased her brow, and she glanced up at Moto.

Looks like she's noticed your glow. Da'fydd told Amber.

Amber made a derisive snort within his mind.

Da'fydd couldn't suppress a slight grin. Even within the confines of their shared telepathic space, Amber's humor and impeccable timing for levity had a way of grounding him. A sense of ease washed over him, a stark contrast to the atmosphere in the meadow that had become suddenly charged with the presence of so many formidable women.

"What happened in the energy?" Kaily tersely demanded of Da'fydd.

Da'fydd favored Kaily with a smirk. "The completion of the bonding ceremony. Isn't that what you wanted, Kaily?"

Kaily favored him with a glare before turning her attention to Ravenna. "Who are you?"

Ravenna didn't answer. She glided across the meadow, rapidly closing the gap between them.

Da'fydd noticed the other women move closer, forming a tighter circle around the five of them, although still some distance away.

Ravenna inclined her head towards Da'fydd. "Princeling."

Da'fydd's eyes narrowed at her nickname for him. "Huntress." He did not incline his head.

Ravenna turned her attention to Amber. "You are glowing, my dear."

"So it would seem." Amber returned the Huntress' gaze with a warm smile. She had an innate fondness for Ravenna; the woman exuded an empowered grace which she deeply admired. "Do you know why?"

Ravenna gave her a single nod of her head. Her eyes left Amber to focus on Kaily. "You have Morgana's memories?"

Kaily hesitated before nodding, her eyes clouded with a disquiet that the simple curve of her frown could not fully express. "Yes."

"Have you mastered the retrieval of them?" Ravenna moved closer to Kaily. Although, Da'fydd didn't think Kaily nor Moto was aware of the Huntress's movements. They were subtle and graceful.

"They surface when they are needed."

"Ah," Ravenna replied with a knowing nod. "You have not mastered their retrieval."

Kaily opened her mouth.

Ravenna held up her hand. "That fact is not open for debate. If you had, you would know who we are." She waved her hand to encompass the women who'd entered the clearing with her.

Kaily's eyes moved over the others.

"We thank you for stepping into the role of High Druidess, but it is time to relinquish that role to the true High Druidess."

Kaily glanced at Amber. "The true High Druidess? I don't understand."

"Clearly," Ravenna replied.

Da'fydd had been on the verge of making the same observation aloud. It was probably better it came from Ravenna rather than himself.

Amber's posture tensed within Da'fydd's arms. *Ravenna's referring to me, isn't she, Da'fydd?*

I believe so. Da'fydd replied.

Because of the glow? Amber asked.

Probably, and the sound when we emerged from the energy into the clearing here. Did you hear it? Da'fydd asked.

Amber nodded.

"Assuming you're talking about Amber," Kaily's eyes slide to the woman engulfed in Da'fydd's arms. "What makes you believe she is the true High Druidess, and I am not?"

Ravenna smiled at the question. It was the type of smile one would favor a child with. "Celtan has chosen." Ravenna held out her hand to Amber.

Amber glanced up at Da'fydd, whose eyes locked with Ravenna for a while before he finally relinquished his hold. Amber held the edges of her cloak together as she stepped out of Da'fydd's embrace. She didn't need to glance back to know that Da'fydd did not display the same level of modesty she had.

Amber placed her hand in Ravenna's who drew her closer to the center. The golden aura surrounding her grew more intense as she neared the center of the meadow where the stone basin stood.

Ravenna stopped in front of the basin. "Hold your linage stone over the water within this stone bowl."

"I don't have it."

Ravenna's eyes landed on Da'fydd. She remained silent, waiting.

Da'fydd shifted to position himself next to Amber at the stone basin, his movements deliberate and fluid. Kaily and Moto joined them, each taking their respective places around the basin's edge. Without breaking the solemn silence, Da'fydd passed the lineage stone to Amber, his eyes locking onto hers for a brief, charged moment.

Amber glanced expectantly at Ravenna.

"Place it on the surface," Ravenna commanded.

"It will sink," Amber countered.

Ravenna smiled at her. "Will it?"

Da'fydd glanced at the other Druidesses as they closed ranks around them, still maintaining a perfect circle.

"Go ahead," Ravenna encouraged.

Amber held her lineage stone over the surface. Her eyes locked with Da'fydd's as she let go. Her eyes drifted back to the basin. On the surface of the water, her stone floated. She jerked back in surprise. A slight laugh escaped her as a frown furrowed her brow. Before long, the water in the basin began to glow with threads that matched the crimson and gold threads in her and Da'fydd's cloaks. A faint hum started low and grew in intensity.

Da'fydd and Ambers' gazes shifted toward the Stone Pillars that seemed to vibrate and shimmer with the energy of Celtan.

Ravenna turned her attention to Kaily. "Place your lineage stone on the surface within the basin."

Kaily shook her head. "I don't have a lineage stone."

Ravenna's head snapped up in surprise. "In truth?"

"In truth. I have a talisman." Kaily glanced at Moto.

A frustrated sigh escaped Ravenna. "We will correct that in the future."

Da'fydd and Amber swore they heard Ravenna mutter something about Gregori interfering where he should not, but neither was certain.

"How does all of this answer my question about how you know Amber is the High Druidess and not me?"

Ravenna studied Kaily. Her eyes shifted to Moto. "Kahoali, how do you know a new Queen has been chosen?"

Moto crossed his arms. "Ki tells us."

"Has your bonded mate witnessed the telltale signs?"

Moto glanced at Kaily before answering. "We have."

"Sari," Kaily murmured so quietly that Da'fydd and Amber almost missed it. Kaily's eyes shifted to Moto. "The glowing and eyes."

Moto gave her an almost imperceptible nod.

"I understand," Kaily told Ravenna. "How do I transfer Morgana's memories?"

"You do not!" A booming voice rang out, interrupting and surprising those gathered around the basin and the others within the clearing.

An imposing male moved with purpose towards those around the basin.

The women and Ravenna bowed low to the newcomer. "Honored One," Ravenna greeted.

"Huntress," he returned his greeting. "You may call me Kensho."

Ravenna nodded in acknowledgment.

Kensho took each into his gaze as his eyes landed on those within the Stone Pillars. His gaze lingered on Amber and Da'fydd longer than the others before he turned his attention back to the group. He first addressed Kaily and Moto. "I know neither of you wished for this responsibility of bringing order back to Celtan. A task thrust upon you by one who should not have." He gave a slight shake of his head. His eyes shone with amusement and frustration that neither Da'fydd nor Amber could decipher. "For a time, you must remain in the position that Gregori placed you." His gaze drifted to Amber and Da'fydd. "As much as taking a back seat will rankle you both; you must maintain the appearance of before." He waved his hand over the basin, picked up Amber's lineage stone, and handed it back to Da'fydd, who pocketed it. "When the time is right, you will bring Celtan back to its proper place at the Center of the Universe and reverse the damage that has been wrought." He glanced at Ravenna and the other women. "You have maintained your secret for a long time and must do so a while longer. However, guide Kaily and Moto as you would the true High Druidess. They will pave the way for a time."

"As you wish," Ravenna respectfully replied.

"Now," Kensho focused his attention on Amber and Da'fydd. He waved his hand, and the glow subsided. "This illusion will help hide your true identity until it is time. Your eye coloring will remain changed. While the eyes can be shielded, they cannot truly be hidden. No worries. Too many have forgotten and will not suspect or know the truth until it is time to reveal the change."

"How will we know when the time is right?" Da'fydd asked.

Kensho tilted his head at Da'fydd before answering. A smile slid across his features. "You'll know." He turned his attention back to Ravenna.

Amber brushed her hand down Da'fydd's arm. *Don't anger him.*

He should not anger me. Da'fydd countered.

Amber could sense his irritation rising. *Do you not sense his power?*

Da'fydd gave her a mental sigh. *I sense it.*

"Bring the Druids under control before they ruin this world beyond repair."

"Without revealing myself?" Ravenna arched a brow at Kensho.

"Precisely!"

Ravenna shook her head. "You ask much, Honored One."

"Not more than you are capable of, Huntress." Kensho laid a hand on Ravenna's shoulder. "Guide Kaily, and through her, the way is prepared."

Ravenna gave him a nod of understanding.

Kensho moved to stand before Kaily and Moto. He laid a hand on each of their shoulders. "Be at peace concerning Sari and Niele."

"Where are they?" Moto demanded.

"Safe," Kensho replied.

Kensho met Moto's eyes with an authoritative glare, effectively silencing any brewing disputes. Without acknowledging the unspoken queries evident in both Moto and Kaily's expressions, he shifted his attention to Da'fydd and Amber. A smile crossed his features before he vanished from sight.

Amber and Da'fydd exchanged glances, as did others within the clearing. Da'fydd looked to Ravenna. "Now what? And who was that?" Da'fydd demanded.

Ravenna smiled and glanced at the ground. She looked back up and met Da'fydd's eyes. "Now, we prepare the way."

"And my other question?" Da'fydd demanded.

Ravenna's smile widened. "You have more important things to attend to than seeking answers to such a trivial question." She waved her hand.

Before Amber and Da'fydd knew what had happened, they found themselves standing in the middle of Da'fydd's chamber.

"Did you know she could do that?" Amber asked, her eyes reflecting just how startled the sudden location change had caused her.

"No," Da'fydd's reply was tight with anger.

"Guess we do now." Amber wrapped her arms around herself and turned to take in the chamber. A chill prickled goosebumps on her arms. The pups lifted their heads from their comfortable bed. She noticed fresh food and water had been placed for them. One of the servants must have been in recently.

Da'fydd moved to stand behind her and pulled Amber against his chest. "We do."

Amber glanced up at him over her shoulder. "What do we do now?"

Da'fydd gave a slight shake of his head. "Well, my High Druidess," he began as he turned Amber to face him. "You have some grand plans for our Lailoken region. You did say you want this region to be a shining jewel of Celtan."

Amber smiled and shook her head. "Now, you're on board."

Da'fydd leaned down and placed a kiss on Amber's lips. "Always, my little bird."

Amber smiled up at him. She lifted her hand to caress his cheek. The light shining from her eyes made Da'fydd's heart swell. "I never dreamed my life could be this..." Amber shook her head.

"Full?" Da'fydd offered.

Amber shrugged. "Maybe. My life has always been about survival," she shrugged again. "I don't know, it's all so overwhelming."

Are you afraid of the future, my Amber?

She shook her head without hesitation. *Not with you by my side.*

From the Author

If you've come this far with me, walked through the mazes of sorrow and love, and stood at the crossroads where destiny meets choice, I want to extend a heartfelt thank you. Your journey with my characters has granted them life beyond the pages of **Destiny Reclaims HER.**

By now, I hope you're as entangled in the webs of this Universe as I am while creating these stories. I have more tales to weave, more characters to introduce, and a Universe that's ever-expanding. But to make that happen, to push this Universe past its potential, I need your help.

If this story touched you, thrilled you, or even made you pause and ponder, please consider leaving a review or rating on Amazon and/or Goodreads. It doesn't have to be an essay, although those are always welcome! Even a sentence or a star rating can make a world of difference. Reviews breathe life into the stories we love and the characters we cherish. They guide me as an author and help fellow readers discover worlds they might otherwise miss.

Become a part of this Universe's destiny. Share your thoughts, and let's make this a reality that expands beyond the confines of paper and ink, or electronics and screens.

Wishing you Journeys as captivating as the one you've just finished!

Your Humble (or maybe not so humble) Creator of Universes,

Machelle Hanleigh

www.machellehanleigh.com

www.ingramcontent.com/pod-product-compliance
Lightning Source LLC
Chambersburg PA
CBHW021131260626
47169CB00005B/1563